VACCINIZED

Dave Klapwyk

Klyk Publishing

978-1-7390761-0-8

Cover Design by Super Dave

CHAPTER 1

"Hello, Sophie."

Hudson sat perched on the edge of the cream leather couch, staring into the tablet. His stocky fingers awkwardly gripped the thin screen, trying not to break it or accidentally press something.

"Hello, Hudson!" his wife squeaked from the tablet.

Even in a drab grey hospital uniform, Sophie was beautiful. Her normally golden blond hair was now greasy and limp, and dark moons drooped below her honey-coloured eyes. Her pained smile appeared, but quickly fell when she gasped for oxygen. A white surgical mask clung to her chin.

"Hey, sweetheart," Hudson replied. A wave of emotion threatened to erupt from his throat, but he swallowed it.

A voice beside Sophie said something that Hudson couldn't decipher.

"If you don't want what I have, leave the room," she yelled firmly. "It's cruel enough that you won't let my husband see me. Now you want me to cover my face when I talk—"

Her voice petered out as if she had run out of gas. The view of her face jerked away. The dull glow of a diffused fluorescent light on the intensive care ceiling appeared on the screen.

"Sophie? Are you there? What happened?" asked Hudson, with a hint of panic in his voice.

The image panned haphazardly for a few seconds before stopping on Sophie's face.

She took a deep breath from an oxygen mask before pulling the contraption off.

"Sorry, hun," she said, still out of breath. "Yelling takes

everything out of me."

"I wish I could be there." His voice almost cracked.

Her eyes panned around the room, and she leaned towards the screen with a serious expression. "If I don't make it, I need you to do something for me."

"What? No, you *are* going to make it. I—"

"Like I've been telling you, I don't think this is right. They vaccinated me, and there's something wrong with..." Her voice trailed off.

He wasn't sure if she was out of breath or words.

"I thought you had Covid?"

She rubbed her bandaged shoulder. "I took it out yesterday and put it—" Then she ran out of breath. She pressed the oxygen mask to her face and took three deep breaths before continuing. "It's where we met, under the..." She forced the words out as if her body was trying to force them to stay in her throat. After mumbling something unintelligible, she took a couple more breaths from the oxygen mask.

"What are you saying?"

"Talk to pretzel, six, sixty-six..."

Her eyes widened with fear. The oxygen mask appeared on the screen and fell to the side. Sophie's arm swung around, and she gasped for air. The image swung wildly before settling on the bed. Behind a fold of white sheet, the side of her face was barely visible. The focus alternated between the sheet and her face. Her mouth gaped open, her eyes frozen in time. A small tear dribbled down her cheek. The screen continued to switch the focus from her face back to the sheet. A high-pitched warning bleeped incessantly.

"Hey!" Hudson stood up and shook the tablet. "Sophie, sweetie? What's going on?"

More voices came through the tablet.

"Get that oxygen mask back on her."

"She's not breathing."

"I need 1 milligram of epinephrine—"

"Turn that thing off..."

The tablet screen darkened except for *No Connection* in small red letters in the centre of the screen.

Hudson yelled and flung the tablet across the room. It bounced off the wall and landed face-down on the carpet. The cartoon eyes on the elephant sticker on the back of the tablet stared up at him. He snatched the telephone off the side table and mashed at the keypad. The frustratingly slow chatbot at 411 eventually gave him the number for the Wanigas General Hospital.

The hospital's phone system was as annoying as the phone directory. After repeatedly pressing '0' after every prompt, a live person finally came on the line. However, she insisted she had no information about Sophie.

"She's in surgery right now," said the receptionist. "But I can get the doctor to call you as soon as they're—"

He slammed the phone down before she finished. Hudson missed the old-fashioned phones he could slam down to hang up. Instead, he picked up the phone and poked at the 'talk' button.

For a moment, he stood in the middle of the silent living room, seething with anger.

"Screw it!" he shouted at the wall. He threw on his shoes and stormed out the door.

Outside, the warm fall afternoon had turned into a cool evening. The neighbour blasted leaves with his blower that sounded like a jet engine. Mr. Hoefstetter looked like he was 102.

Every slow, steady step appeared to be his last. Despite the appearance of imminent death, he relentlessly tended his precious yard and gardens.

Hoefstetter turned his blower off and tilted his head. "Everything okay, Hudson?"

"Nope," yelled Hudson as he climbed into his Ford F-150.

The tires screeched as he tore out of the driveway. Oak and maple leaves swirled in his wake as he sped from the suburb.

Wanigas General Hospital was on the far side of town, but it took him less than 15 minutes to get there. He parked in the emergency unloading zone and burst through the front doors.

A man in a grey fedora argued with a masked nurse behind a table. Hudson strode by them.

"Sir, you have to wear a mask," her muffled voice said through her mask.

"I'm here to see my wife," he said without stopping.

"Visitors are not allowed, sir. Unless you have an emergency—"

"This is an emergency. My wife is dying."

Fedora man said something he couldn't hear.

Hudson marched down a short hallway to the reception area.

"Where's Sophie Finlay?" he demanded of the nurse sitting behind plexiglass.

"Where's your mask?" she asked.

"Where's my wife?" Hudson pounded his fist on the counter.

The woman's eyes widened, and she stepped back. Hudson was an imposing figure in his normal state. His six-foot-two frame, bulging biceps and rugged face made many small children cower when he smiled. And when he was angry, most sane adults quivered in fear.

She grabbed the phone and talked urgently into it. A hand touched his elbow, and he swung around with a grunt.

A white mask dangled from the finger of the woman from the front door.

"Everyone must wear a mask," she said with a trembling voice.

"Where's the ICU?" he yelled.

She raised her hand slowly and pointed at the hallway to the right.

Leaving her standing with the mask still in her hand, Hudson ran into the empty hallway. Following the signs for the ICU, Hudson stormed through the hospital.

Once in the Intensive Care Unit, he began searching the rooms. A tall doctor with a serious face stood in front of him.

"You're not supposed to be here," said the Doctor.

Hudson's imposing figure appeared to have no effect on him.

"I'm looking for my wife, Sophie Finlay. I was on a video call with her when—"

A hand grabbed Hudson's elbow, and he swung around. The

orderly was an inch taller than Hudson and about 40 pounds heavier. One of his massive hands clamped down on Hudson's arm. Although the man wore a mask, Hudson assumed he had a menacing grimace behind it.

He turned back to the doctor. "Please, tell me where my wife is..."

The doctor shifted in front of an ICU room door. "I'm sorry, she's not—"

"She's in there, isn't she?" he demanded.

Behind him, the orderly pulled at his arm.

Hudson turned and slammed his fist into his face. The man's iron grip loosened, and Hudson pulled away. He shoved the tall doctor aside like he was a stalk of wheat and exploded into the room.

A crisp white sheet covered most of the body on the bed. Wisps of Sophie's greasy blond hair snaked out at the top.

All of Hudson's fury and frustration melted into an anguished agony of despair. He stumbled to the bed and collapsed onto his wife's cold body. Hot tears streamed down his cheeks.

The hefty orderly ran into the room, cupping his bleeding nose. He opened his mouth to speak, but stopped when he saw Hudson weeping uncontrollably.

The lanky doctor entered the room. "Take that man out of here *now*. He's not wearing a mask and—"

"Let him be," said the orderly.

CHAPTER 2

Two weeks later, in the middle of a sunny afternoon, Hudson lay in bed, staring at the ceiling.

The phone rang.

Hudson rolled over and covered his head with his pillow.

It rang again.

It could be his older brother, Jeffery, again.

It kept ringing.

He pushed himself to a sitting position and rubbed the sleep from his eyes.

The ringing echoed loudly again in the empty house.

Jeffery called yesterday to offer his condolences, and it wasn't like him to call two days in a row. It wasn't normal for him to call more than once per year.

When he stood up, Hudson's legs wobbled for a moment as if he were standing on a floating floor. The room seemed to tilt on its axis before he regained his sense of balance.

Hudson lumbered through the hallway as the ringing grew louder. The pungent stench of rotting food assaulted his nostrils as he shuffled into the kitchen. He reached for the phone and knocked a plate of stale cookies into the sink with a clang.

"Yeah," he barked into the receiver.

"Hello, Mr. Finlay?" said an annoyingly friendly male voice he didn't recognize.

"That's me." He tried to blink the grogginess away. "Who's this?"

"My name is Stanley Schmidt. I'm from Schmidt Funeral Home. Is this a bad time?"

"This is a horrible time. My wife died."

"I understand that, sir, and I know you're grieving, but we need to discuss final arrangements for your wife."

Hudson sighed. "Right."

"At this point, I would suggest cremation and—"

"Why cremation? I wanted to bury her in the cemetery next to her parents."

"It's been over a week, Mr. Finlay and—"

"Yes, I've been preoccupied."

After the incident at the hospital, the police charged Hudson with assault and battery. He spent a week in jail before his lawyer convinced the district attorney to drop the charges, citing extenuating circumstances. The doctor and orderly at Wanigas General agreed not to pursue the matter.

"I understand sir, but it's been too long, and her body is . . . It would be best to have a cremation. You can still have a celebration of life service. I'm sure Mrs. Finlay has family that would like to pay their respects."

"Am I allowed to *have* a funeral?"

"Under the current rules, you can have a service with ten close family members—"

"That's not right." Hudson's voice rose in anger. "First, they won't let me near my wife when she's dying, and now I can't have a proper burial? What happened to living in a free country?"

"These are desperate times, Mr. Finlay. The pandemic has caused much strife in—"

"The *pandemic* has caused strife, or is it the Draconian measures?"

Hudson wasn't sure what *Draconian* meant, but it was something Sophie used to say. All he knew was that life wasn't fair, and it seemed like the world was against him.

"I don't make the rules, sir. Did you still want to have a service?"

Sophie was an only child, and her parents were both passed. Current restrictions made travelling difficult for his brother and many of their friends. Some had already told him they would pay their respects when "things have calmed down."

"There's no point," he answered.

"Okay," said Schmidth, "We will perform the cremation, and you can make an appointment to pick up the urn and her personal effects."

"Can I at least see her one more time before you…"

"Too much time has gone since she passed away, and her body isn't a condition conducive to viewing anymore."

"I don't care!" he yelled. "I want to see Sophie."

The doorbell chimed. The electronic bells rang a cheerful tune that echoed through the quiet house. After Hudson installed the doorbell a few years back, Hudson and his wife had a long, playful argument over which tune to use. He wanted the deep resonating gong, but she insisted on a happy sing-song tune. Eventually, he relented, allowing her to have her stupid, cheery tune. It was the first time he heard the doorbell since she died. He wasn't sure if the sound made him angry, sad or both.

"Yes, I understand that sir, but—"

"Hang on," Hudson interrupted. "Someone's at the door."

He set the phone down and pounded out of the kitchen.

The doorbell got one more irritating diddy before he swung open the door.

A blue cloth mask covered Mr. Hoefstetter's face, and he stood two steps back from the front stoop. "I'm sorry to bother you, Hudson," he said in a muffled voice through his mask. "I know this is a difficult time, but the leaves in your yard are piling up. If you leave them too long, mildew will start growing and moles will make tunnels. Also, they are blowing into my yard."

Wisps of his grey hair waved in the wind. The blue mask made it impossible to tell if he was concerned, angry or happy.

"I've been a little preoccupied," Hudson scowled. "My wife died, and I was in jail for a week."

The man's entire upper body bowed as he nodded vigorously. "Yes, I heard. If you don't mind, I would like to help."

"Go nuts," Hudson hissed and slammed the door.

When he picked up the phone, Dr. Schmidth was gone. He considered calling him back but changed his mind. Instead, he opened the fridge in search of sustenance. A wave of noxious fumes assaulted his nasal passages. He braved the stench and poked his head inside. He found a carton of lumpy milk, a fuzzy blue sandwich, enigmatic leftovers in red plastic Tupperware and limp purple carrots marinating in a mysterious brown liquid in the vegetable drawer.

As his appetite vaporized, he shoved aside the orange juice with green floating fuzzballs and reached for a tall can of beer.

In the living room, he slumped onto the couch and cracked the can. A yeasty spray showered the elephant-shaped pillow beside him, and he slurped up the bubbly beer erupting from the can before it spilt onto his lap.

He leaned back and exhaled. The house was dead silent.

There were moments in life when he enjoyed the silence. Like sitting in a camouflaged hunting stand, waiting for the appearance of a 12-point buck. The only sounds were the faint rustling of oak leaves or the chirp of a lone black-capped chickadee.

However, this was not the calming quiet of nature. The hushed house was a cruel reminder of a home once filled with the clamour of a happy, busy life.

The Covid restrictions had already sucked most of the joy out of the house — no chatter of friends at their annual Christmas party. No morning scramble to eat breakfast, kiss his wife, find the keys, or argue over how the utensils go in the dishwasher before dashing off to work. There was no chatter of a Super Bowl party interspersed with raucous cheering and thoughtful debates over who was the greatest quarterback of all time. No returning from work, walking into the living room, only to be ambushed by a giggling Sophie from behind the couch as she slammed the elephant pillow at his face.

It all disappeared when the government shut down society, hoping to stop a pandemic. Sophie insisted the elites had engineered the virus and resulting shutdown to control the population and manipulate its citizens. She was deep into a lot of conspiracy theories. Hudson didn't know what to believe.

What he knew was that she was gone, and this house was as void as his soul. Early in the pandemic, the auto plant laid him off, but she was a firefighter and kept working. Although he spent many days alone, waiting for her to come home, it never seemed *this* quiet.

The muted house tightened its cruel grip as he guzzled the rest of his frothy beer.

The sound of a four-stroke lawnmower engine broke him from his silent, depressing funk. Out the front window, Mr. Hoefstetter waved from atop his riding mower as he drove by.

A hint of regret nudged at Hudson.

He closed his eyes and leaned back. The lulling hum of the engine outside distracted him from the oppressing silence of the empty home.

He conjured a Sophie visage in his mind. He pictured her charming smile, alluring golden hair and piercing eyes the colour of honey that could penetrate his heart with just a glance.

With the half-empty can of Bud still clutched in his grasp, he drifted into dreamland.

CHAPTER 3

Sophie tucked a tuft of unruly hair behind her ears, wiped a hand on her apron, and grabbed an oven mitt covered in tiny pink elephants. She opened the oven, pulled out a tray of cookies, and set it on the marble counter.

The sweet aroma was irresistible. He reached to grab one, but Sophie smacked his hand.

"Don't touch them with your filthy hands."

"They're not filthy."

"You worked all day on greasy, dirty cars."

"It's a clean auto manufacturing facility, not a mechanic's shop," he said with a pout.

"Why don't you do something useful and start cooking the meat?"

He opened the fridge and pulled out a plate with two thick red steaks.

"Are we going camping again on the July 4th weekend?" he asked.

"Yes, but you can't bring your gun this time."

"How am I supposed to bring home the meats if I can't bring my gun?"

"You can fish, but no hunting. If you want to hunt something, it should be the criminal organization called our government."

The comment surprised Hudson. Calling the government a criminal organization was nothing new, but promoting violence wasn't in her playbook. Also, he didn't think they *could* camp under the current restrictions, and wasn't it autumn? Independence Day already passed, didn't it?

"What are you talking about?"

"I warned you about them," she scowled. Her once smooth blond hair was stringy and greasy. Dark circles hung beneath her eyes, and her baking apron was a hospital gown.

He dropped his plate, which shattered on the ground. Blood pooled at his feet.

"They put it in me, but I took it out!" she hissed.

"What's wrong with you?" He reached out to her, but she swatted him away.

"You can't touch me," she said through an oxygen mask. "They won't let you."

She grabbed the baking tray and held it out. "Here, have some cookies!"

However, it wasn't cookies. Instead, a mound of pretzels filled the tray.

"What...?"

He watched the tray fall to the floor and spill the pretzels onto the raw steak. When he looked up, she was gone. A steady beep of a heart rate monitor emanated from the tablet on the counter. He picked it up and gasped in horror at the frozen image of a covered body on a hospital bed. The beeping sped up and then flatlined.

"Sophie? Is that you? I thought we were going camping?"

Suddenly, she sat up, and the white hospital sheet fell away. Rotting skin sloughed off her face, and she glared at him with dead eyes.

"I took it out," she said in a zombie monotone. He dropped the tablet, and it landed in the pretzels.

A decaying hand reached through the tablet and retrieved a pretzel. She held it up to her rotting face and screeched like a witch on acid. “Talk to the pretzel!”

Flames appeared on the pretzel and quickly spread to Sophie.

“What’s happening to me?” she cried. Fire consumed her body, and her skin melted away.

Hudson felt for the keys in his pocket. “I’m coming, Sophie. I’m coming.”

His feet slipped on the bloody steak when he tried to rush out of the kitchen, and he slammed onto the floor. When he sat up, steak blood covered his legs.

He tried to scream, but nothing came out.

Hudson woke up confused. His lap was wet, and he was on the couch in the living room. It took him a moment to adjust to his waking reality. He tossed the empty beer can across the room. It knocked over a glass elephant figurine and a frame with a photo of him and Sophie sitting around a campfire.

The can settled on the floor, and silence retook the house.

“I gotta get out of here!” he announced, wiping the tears and sweat from his face.

He spent the rest of the day helping Mr. Hoefstetter clean up the yard. That night, after three more beers, he had a decent, dreamless sleep.

CHAPTER 4

Early the next morning, Hudson drove his pickup twenty minutes north of Saginaw to Schmidth's funeral home. The large, white brick building didn't look like a funeral home. Although he wasn't sure what a typical funeral home was supposed to look like. Long, dark windows lined with identical planter boxes flanked a covered entrance. The black decal on the glass door said he was entering Schmidth Funeral Home and Cremation Service.

A man in a grey fedora exited the front door, walked quickly past Hudson, got into a blue SUV and drove away. Hudson thought he recognized the man, but couldn't remember where. He exited the truck and walked inside.

The interior was almost as eerily quiet as Hudson's house. Mr. Schmidth glanced up from a hushed conversation with a sobbing elderly woman and held up his finger. He said something to the woman, who nodded as she sat on an antique wingback chair and continued crying. The funeral director padded across the plush azure carpet to Hudson. When Hudson was still a few steps away, he pointed to the box of surgical masks on the glossy side table and smiled.

"I thought we didn't have to wear these anymore." His booming voice seemed to rattle the man, who pushed his finger to the lip area of his mask.

"This is a funeral home, sir," he said in a whisper. "Please keep your voice down."

Hudson rolled his eyes and strapped a mask over his face. "Are we going to wake the dead?" he mumbled.

Schmidth adjusted his tie and raised his chin. "What can I help you with, sir?"

"My name is Hudson Finlay." He held out his hand briefly before remembering people don't shake hands anymore. "We spoke on the phone yesterday."

"Of course, Mr. Finlay. Right this way, please."

He led him down a wide hallway lined with intricately detailed wood panel walls to a small, gaudily decorated room. Inside, he reached onto a shelf and pulled down a silver urn and held it out.

Hudson stepped back. "What is that?"

Schmidth lowered his head and spoke in a soft tone. "It's the remains of your loved one, sir." He still held out the urn, urging Hudson to take it.

"I told you I wanted to see her one last time!" He folded his arms and glared down at the man.

"As I said on the phone – it's been too long, and the body was not in a condition conducive to viewing." His voice was still soft but quivering slightly. "I'm very sorry for the miscommunication, sir."

Hudson snatched the silver urn out of his hand and turned away.

"I know this isn't a good time," Schmidth called after him, "but there is still the small matter of your bill."

"You can do the same thing with that bill that you did to my wife," he called back as he stormed past the weeping widow. He threw open the front door, burst outside and slammed into a woman attempting to enter the building. Sophie's ashes almost emptied into the parking lot, but he pressed the urn to his body as if receiving a touchdown pass.

"Oh, I'm so sorry," the woman apologized. She was in her late fifties, with greying hair, faded jeans and a ruffled blouse. Her face looked vaguely familiar.

Hudson shook his head. "No, it's my fault. I should watch where I'm going."

"Hudson Finlay?" the woman raised her eyebrows. "You're Sophie's husband, right?"

"Yes...and you are?"

She pointed at herself. "Ursala...Ursala Janwick. We met over a tablet a couple of times. I was Sophie's nurse."

Hudson nodded slowly. "Right."

She pointed at the silver urn. "Is that...Sophie."

He nodded.

"I was working when she came into emergency. It's not right that they wouldn't let you see her. I'm so sorry for your loss — losses. It shouldn't have happened. Let me know if there is anything I can do."

"Thanks."

They stood for a few awkward seconds before Hudson asked. "Why are you here? Did you lose someone too?"

"My grandfather died yesterday..."

He wasn't sure what to say. This was an awkward social moment he would have normally turned to Sophie to intervene. "I'm sorry for your loss."

It was an expression he had heard a lot lately.

Ursala nodded. "Thanks. It was his time to go. I'm sure this is nothing like what you must be going through."

He couldn't think of any decent response. "Well, it was nice seeing you again, but I should get going."

"Okay. I'll see you around sometime."

"Yeah."

As he reached the pickup, Ursala called back from the funeral home doorway. "I meant to ask you...Do you know anything about the cut on her shoulder?"

She pointed to her upper arm.

"No. What cut?"

She let the door close behind her and walked closer to Hudson. "She was bleeding from her shoulder when she came in. I asked her about it and she just said she cut it."

"Cut it on what?" he asked.

She shrugged. "Sophie didn't say, and it didn't seem important. Later, after they moved her to intensive care, I changed the bandage. It was a sizable slice that probably should have been disinfected and stitched."

"She didn't tell me anything about getting cut," said Hudson.

"I suppose it doesn't matter anymore."

As she turned to leave again, Hudson asked, "Do you know anything about a pretzel?"

"You mean like the snack?" asked Ursala.

"Before she died, she said something about a pretzel and a bunch of numbers. Do you know anything about that?"

Ursala shook her head. "She had a lot of drugs in her system. I'm sure it means nothing."

"You're probably right. What did you mean *it shouldn't have happened*?"

"Sophie was healthy, strong and even had the vaccine and two boosters. Maybe it was the infection in her arm or an adverse reaction to Covid-19, but something didn't seem right about her case."

"That's strange."

"Anyway, I suppose it doesn't matter now." She reached out, touched his arm and looked into his eyes. "She loved you, Hudson...a lot."

CHAPTER 5

One year later, at the Wanigas Private Academy, a group of twenty-three students listened as their teacher strolled between the row of desks.

"Please do not turn over your test papers until I say." Mr. Tartsmeyer said as he slapped the history test onto Reggie Hargreaves' desk.

Reggie tapped a finger on the laminate and waited. At the desk beside him, his best friend, Carter, whispered, "Did you study?"

"Oh yeah," Reggie smirked.

"You have forty minutes to complete the test. That is enough time for those that paid attention and completed the reading assignments. I know Shakespeare is heavy reading, but Grade 11 is not supposed to be easy."

He stood at the front of the class and waited for silence before he spoke again. "You may begin!"

The room erupted in a flurry of paper shuffling, groaning, and anxious sighs.

Reggie brushed his unruly brown hair from his face and slowly turned over the test.

Ten minutes later, he stood up and walked to the front of the class. Mr. Tartsmeyer noticed him as he approached and slammed his laptop shut.

"What are you doing, Reggie?"

He placed his test papers on the desk and smiled. "I'm done."

His teacher sighed. "If you don't know some answers, maybe you should think about them a little longer. You still have thirty minutes."

Reggie turned and sauntered back to his seat. "I don't need more time."

Carter looked up from his test and shot him an inquiring look. Reggie just smiled and shrugged.

"Your funeral," said Mr. Tartsmeyer and opened his laptop again.

Reggie leaned back in his seat, reached into his bookbag and pulled out his phone.

"No phones in class!" Mr. Tartsmeyer's eyes peered over his laptop screen.

"Why not?" asked Reggie. "I'm done with my test; you're not teaching and I'm bored."

"You should be studying for your remake test," suggested Mr. Tartsmeyer.

"I don't have to because I aced this one."

"Not likely. Put your phone away, *now*."

A moment later, Reggie pulled out his laptop and opened it on his desk.

"What are you doing?" His voice was an octave higher this time.

"I'm researching the origins of the phrase, *idle hands are the devil's workshop*. Did you know although this is commonly attributed to the Bible, the exact usage—"

"I don't care if you're attempting to translate the dead sea scrolls. I told you that no electronics are allowed in class."

"My mistake - I thought you told me to put my phone away."

Mr. Tartsmeyer took a deep breath and took off his glasses. "No laptops, no phones, no tablets, no pagers. No electronic device of any kind. Just sit there and think about how you might study better for the next test."

"What's a pager?"

"Just be quiet and study."

"I don't need to study, I—"

Mr. Tartsmeyer held up his pointer finger and gave his meanest death stare. "Don't test me."

"Why not? You tested me…" Reggie mumbled.

Carter chortled through his nose but didn't look up from his test.

"What did you say?" yelled his teacher.

"Can I take a nap?"

"You can do what you want as long as you do it quietly without disturbing your fellow students."

Mr. Tartsmeyer reached over his laptop and grabbed Reggie's test. For the next few minutes, he studied the papers, his face a scrunched look of consternation.

Twenty-seven minutes later, Mr. Tartsmeyer clapped his hands. "Pens down. Please bring your tests to my desk."

The bell rang as the students jockeyed to the front. Carter ducked down and jotted a last answer before standing up.

"How did you finish so fast?" he whispered to Reggie.

"I did some clever studying," Reggie answered with a coy smile.

"Did you cheat?" he asked in a stern whisper.

"Someone did." Reggie stood up and headed towards the door.

"Not you, Reggie Hargreaves." Mr. Tartsmeyer pointed at him with a bony finger. "You and I are going to have a little chat with the principal."

Ten minutes later, Reggie sat across the desk from Principal Justine. Beside them, Mr. Tartsmseyer remained standing with a stern look.

Principal Justine leaned back and smiled. All the teachers, councillors, janitors and even those working in the cafeteria used their last name preceded by either Ms., Mrs., Miss or Mr. However, their principal preferred her moniker to be her first name, preceded by *principal*. She was desperately trying to be a principal that all the kids loved, and she hoped that using her first name would help them see her as an ally rather than an oppressor. She kept her hair in a tight ponytail and often wore jeans that were too tight for someone her age.

"Why don't you have a seat, Mr. Tartsmeyer?" She pointed to the chair beside Reggie.

"I prefer to stand." He folded his arms in defiance.

"Yes, but I'd prefer you to sit." Her neatly trimmed eyebrows raised, waiting for him to comply.

After a moment, he sighed, then grabbed the chair. It made a loud scraping sound as he moved it from beside Reggie to a spot beside the desk.

Principal Justine's painted eyebrows fell back to their default position.

"I understand we have an issue with a test," she said, looking at Reggie.

Mr. Tartsmeyer leaned forward as if trying to intercept her gaze. "He *cheated* on the test."

Her eyebrows scrunched down as her gaze remained on Reggie. "Is that true?"

"Maybe."

The eyebrows raised again in surprise. Watching her eyebrows was akin to watching a yo-yo.

"No *maybe* about it," said Mr. Tartsmeyer. "There is *no* way that he completed that entire test in just ten minutes and got every question perfect without cheating."

"How long did it take you to create this test?" asked Reggie.

"It took many hours," he answered. "But what does that have to do with anything?"

"What is the punishment for cheating on a test?" Reggie reached into his book bag and retrieved a half bag of pretzels.

"What are you doing?" asked Mr. Tartsmeyer. "You can't eat in the principal's office!"

"This is lunch period," said Reggie, tossing a stick into his mouth. "I'm hungry, and a growing, learning young man needs his sustenance."

"You can't—" yelled Mr. Tartsmeyer, but the principal held up her hand.

"Let him eat." She turned back to Reggie. "You can have your snack, but I need you to explain yourself. Did you cheat on the test?"

"I did not have any notes beside me. I didn't sneak a look at my books. I didn't use my phone."

"Yes, but did you cheat?" she asked. "You can tell us. I'm sure you have a valid explanation for why you may have felt the need to cheat. If you need help or tutoring or assistance discovering your individual learning mode..."

"I don't need tutoring or help. I am smart enough."

The principal clicked on her mouse and looked at her screen. "I see that you have A's and B's in all your classes..." She looked up at him with a single eyebrow raised. "You're not cheating in all your classes, are you?"

After swallowing another pretzel, he answered, "No, I'm not cheating in the other classes."

"So, you admit it!" yelled Mr. Tartsmeyer. "You *did* cheat on this test!"

"Before I answer that question, let me ask *you* something." Reggie pointed a pretzel at both of them. "What is the punishment for cheating on a test?"

"Immediate expulsion!" Mr Tartsmeyer jumped to his feet. "This school has a zero tolerance for cheating."

"Sit down," said Principal Justine in a calm voice. "Let's not get dramatic."

He reluctantly returned to his chair.

"It is true, we have a zero tolerance for cheating," she said in a calm voice. "But since this is your first offence, I'm sure we can work something out if you are honest."

"You can't reward him for admitting he cheated," demanded Mr. Tartsmeyer. "We must expel him!"

"According to the board, the consequence for cheating is a three-day suspension, followed by an ethics and morals training session."

"Is plagiarism considered cheating?" Reggie rubbed his hands, dusting off the pretzel crumbs.

"Yes!" They answered simultaneously, although with distinct tones. Mr. Tartsmeyer's was forceful, while Principal Justine's was tentative.

"And there are no exceptions, correct?" Reggie pulled out a set of stapled pages from his bag.

"No," his teacher answered quickly.

The principal shook her head in agreement.

Reggie held the pages close to his chest. "So, if anyone at this school cheats on a test – including plagiarism – they are immediately suspended for three days?"

"Absolutely!"

"That is the policy."

Like a chess player that knows he's trapped his opponent, a smile grew on Reggie's face.

"I found this interesting test online last night," he said, handing the papers to Principal Justine.

Her brows furrowed again as she took the papers and studied them. Mr. Tartsmeyer rose from his chair and looked over Principal Justine's shoulder.

"You cheated by finding the test online?" he asked.

"That is a test I found from a school in southern California." Reggie resumed snacking on his pretzels as he spoke. "It is from four years ago. It appears Mr. Tartsmeyer did not write that test. He plagiarized it. As you both agreed, *that* is a form of cheating, which this school has zero tolerance for."

Mr. Tartsmeyer squirmed in his chair. "I may have borrowed some ideas from other teachers...there's no harm in that..."

Reggie stuffed the pretzel bag into his backpack and stood up. "I guess I'll see you in three days, Mr. Tartsmeyer."

As he reached the door, Principal Justine called, "Not so fast, Mr. Hargreaves!"

CHAPTER 6

"What are you in for?" asked Carter.

Later that day, after school, Reggie sat in the math room with four other students. Apparently, Mr. Tartsmeyer's test pilfering was not a punishable offence. Reggie argued that as part of his studying, he had inadvertently come across the test and thought it was relevant to the class. How was studying for a test cheating? What rule was it breaking? After a lengthy and sometimes heated discussion, Principal Justine gave Reggie a one-week detention. It was worth it just to see Mr. Tartsmeyer squirm.

Three of the students sat spread out amongst the two dozen seats. Reggie and his friend Carter sat next to each other at the back of the class. The young teacher at the front of the room napped with his head buried in his arms. Reggie couldn't recall his name.

"I embarrassed our English teacher," said Reggie, smiling.

"You mean *Farts*meyer?" croaked Carter. His voice echoed across the room.

The young teacher at the front looked up from his nap for a moment before dropping his head back down.

"I found a copy of the test he plagiarized and told the principal," Reggie whispered.

"Is that how you finished so early?"

Reggie nodded.

"How did you find a copy of the test?"

"I have my ways." Reggie leaned back, combed his long hair behind his head, and smiled.

During the Covid lockdown, he got bored with the endless online classes, annoyed with technologically inept teachers and tired of the inadequate online instruction. One of the few advantages of attending a private school was the advanced curriculum. However, that advantage dissipated when the schools closed and the students had to fend for themselves from home. Reggie's intelligence was above average for his age and to prevent himself from losing his mind, he delved into the world of computer programming, coding and eventually hacking. By the time classes resumed after the pandemic, he had become an adept hacker. Using his newest algorithm, Reggie attempted to hack into the school network and found a weak link in Mr. Tartsmeyer's password choice. He inadvertently stumbled across his teacher's test and exam directory. Wanting to expose his history teacher's lazy teaching methods, he performed a quick internet search and found the original test.

"Why are *you* in detention?" he asked.

Like Reggie, Carter was an 'A' student, especially in the science classes. However, he did not share Reggie's contempt for authority. It was unlike him to step out of line.

"After finishing my lab in Chemistry, I conducted my own little science experiment," he said with a wry grin.

Reggie leaned forward. "What did you do?"

"Using some potassium nitrate, sulfur and charcoal, I made some black powder. I didn't expect it to work so well. It burned through the lab counter before the teacher sprayed it with the fire extinguisher. You should have seen the white flames!"

Suddenly, the door to the classroom swung open. All eyes stared at the big man with grey coveralls standing at the door with a yellow bucket and a mop. Dark bags hung under his dismal eyes. He looked at the half-asleep teacher with a grim expression. "Sorry, I didn't know anyone was in here."

"It's fine," said the teacher, rubbing his eyes. "It's just detention hall."

"I'll come back," offered the big man. He turned and slowly rolled his bucket out of the room.

Before he disappeared, Reggie noticed an elephant sticker on the wooden mop handle.

"Who was that guy?" he asked Carter.

"That's the janitor."

"Really?" asked Reggie.

"I heard he used to work at the auto plant, but they fired him during Covid."

"He doesn't look like a janitor. I wonder..."

Reggie squinted and stared ahead at the closed door where the janitor had stood seconds before.

"Not this again," said Carter. "Whenever you have that faraway look, it means one of two things–you're dreaming up a new coding program, or you think you've uncovered more evidence of government oppression."

Reggie didn't respond, so Carter continued. "Since we're not allowed electronic devices in detention, it must be the janitor. You think that because he looks like a wrestler, he must be a plant by the government to spy on wayward students. They discovered you are a dissenter that believes the government engineered the virus to control the population and create a socialist world order. The elites sent a spy to infiltrate Wanigas Private Academy to assassinate one of their greatest adversaries."

Reggie looked at his friend. "I know you're mocking me, but you know some of that's true."

"The janitor is an assassin?"

"No, you moron, the other part."

"What *are* you thinking?" asked Carter.

"Do you know if he has kids?"

Carter shrugged. "I don't think so. My mom said he lives alone on the west side of town."

His mother was head of the parent advisory committee and prided herself on knowing everything about everybody at the school.

"She says that after his wife died of Covid, he became angry and depressed. They fired him at the auto plant, and he got a job mopping floors here."

"Did you see the elephant sticker on his mop?" asked Reggie.

"Why? Is that the secret symbol of the elites?"

"Not exactly..." Reggie raised his hand and spoke loudly. "Excuse me, sir?"

"Yeah?" answered the teacher.

"I have to use the bathroom."

"Can't you wait twenty minutes?"

"No, I drank a lot of water and I have bladder issues," Reggie lied.

The teacher waved his hand. "Go ahead, but be back in five minutes."

"Thanks," he answered and stood up.

"What are you doing?" Carter whispered.

"If the assassin succeeds, avenge my death," said Reggie smiling as he walked away.

Carter folded his arms and shook his head. "Very funny."

"Five minutes," the teacher called as Reggie left the classroom.

To the left was the water fountain and boy's and girl's washrooms. Beyond them was a long, empty hallway. To the right was a short stretch of hall flanked by grey metal lockers. Reggie's footsteps echoed in the empty school as he turned right. At the tee in the hallway, he looked in both directions but saw no one. He listened for a moment. The faint rattle of rolling wheels emanated from the right, and he walked in that direction. Further down the corridor, past the math and computer classes, he found the janitor rolling his pail into the music room.

"Hey, wait!" called Reggie, but the man disappeared into the classroom.

Reggie chased after him and stepped inside the room.

"What do you want?" The janitor did not look up. He pulled the dripping mop from the bucket and placed the sopping white cotton yarns into the ringer. The mop's head squelched as he pushed the handle down. Once he had squeezed enough grey water out, he released the ringer handle and pulled out the mop. He slopped it on the floor, splashing water onto Reggie's new shoes.

Reggie took a step back. "Are you Elephant, zero, five, eleven?"

The man moved the mop across the floor in long sweeping motions. "No, I am not an elephant. You should go back to class."

"Classes are over. I'm in detention."

"That's nice. Go back to detention and leave me alone."

Reggie squinted his eyes. "Are you sure you're not Elephant—?"

"Beat it, kid."

"I'm Pretzel, six, six-sixty, except the *z* is a dollar sign."

The janitor paused mopping ,and faced Reggie. His imposing figure and annoyed expression made Reggie take a step back.

For a moment, they stared at each other in silence.

Finally, Reggie spoke.

"Sorry, my mistake. I thought you were someone else."

He turned and left the room.

"Did you get lost?" asked the teacher when Reggie returned.

"Sorry, it's that time of the month." Reggie placed a hand on his stomach.

The teacher rolled his eyes. "Sit down before I give you another detention."

"Where did you go? What happened?" Carter asked when he returned to his seat.

"I went to the washroom, where I experienced an extraordinarily large bowel movement. It was bigger than—"

"Shut up." Carter slapped Reggie's arm. "Seriously, what happened?"

"I talked to that big janitor guy."

"Why?"

"I thought I knew him." He turned to his friend. "He's not a very nice man."

"My mom says he used to be a boxer. She told me not to go near him because he's dangerous. Apparently, he was charged with assault for almost killing a doctor at the hospital."

"He *is* kind of scary."

After detention was over, Reggie and Carter stood atop the concrete steps outside the school. They both stared at the janitor leaning against a fat oak tree next to the sidewalk.

"Is he looking at us?" asked Carter.

"I think so," Reggie answered.

"Do you want a ride?" Carter asked. "My mom's picking me up. She won't lecture me on the importance of behaving in school if you're with me."

"Nah, I'm good. I'm going to go talk to him."

"Your funeral . . ." said Carter as Reggie plodded down the steps.

A cool autumn gust tore a collection of leaves from the almost barren tree and sent them showering onto the grass around the janitor.

Reggie left the sidewalk, waded through the leaves and stopped a few safe paces from the man.

Without his baggy coveralls, the man looked even more imposing. His bulging biceps stretched his dirty white t-shirt.

"Who is Elephant, zero, five eleven?" the man asked.

"If you don't know, it doesn't matter," Reggie answered with more confidence than he felt.

"What about pretzel? Is that a nickname or something?"

"It's a handle?"

"A handle to what?"

"A social media handle."

"Did you know Elephant, zero-five-eleven?"

"What do you mean *did* know? Did the government eliminate him?"

The janitor shook his head. "Never mind. It doesn't matter."

He turned and walked away.

"Wait!" Reggie called. "Something *did* happen to him, didn't it?"

He ran to catch up. His feet kicked up red, green and brown oak leaves. The wind snatched them and sent them floating away.

While maintaining a safe distance, Reggie walked beside him.

The man walked with long, quick strides. Reggie was almost jogging to keep pace.

"He's dead, isn't he? Did he talk about Pretzel, six-sixty-six?"

"I don't know what you're talking about." He stared forward without expression.

"Yes, you do. Otherwise, you wouldn't be waiting for me outside the school."

"I made a mistake."

"Did he find the implant and remove it? Did he take it out, and that's why—"

He stopped abruptly and glared at Reggie. "What did you say?"

Reggie was relieved to stop and catch his breath but nervous about the look on the janitor's face.

"I asked if he found the—"

"No, the other part. You asked if he took it out. Took what out?" His voice was stern and loud.

A mother pushing a stroller glanced in their direction and continued walking.

"How can I trust you?" Reggie folded his arms and tilted his head. "You could be one of them."

He flinched when the man held out his hand till he realized he was offering a handshake.

"My name is Hudson Finlay. I think my wife was the elephant handle."

"That's not—" Reggie stopped mid-sentence and shook his hand. "I'm Reggie."

Reggie's hand disappeared in Hudson's massive grasp, and he tried not to grimace under the strain of the firm grip.

"Elephant zero-five-eleven was a woman?"

"What did you mean, *did she take it out*?"

A man in a suit and tie walked by. His long brown scarf twirled in the wind behind him.

Reggie looked at the man and then at a woman walking her poodle.

"We shouldn't talk here," he said. "They could be listening."

"Who? There's nobody here."

"If they killed her, then she was onto them. We should go somewhere secluded to talk."

Hudson pointed to his pickup truck in the school parking lot. "Why don't we go back to my place, and we can—"

"Do I look stupid? A burly stranger invites a cute teenage boy to his home is the opening scene to a million crime dramas."

"Trust me, you're not that cute."

“I am not going anywhere with you.”

Hudson took a deep breath and exhaled slowly. “Can we meet at the Miss Wanigas Diner? It’s a public space where there will be plenty of witnesses to your murder.”

“Was that a joke?” Reggie asked with exaggerated astonishment.

“If you meet me there in ten minutes, you’ll find out.”

CHAPTER 7

Hudson sipped his black coffee and stared out the dirt-streaked window of the Miss Wanigas Diner.

"Can I get you a refill?" asked the dark-haired waitress standing next to his booth.

He nodded and slid his half-empty mug towards her.

"Can I get you something to eat?" She asked as she filled his mug. "We have all day breakfast."

"No, thanks," he replied, still staring out the window.

"Are you waiting for someone?"

"Yeah."

"If she doesn't show, *I* can keep you company," she said with a smile before moving to the next booth to take their order.

From his seat at the window, Hudson could see everyone coming before they entered the diner, so when Reggie appeared beside him, he almost spilled his hot coffee.

"How did you...?" He looked behind Reggie as if he was looking for the teleporter.

Reggie slid onto the bench opposite Hudson. "I came in the back."

"Why...? Never mind. Can you please tell me what is going on? How did you know my wife, and what did she have inside her?"

The waitress returned and smiled at Reggie.

"Would *you* like something to eat or drink?" she asked, placing two menus on the table.

"Hello...Caitlin," Reggie read on her name tag, his gaze lingering on her plunging neckline.

"Did you want a burger or something?" Hudson asked. "I'm buying."

After tearing his gaze from Caitlin's ample bosom, Reggie looked at the menu.

"Do you have anything *not* deep fried?"

"We have a hot beef sandwich or a cheeseburger..."

"I'm a vegetarian."

"A grilled cheese?" she suggested.

"I'm lactose intolerant."

"Toast with jam?"

"Is it gluten-free?"

"This is a diner, not a health food emporium. How about a salad?"

"Do you have a couscous salad?"

"We have Ceasar or garden."

"I'll take a garden salad with low-fat raspberry vinaigrette. You *do* have low-fat dressings, right?"

"Of course."

Hudson couldn't tell if she was being serious or sarcastic.

"I'll have some pancakes and sausage," he said.

She took the menus and smiled at Hudson. "Thank you. It'll be a few minutes."

"That chick was hot," said Reggie after she left. "But I think she was into you more than me."

"I can't imagine why."

"If I had muscles like yours, I bet she would be *so* into me," he said and flexed his skinny biceps.

"I'm sure she would, Reggie. Now focus! Tell me what you know."

"Right!" Reggie broke from his mini daydream and looked at Hudson. "It's a bit of a long story."

"Then you should get started right away."

Reggie took a breath and began. "I often browse certain chat rooms and various social media sites. I have a *lot* of friends and followers. Some things we talk about are the latest Python modules or coding exploits."

"What are those?"

"Its just hacker speak. Don't worry about it. My other passion is uncovering the truth behind things like the corrupt authoritarian socialist world government, the International Economics Congress and the Great Reset."

"Wow! Paranoid much? Get to the part where my wife enters the picture."

"On one of those forums was a discussion about how there are trackers in the vaccines that..."

"Hold the phone there, Fox Mulder. Do you have any idea how ridiculous that sounds? If the government wanted to track us, wouldn't it be easier to use our phones? Aren't they already doing that, anyway?"

"Possibly. There could be other reasons for a tracker. All I know is that people like your wife and myself believed it was true. Videos were going around that showed people using magnets to detect the implants in their arms."

Hudson folded his arms and leaned back. "This I have to see. Let me see you stick a magnet to your arm."

"I tried, but it didn't work on me. Only certain people can get a magnet to stick to their arms."

"That's impossible."

"Your wife tried it, and it worked."

"How do you know?"

"She told me."

Hudson adjusted his position in the booth. "What are you talking about?"

"Elephant, zero, five, eleven never uploaded photos or videos, but she insisted that the government implanted something in her arm."

"You mean some secret agent shot her with a dart gun or something?" His face contorted in an expression of disbelief.

"No, you idiot. The vaccine."

Hudson reached across the table and grabbed a handful of Reggie's hoodie. He pulled the teenager halfway across the table. "Don't *ever* call me an idiot," he growled.

"Hmm-mm." The waitress cleared her throat as she approached the table.

He released his grip, and Reggie fell back to his seat.

"Here's your water," Caitlin said with a nervous smile. "I'll be back in a few minutes with your food."

"Sorry." Reggie smoothed his wrinkled hoodie. "Don't take things so personally. I'm just tired of people being so ignorant about what is really going on in the world. People believe anything the government says. *Covid is deadly, so everyone stay home. Don't go to work. Don't go to school. Don't go to church. Wear a mask. Take the vaccine. Take the booster. Take another booster.* Where does it stop? How far can the government go before people question their motives? This is supposed to be a free country, not an authoritarian—"

"Stop!" Hudson's deep voice resonated through the diner.

Some customers turned to look.

Hudson lowered his voice. "You are worse than my wife with the crazy conspiracy theories."

"Unlike some sheeple, she understood the truth about—"

"You're veering off course again." Hudson held up his hand as if stopping traffic. "Tell me about my wife. Did she really find a tracker in her arm?"

"She said when she placed a rare earth magnet on her shoulder, there was some pull."

"And then what?"

"And then nothing." Reggie held up his arms. "That was her last entry. I never heard from her again. I tried contacting her and even used my elite hacking skills to track her, but all I found was that she was local. When I saw the elephant sticker on your mop, I took a chance that you might be Elephant, zero, five, eleven. Why *did* she use an elephant as her handle?"

Hudson put his head in his hands and stared down at the table.

Reggie spoke again, but this time in a quiet tone. "I heard she died of Covid. Did—?"

"Before she died," Hudson interrupted, "Sophie said she *took it out.*"

"Took what out?"

"I have no idea." Hudson's eyes widened, and he held out his hands. "I assumed she was talking gibberish from the drugs."

Reggie leaned forward and whispered. "Was there a mark on her arm?"

"There was a cut. Her last words were talk to pretzel six, sixty-six."

Reggie pointed at himself. "That's me! I knew it! What else did she say?"

"Not much..."

"Gentlemen." Caitlin stood at the table with a plate in one hand and a bowl in the other. "One vegetable salad with raspberry vinaigrette and one order of pancakes."

She placed their food on the table. "Let me know if there's anything else you need."

After she left, Reggie asked. "That's it? She said nothing about the tracker or—"

"I don't think so..." He forked a sausage and took a bite.

"What about the cut on her arm? What did she say about that?"

"Nothing. I didn't ask."

"How could you not ask? You're sitting at her bedside. You see a bandage on her arm, but you don't—"

"They wouldn't let me into the hospital," he snarled. "As I watched her die on my tablet, it never occurred to me to inquire about her bandaged arm!"

Reggie took a tentative bite of lettuce. "Sorry, I didn't mean to..."

"Don't worry about it."

Nothing was said for the next few minutes as they ate their food. Reggie broke the silence. "Do you realize how huge this is? She had proof of a tracker in her arm. We should go public with this."

"With what? There's no proof – no evidence of anything."

"What if you request an autopsy? If they exhumed her body and checked her arm."

"Even if they found a scar on her arm, it isn't proof of anything. Besides, the moron at the funeral home cremated her."

"What do you mean, moron?"

"I asked to see her one last time, but they cremated her before I got there."

"That's strange."

"You know what else is strange?" Hudson pointed a fry at him. "On my way out of the funeral home, I met Ursala. She was Sophie's nurse at the hospital, and she told me about the cut on Sophie's shoulder."

"And you didn't find that strange?"

Hudson shrugged. "I guess, but I figured she cut herself at work or while slicing carrots or something."

"How do you cut your shoulder by accident?"

"Wait!" Hudson held up a forkful of syrupy pancake. "Now I remember! Right before she died, Sophie said *it's where we first met under the...*"

"Under what?"

"I don't know. She was struggling to breathe...there was an oxygen mask and..."

Reggie dropped his fork. "She found the tracker, cut it out and hid it!"

"I don't know." Hudson stared into space, thinking.

"Even if you don't believe in her crazy conspiracy theories, you have to admit the evidence is stacking up like your refined carb pancakes! On her deathbed, she tells you she cut something out and put it somewhere. A nurse confirms she had a cut on her arm. Then she dies, and the coroner cremates your wife before you get to inspect the body."

Hudson nodded. "It *does* sound strange."

"Well?"

"Well, what?"

"Well, where did you first meet?"

Hudson pulled out two wrinkled twenties, set them on the table and stood up.

Reggie's mouth hung open. "Where are you going?"

"It was nice meeting you. Thanks for talking with me."

CHAPTER 8

Outside Miss Wanigas Diner, Hudson got in his truck and turned the key. The six-cylinder engine roared to life, and the muffler let out a puff of black smoke before the engine calmed down.

He moved the shifter in reverse and let off the brake, and the passenger door opened.

"You can't leave without me." Reggie hopped beside the reversing vehicle, trying to jump in.

"Yes, I can. Get out of my truck."

"Stop!" Reggie demanded as he awkwardly tried to get his second foot through the open door while the truck was still backing up. When Hudson shifted into drive, Reggie almost made it inside the vehicle. Instead, he fell but desperately clung to the inside door handle. Both feet dragged for several feet before his grip slipped, and he fell to the road.

Hudson accelerated and drove half a block before stopping. He looked behind him and watched Reggie stand up and flip him the middle finger.

Hudson reached over and closed the passenger door before driving away.

It took him less than ten minutes to reach the bridge over Wanigas River. He crossed it and drove down a short stretch of road before pulling into Legan Shipping Company. The sprawling warehouse edged onto the river on one side and an extensive park on the other splayed out from the other. Hudson drove past the entrance along a short laneway past the loading docks and parked on a large, empty concrete pad. Beyond the pad, an asphalt trail ran parallel to the river. A short pathway led from the pad to a fire training tower.

He leaned his head back and sighed as he membered a summer evening eleven years ago.

Before Sophie died.

Before Covid.

Before they were married.

Before they had even met.

It was a hot, late summer evening when a younger, happier Hudson jogged on the river trail. Rivulets of sweat dribbled down his face and he panted heavily as his feet pounded the asphalt trail. The river looked enticing, and he considered veering off the trail and jumping in. However, the river was not a chocolate brown colour because it flowed with a sweet liquid confection, and he continued running.

He was only halfway along his regular loop, but it was exceptionally hot, and he was not sure if he could complete it. With teeth gritted, he pushed forward, ignoring the slight nausea in his stomach.

The world spun, and he careened off the path, stumbling and landing face-first in the grass. The world darkened, and he passed out.

When he awoke, an angelic vision of a woman in a large, black firefighter's helmet looked down at him. Her bright honey eyes twinkled in the late afternoon sun.

"Can you hear me?" she asked.

"Have I died and gone to heaven?" he croaked.

Her laugh caused the butterflies in his stomach to take flight. "No, you are suffering from heat exhaustion."

She propped him up with surprising strength.

"I'm okay," he said, rubbing the sweat from his eyes.

"Drink," she ordered and held out a water bottle.

The cool water slid down his dry throat, and he finished the bottle greedily.

"I'm sorry." He handed the empty bottle back to her. "I finished your water."

"That's okay." Her face glowed with a smile.

Hudson stood up slowly.

"You shouldn't get up yet..." she began, but he was already on his feet.

He wavered for a moment until the world stopped spinning and then held out his hand.

"I'm Hudson."

Her hand was as hot and sweaty as his and almost as calloused. Unlike most women he met, her grip was firm.

He looked at her with a puzzled expression. She wore a heavy tan firefighter's coat with reflective stripes, matching trousers and black rubber boots. Leather gloves hung from her pocket.

"Where's the fire?" he asked.

She removed her helmet, revealing long, blond, shimmering hair. The butterflies in his stomach fluttered wildly like they were escaping a raging inferno.

"There's no fire," she said.

"Do you always walk around on hot summer days like this? If I collapsed from heat exhaustion in my shorts, you must be on fire in that outfit."

She pointed to the tower behind her. "I'm training."

The four-story firefighter training tower was about twenty feet square and sixty feet tall. The first fifteen feet were concrete blocks, and the rest was steel siding. An opening at each level exposed the stairway inside.

"What is that?"

"It's a fire training tower," she said.

"You climb to the top in all your gear?"

"That's right. I also carry a 58-pound hose bundle."

"Impressive." He looked around. "Where's everybody else?"

"My physical performance test is next week. I came here to practice."

"I jog past here almost every day, and I always wondered what it was."

"Did you want to check it out?"

He would gladly follow her into an active volcano of hot lava. "For sure! Can we go to the top?"

He followed her to the steel door, and they stepped inside.

She stopped at the bottom of the stairs. "Are you sure you're okay to climb all these stairs?"

"I'm fine," he said as he started up. "I'm training too."

"What are *you* training for?" she asked as they ascended the steps.

"I have a boxing championship match in two weeks."

"You're a boxer?"

He turned and smiled at her. "You should come to see me fight sometime."

"I'd like that."

"Race you to the top!"

They spent the next two hours talking at the top of the tower. A year later, he proposed, and they married the following spring.

It seemed like a lifetime ago, but it was ingrained in his memory like it was yesterday. Hudson got out of the car, walked to the training tower and looked up.

The orange glow of the setting sun still glimmered on the treetops. He shook the rusty padlock on the metal door and sighed. After retrieving a rock bigger than a boxing glove, he smashed the lock and stepped inside.

The darkness seemed to envelop him. Hudson fumbled with his cell phone till he found the flashlight app. A mouse squeaked his displeasure at the intruder and skittered away. Floating dust particles sparkled in the cone of light from his phone.

The walk up the four flights seemed to take longer than he remembered. His footsteps echoed loudly on the metal grating as if reminding him he was alone.

At the top, the last vestige of sunlight glistened above the four-foot wall. Graffiti and jackknife etchings covered the unpainted vertical spruce planks on three sides. He looked around, but there was nothing on the metal floor. No 58-pound fire hose, no bottles from partying teens, no blankets from a homeless bed, and no discarded needles. Also, there was no Sophie laughing that her firefighting gear gave her an unfair disadvantage in their race to the top.

He sank to the floor and cried.

It was a mistake coming here. Reliving old memories was like removing a scab. The newly opened wound spilling fresh blood. What was he expecting to find? For Sophie, conspiracy theories were an obsessive hobby. He adored her and never criticized her absurd speculations. But he never let himself get sucked into her wacky world of paranoid delusions. Now he was here because of drug-induced mumbled rambling and some kid that shared her penchant for deluded fantasies.

Through a blur of tears, he saw a fresh drawing of an elephant on a plank near the corner.

Sophie was not an artist or a painter. Their losing streak at Christmas Pictionary was proof of that. However, she had taught herself how to draw a cartoonish depiction of a baby elephant. He blinked away the tears and leaned forward. His fingers slid across the black marks on the rough wood. It *was* her distinctive pachyderm caricature.

The plank moved slightly. He pushed it, and the wood rattled in place. He clawed at the side and pried it off. On a small two-by-four shelf inside, he found a small metal peppermint tin. He picked it up. It felt light as if there was nothing inside, but when he opened it, he saw something. Although it was difficult to see in the fading sunlight, he saw something. It was not much larger than a grain of wild rice. He held it close and squinted. It *wasn't* a piece of long-grain basmati.

Voices startled him, and he almost dropped the tin. He stood up and looked out of the tower, almost expecting to see a man in a black suit with a bulge the size of a pistol under his jacket striding towards him. He was becoming as paranoid as Sophie.

Instead, he watched two women speed walking along the river trail.

With the tin safely stuffed into his pocket, he descended the stairs and returned to his truck.

CHAPTER 9

Hudson turned on the pickup truck lights as he pulled into the Happy Valley Mobile Home Community. His headlight beams stabbed the late evening darkness, and the tires crackled on the gravel drive as he rolled to the back of the trailer park. When he swung into his lot, the beams illuminated a dark figure standing outside his double-wide trailer.

He parked his truck and shut off the engine.

"What are you doing here?" he asked.

"Did you find it?" A single fluorescent bulb mounted above the trailer door dimly lit Reggie's head, but his face was bright with anticipation.

Hudson stepped out of the truck. "Are you stalking me now?"

"Maybe. Why are your eyes red?"

"How do you know where I live?"

Reggie waved him off. "That was easy. I accessed the school employment records and found your address."

Hudson continued past him and unlocked the door. "Isn't it past your bedtime?"

"I'm assuming by your deflections that you found something," said Reggie, following him inside.

Hudson flicked the light on and bee-lined it to the fridge. "I'd offer you a beer, but I'm assuming you're too young to drink."

"Alcohol is toxic to your liver, cancer-causing and—"

"How about some milk?"

"I'm lactose intolerant, remember?"

Hudson cracked open his beer and leaned against the counter. "Help yourself to some water."

"Do you know if your copper pipes have lead solder in them?"

"Probably."

"Never mind, I'm not thirsty."

Hudson grunted and sat at the small dining room table. "Do your parents know you're here?"

"I texted I was out with friends, but my father doesn't care."

Reggie studied the framed pictures on the wall. "Is this her?"

"Yes, that's Sophie."

"Dude! She's hot!"

Hudson debated whether to punch the kid or thank him.

"That's my dead wife you're talking about."

"I know, but she was a serious ten. You really lucked out."

"Thanks, I think."

"What's with the elephant figurines?" Reggie asked, poking at the baubles on a small shelf.

"Don't touch those. She collected elephants."

"Oh."

"Promise not to freak out," said Hudson, setting down his beer and reaching into his pocket.

"No way!" Reggie swivelled around. His jaw hung open as Hudson placed the metal box on the table.

"What is that?"

Hudson opened the tin. "I found this."

"I knew it!" Reggie yelled. He pushed his glasses up his nose and leaned close. "That is a freakin' tracking capsule that your wife cut out of her arm!"

"Back the conspiracy truck up a bit. We don't know what it is."

"Oh, come on! We know exactly what it is." He reached down towards the tin.

"Don't touch it!"

"Where was it?" Reggie asked.

"At the fire training tower."

"That's where you met?"

"Yeah." Hudson took another gulp of beer.

"Were you a firefighter or something?"

"No. She was."

Reggie leaned back. "Whoa! She was a hot and a firefighter!"

Hudson slammed his bottle down hard. Beer erupted from the top and splashed on the table. Reggie jumped back.

"Stop talking about Sophie!" Hudson yelled.

They both stared at the puddle of foamy beer in silence for a moment.

"Sorry," Reggie squeaked. "I didn't mean to..."

"Yeah," Hudson grunted.

After another brief silence, Reggie tentatively reached into his pocket and pulled out his phone.

"What are you doing?" Hudson asked.

"I'm trying to get a better look." Reggie pointed his phone at the tin and zoomed in.

"Let me see." Hudson moved out of his seat and looked over Reggie's shoulder.

They both leaned forward and squinted at the screen.

A flash of light swept across the trailer window, accompanied by the unmistakable sound of a vehicle rolling into Hudson's drive.

Reggie closed the tin. "They're here!"

Hudson held out his hands and shrugged. "*Who's* here?"

"The men in black," Reggie said with wide eyes. "They know about the tracker."

Hudson spread the blinds open and watched two men exit a dark blue SUV parked behind his truck. "It doesn't look like Will Smith and Tommy Lee Jones."

Both men wore dark suits, although it was difficult to decipher what colour through the dark night. The man in the lead wore a fedora.

"That's weird," said Hudson. "I've seen that man before."

"Where?" asked Reggie.

"At the hospital, when Sophie died and again at the funeral home."

"Are you sure it's the same guy?" Reggie stood up and joined Hudson at the window.

"I think so. He's wearing that same stupid hat."

"What do we do?"

Hudson went to the front door and turned the lock. "Do you have the tin?" he whispered.

Reggie patted his jean pocket and nodded.

Three sharp knocks seemed to vibrate the entire trailer. Hudson held his finger up before rushing to the bedroom. He reached under the bed, pulled out a black backpack and swung it over his shoulder.

"Mr. Finlay?" said a gravelly voice outside the door.

"Who is it?" Hudson replied as he walked to the rear of the trailer and knelt in front of a small table filled with books.

"We're investigating your wife's death and have a couple of questions."

"What agency are you with?" Hudson slid the bookshelf over and pulled at the wall panelling.

"The...um...hospital," said the man outside. "This is a routine investigation. Can you please just open the door so we can talk?"

Hudson removed the panel, revealing a hatch the size of a bar fridge. "I'm coming. Let me get my pants on first."

Reggie leaned down and stared at the hatch. "Where does—?"

"Go!" Hudson mouthed the words and pointed.

After a brief hesitation, Reggie crawled through the hatch and dropped to the grass below. Hudson handed him the black backpack and followed. They crawled under the side of the trailer before emerging out the back. Reggie followed Hudson as he shimmied along the trailer and peered around the corner.

"Where are we—?" Reggie whispered before Hudson quickly shushed him.

The two men said something that Hudson couldn't decipher. Through the darkness, the men appeared to be brandishing weapons.

There was a loud crash as Fedora man kicked in Hudson's front door. As soon as the two men burst inside, Hudson ran to his truck, and Reggie followed.

Reggie walked around to the passenger door, while Hudson unlocked the truck box. He pulled out a leather sheath with a hunting knife.

"What are you doing?" Reggie asked in a panicked whisper.

Hudson moved furtively to the blue SUV and stabbed at the front tire.

Suddenly, fedora man stepped out of the trailer. His imposing silhouette stood motionless for a moment.

Hudson froze beside the SUV.

"I found something," said a muffled voice from within the trailer. "I think he went out the back."

As soon as Fedora man returned inside, Hudson ran back to the truck and hopped inside. Reggie joined him and set the backpack on the seat between them.

"Ready?" asked Hudson.

Reggie nodded furiously. Hudson turned the key, and the engine roared to life. The tires spun, sending gravel into the SUV behind them. He drove onto the grass as the two men exploded out of the trailer. The truck's back end fish-tailed on the dewy grass as Hudson flung the wheel hard to the left.

Reggie struggled to slide on his seatbelt as the truck bumped along the grass till they hit the gravel road. The truck tires launched more stones and dust into the darkness behind them as Hudson sped away.

"That was crazy!" Reggie looked out the rear window.

"Are they following us?" Hudson asked, spinning the truck around the corner.

Reggie turned to look and saw headlights swing onto the road behind them. "I think so! What are we going to do?"

"Hang on." Hudson slammed on the gas pedal, and the truck flew out of the trailer park onto the paved road.

The tire screeched, and the back end swung out till he straightened the truck and sped down the dark road towards the city.

"They're still behind us," yelled Reggie.

The SUV bounced out of the trailer park and turned onto the road. At first, it seemed like the SUV might catch up to them. But then the rubber on the front slashed tire thumped loudly on the pavement. The rubber shredded and flew off the rim. A bright shower of sparks lit up the moonless night. The SUV shuddered, then careened into the ditch.

"They're gone!" Reggie pumped his fist. "We did it. I can't believe we did it. That was awesome! It was also crazy terrifying. Who were those guys? Do you think they wanted to kill us? I'm shaking. Are you shaking? I talk when I'm nervous. Where are we going now?"

"Take a breath, Reggie."

He inhaled and exhaled in rapid succession.

Hudson shook his head. "Breath slowly. In through the nose - out through the mouth."

Reggie tried with moderate success to control his breathing. He grabbed the black backpack and unzipped it.

"What's in the bag?"

"It's a bug-out bag."

"I've heard of these," said Reggie, unzipping it. "They're in case of a zombie apocalypse or alien invasion, right?"

"Something like that."

"Cool! Are these air tags? Whoa, that's a lot of cash."

"Do you always go through other people's stuff?" Hudson tried to grab the bag, but Reggie moved it out of reach.

"Ew! Why do you have tampons?"

Hudson leaned over and yanked the bag out of his hands. "Gimmie that!"

He held the wheel with his knee and zipped it closed.

"It was Sophie's," he said setting the bag beside him. "She insisted we have one just in case. I kept it when I moved out of the hours, but more for sentimental reasons than anything else." He cast an accusatory glare at Reggie. "Did you take any of the money?"

"Pffft! I don't need your money."

"Where are we going?" Reggie asked, staring out the window.

"I'm taking you home."

"Home? Shouldn't we plan our next move or something?"

He pulled the tin out of his pocket. "We need to figure out what this is."

"Not tonight. I've put you in enough danger for one day. Where do you live?"

"365 Medina Heights," Reggie answered.

"Oh."

Hudson recognized the street name as one of a few streets on the south end of town featuring opulent mansions and sprawling estates.

The road from Happy Valley Mobile Home Community was dark and quiet until they reached Wanigas city limits. Ten minutes later, the quiet country road gave way to the myriad of streetlights, other cars and businesses of downtown Wanigas. Eventually, they drove through town to quiet, winding Medina Heights Road.

"What are you going to do?" Reggie asked. "You can't go home."

"I guess I'll stay at a motel or something."

"Why don't you stay at my place?"

"Sorry, kid," Hudson said, smiling. "I think I'm a little too old for a sleepover."

"You'll be safe at my place," Reggie insisted. "You can stay in the guest house."

"The guesthouse?"

Reggie pointed ahead. "Up here on the left."

A long 10-foot stone wall ran parallel to the road. Two ornate wrought-iron gates guarded the entrance.

"Two, three, five, seven, eleven." Reggie pointed at the keypad mounted on a metal stand in front of the gates.

Hudson drove up, rolled down his window and keyed in the numbers. "Do you live in a gated community?"

"No, this is my place," Reggie said as the gates creaked open.

"Wow."

Neatly trimmed dogwoods lined the long drive to the three-storey limestone mansion. The Victorian-style home featured canted bay windows, ornate gables and a varying array of steeply pitched roofs that poked into the night sky. To the right, a short drive led to a wide garage with four bay doors. To the left, the road disappeared behind a sprawling, weeping willow.

Hudson drove up to the concrete staircase that led to a hefty oak door entrance.

"The guesthouse is behind the willow," said Reggie. "I'll have the maid bring you dinner."

"What's your last name, Reggie?" Hudson asked.

Reggie pulled the door handle and opened the door. "Hargreaves," he answered.

"You're *that* Hargreaves?" Hudson raised his eyebrows. "The CEO of Nanotech?"

"Yep." He handed Hudson the tin. "Don't go anywhere without me tomorrow."

CHAPTER 10

"Where have you been, young man?" asked Lawrence Hargreaves. "It's past midnight."

He loosened his navy-blue necktie and gave Reggie a stern look.

Reggie closed the large wooden door behind him. "Since when do you care, Dad?"

"Answer the question," he demanded.

"I was out with friends."

His father looked over his shoulder as if he could see through the door. "Who was that in the truck?"

"A friend. I told him he could stay at the guest house. A couple of goons broke into his place."

"What were you two doing?"

"What's with the sudden interest in my life? You're gone almost all the time. Now you want—"

"You know I'm busy at work. I have thousands of employees worldwide that—"

"Yes, I know. I've heard this speech a million times. People depend on you, and you have responsibilities. What's your point?"

"My point is, I don't always have time to hold your hand and walk you to school or take you out for ice cream after you get an 'A' on your exam."

Reggie rolled his eyes. "No father holds their teenage son's hand and takes them to school and I'm lactose intolerant. Of course, you would know that because *you're my father*."

Mr. Hargreaves grabbed Reggie by the collar. "You need to learn to respect your father."

He pulled his hand back as if to strike him.

Reggie held out his chin defiantly. "Do it! Smack me around. You think everyone is subordinate to you. All your employees show you respect and deference. If they don't, you simply fire them, but I don't work for you."

"I'm your father!" he shouted. "I deserve your respect!"

Reggie shook away from his father's grasp. "And I'm your son and I deserve your love, but you love your job more than me. I wish my mother was here because you're a pathetic excuse for a father."

Lawrence Hargreaves swung his right hand fast. It impacted Reggie's face with a smack that seemed to echo across the cavernous entryway.

"Don't speak to me like that and don't *ever* say that I don't love you! I raised you, I put a roof over your head. I put food on your table. I remember when you were a little boy..." His voice cracked, and he swallowed.

"I'm not a little boy anymore." Reggie rubbed his aching chin. "And if this is how you show your love, I don't want it!"

He stomped up the wide staircase, but his heavy footsteps barely made a sound on the soft silk carpet and thick oak treads.

"I'm sorry, Reggie," his father called after him. "I've had a long day and..."

Reggie heard little else as he stamped down the hallway to his room. The door slammed shut with a satisfying crash.

He dove face-first into his bed, pounding his fists into the mattress. Tears spilled from his eyes.

Twenty minutes later, he sat on the edge of his bed and wiped his tear-stained cheek, then reached under his bed and pulled out a half-empty bag of pretzels. He breathed slowly – in through the nose and out through the mouth and nibbled on a pretzel. That's when he remembered Hudson was in the guest house.

He stood up abruptly and left his room. In the hallway, he stopped and listened. His father's deep muffled voice sounded like it was coming from somewhere downstairs. He continued through the hallway and down the stairs. In the kitchen, he found the maid.

She offered him a pained smile. "Are you okay? Does it hurt? Can I get you some ice?"

"No, thanks, Maria. Is there anything to eat?"

"There's some vegan stew in the fridge. Your father ate all the kale salad, but I can make you some more if you like."

"Nah, the stew is fine."

She opened the fridge, pulled out the dish, and spooned out a generous portion into a bowl.

"Can I get a second bowl? I have a friend staying overnight in the guest house."

After she microwaved the food, Reggie took them and the utensils and headed to the back door. Along the way, he heard his father talking in his study. He slowed as he walked by the partially open door.

"I know," his father said. "I will find out if he has it in the morning. He's not going anywhere tonight."

His father paused as the person on the other end of the phone spoke before talking again.

"It doesn't matter. It's a tracker, so we can track it. He's my son! He's not going to...Hang on a second..."

His father's dress shoes clacked on the hardwood as he walked towards the door. Reggie quickly turned and walked around the corner. Behind him, the study door locked.

He continued to the back door and outside to the guest house.

The cool autumn air felt refreshing as he crunched through the fallen leaves in the darkened backyard. Since both hands each carried a bowl, he knocked on the guest house door with his foot.

Hudson opened the door. He still had his shoes on, and everything in the small room remained untouched. The pillows on the couch sat neatly in the position where Maria had set them, and the bedsheets were still neatly tucked under the mattress. Even the floor looked clean.

"Are your parents' home? I should talk to them about staying here..."

"Don't worry about it." Reggie set the bowls on the small dining table. "I already told my dad."

"Are you okay?" Hudson leaned forward, looking at Reggie's face. "You look like you've been crying, and your chin is purple."

Reggie pulled out two spoons from his pocket, set them on the table and slid out a chair. "I'm fine. Sit down and eat. Maria makes the best lentil stew, and you must be starving."

"This doesn't feel right." Hudson paced beside the table. "I shouldn't be here."

Reggie dug into his stew. "What are you talking about? Those guys probably trashed your place. Where else could you go?"

"I don't know. A hotel or something?"

"What's wrong with this place?"

"It seems awkward for a grown man to have a sleepover at a teenager's house."

"I'm assuming by your current level of housing and your employment as a janitor at the school, that you are not as financially stable as my family is."

"I lost my job during Covid and the janitor's job at the school is barely a paying job. That's hardly my fault."

Reggie swallowed another mouthful. "I never said it was. All I'm saying is that you can't afford to stay at a hotel and this place is free."

Hudson sighed, pulled out the chair, and sat down. "I'm not poor."

"Of course not," said Reggie.

Hudson picked up a spoon and took a scoop of stew. After a few swallows, his face soured.

"What is this?"

"Curried tomato lentil stew. It's great, isn't it? I think it's the fresh cilantro that gives it that citrusy flavour."

"Where's the beef chunks?"

"This is a vegan dish."

"Hmm."

"What's your issue with vegans?"

"I have no problem with vegans." Hudson sloshed his spoon through the colourful dish. "Cows are vegans too."

Reggie finished his stew and sat up. "What are we going to

do tomorrow? We have to find someone who can look at our tracking capsule up close."

"*We* are not doing anything. *You* are going to school. If I find out anything about what we found, I'll let you know."

"You can't push me out of this."

"I don't want you involved. After last night…I don't want you in danger."

"It's too late for that. I heard my father talking. He knows about the tracker."

Hudson's dropped his spoon on the table. "What?"

"I heard him speaking with someone on the phone. He's looking for the tracker and he knows I have it."

"How is that possible? Did you tell him something?"

"I didn't tell him anything, but I think he's involved."

Hudson shook his head. "His company made this didn't it? I knew Nanotech was a high-tech company, but I thought they were into software and networks and stuff."

"They're into a lot of things, including pharmaceuticals, biotech and even private military."

Hudson looked suspiciously out the window. "Is he going to send someone to kill me while I sleep?"

Reggie smiled. "Now you're almost as paranoid as a conspiracy theorist."

"I'm serious." Hudson's brows furrowed. "Am I in danger?"

"You recovered a top-secret injectable tracking device, and two henchmen broke into your trailer. Of course, you're in danger."

Hudson stood up and peered out the window into the dark night. "I should leave."

"My father has lots of secrets and is a very dangerous man, but he does not make rash decisions. He is a clever, patient man. He doesn't know if we have the tracker, and I think he'll watch and wait till we are off his property before he makes a move."

"What about you? Are you in danger?"

"He would never hurt his own family."

Hudson raised his eyebrows. "Are you sure about that?"

Reggie rubbed his chin. "He can be a little rough sometimes, but he would never really hurt me."

CHAPTER 11

At 5 o'clock the next morning, Hudson woke in the guest house slightly confused until he remembered he was in the Hargreave's guest house. Before Reggie woke and offered him non-fat yoghurt with fruit, Hudson got into his truck and drove into town. He headed straight to the Wanigas diner where he ordered the Michigan Big Breakfast special. After three eggs, two bacon strips, three sausage links, two slices of peameal bacon, home fries, toast, orange juice and a cup of coffee, he finally satiated his appetite.

Afterwards, Hudson drove to the Wanigas Private Academy. Few students were at school this early, and only a few teachers and staff showed up before 7 o'clock in the morning. He looked around for anyone following him before climbing the steps into the school.

"Good morning, Mr. Finlay," said the math teacher, Mrs. Janes.

Hudson smiled and continued to the stairwell. He climbed to the third floor, walked down the hallway and turned into another corridor before he found what he was looking for.

He pulled out a massive cluster of keys from his pocket and unlocked the science lab door. Inside, he located a black and white microscope and pulled out his tin. After carefully removing the capsule from the tin, Hudson tried to place it on the microscope. However, there was no place to put it. Then he remembered he was supposed to use a glass slide. He searched five drawers before he found a blank one. He set the capsule on the slide and slid it under the lens. When he looked through the eyepiece, all he saw was blackness. He adjusted the focus ring but still could see nothing. Again, he adjusted the focus ring, but it became stuck and there was a cracking sound. The glass slide lay shattered on the table.

"What are you doing?" asked Mr. Gortsmeyer. The science teacher stood in the doorway in his bow tie and thick-rimmed glasses.

"Sorry...I was trying to see something...I think I broke your microscope...."

Mr. Gortsmeyer walked over. "It appears you have broken a slide. Let me help you. What are you trying to look at?"

"It's nothing. I found a little thing and..."

"If you're trying to see a little thing, then this *is* the instrument to use." He pointed to the capsule on the table amongst the shards of glass plate. "Is that what you're looking at?"

Hudson bit his lip. "Yeah."

"Hmm." Mr. Gortsmeyer reached into a drawer and pulled out a set of small tools and a glass slide. After putting on his glasses, he used a tiny pair of tweezers to pick up the capsule and gently place it on the slide. After rolling the lens back up, he placed the slide underneath and pressed a button on the bottom. A bright light illuminated the slide from below.

"Okay, let's see what we've got here." He peered into the eyepiece and adjusted the course focus and then the fine focus.

"There." He stepped back and pointed at the microscope. "Take a look."

Hudson leaned over and looked through the eyepiece.

A small copper-coloured cube sat on top of a slightly larger shiny black cube. No letters, no numbers, no wires, no markings. Just two different coloured cubes.

"What is it?" asked Hudson.

"I was going to ask you the same question. Where did you find it?"

"Is it possible for someone to inject this into someone?"

"Injected? How?" He removed his glasses and let them hang from their silver chain around his neck.

"With a needle – like the ones they used to inject the Covid vaccine."

"That's an odd question."

"Sorry, I guess that's stupid, right?"

"Absolutely not! I always tell my students there are no stupid questions. Like Albert Einstein said, 'The important thing is not to stop questioning.'"

Mr. Gortsmeyer reached into another drawer and pulled a digital vernier caliper. He put his glasses back on and carefully used the tweezers to place the tracker inside the vernier's jaws.

"Hmm...this is just over two millimetres or just over three thirty seconds of an inch. A hypodermic needle for injecting is probably between 22 and 25 gauge which is *less* than a millimetre, so no, I don't think this would fit through the shaft."

"But is it possible with a larger needle?"

Mr. Gortsmeyer held up his glasses as if they helped him think. "Perhaps, if you used a 12-gauge needle, but those are for intramuscular or subcutaneous injections, not vaccines."

"So, it's possible?"

"Yes, but what is this? Where did you get it and why do you want to inject it?"

"One more question, Mr. Gortsmeyer. If it were injected into someone without their knowledge, could it harm them?"

"Possibly. It could cause an infection. You're not considering injecting this, are you?"

"No."

Hudson heard the rumble of the school bus's diesel engine outside.

"The kids are here." Mr. Gortsmeyer walked to the window and looked outside as the bus hissed to a stop. "I have to get ready for class—hey they can't park there. That's the bus unloading zone."

Hudson joined him at the window and looked out. In front of the bus, a blue SUV sat parked in front of the *no parking* sign. The car was tilted at a strange angle towards the front driver's side tire, which was smaller than the others. Two men in suits stepped out. One of them wore a grey fedora.

"I have to go too."

Hudson swept the tracker back into the tin and shoved it in his pocket. "Thanks for your help, Mr. Gortsmeyer."

Before the science teacher could respond, Hudson was already flying out the door. He raced through the hallway and down the stairs. His face scrunched into a fierce mask of determination. As he marched towards the front door, Reggie intercepted him.

"You need to go back." Reggie held out his hands as if to stop him. "They're here. We have to run."

"I'm not running," he said, still staring and walking forward.

"What's going on? Why do you look like you're about to rip someone's head off?"

"Because I am."

"What's going on? What happened?"

"They *are* involved in Sophie's death, and I intend to find out how and I'm going to hurt them."

"There are two of them and only one of you." Reggie adjusted his backpack and struggled to keep up with Hudson's ardent strides.

"I like those odds."

"That sounds like a cheesy superhero movie quote, but this is the real world and those are—"

"Good morning, Mr. Fin—" Principal Justine's glowing smile fell when she saw the fire in Hudson's eyes. "Is everything okay?"

The man in the grey fedora and his companion burst through the front doors of the school.

Hudson stopped mid-stride as he and the men made eye contact. "I have some personal business to take care of."

"Who are they?" Principal Justine pointed to the two men. "Do you know them?"

"They are going to help me with an issue in the gym." He nodded at the men, before turning and walking down the hallway towards the auditorium.

"What issue?" she asked.

"Yeah, what issue?" Reggie chimed.

The two of them struggled to keep up with Hudson.

"It's about a mess in the gym," said Hudson as they reached the gym doors. "Please let those men in, but I need you to stay out till we complete our business."

Justine peered through the open door. “What mess?”

“Please stay out!” His piercing glare convinced both of them to comply.

The Wanigas Private Academy gymnasium doubled as a sports centre and an auditorium, with two basketball nets and a black curtained stage. Two girls practicing their jump shot looked up when Hudson entered.

“You two! Out of the gym now!” he yelled.

They dropped the basketball and ran to the doors on the opposite side of the gym as the ball rolled into a corner. Hudson grabbed two metal chairs from the stage and followed them. Once they were out, he stuck a leg of one chair through the door handles.

The other doors opened, and the two men padded in. With a chair in one hand, Hudson walked by them and locked the other doors with the chair.

The two men in dark blue suits waited in the centre circle with their hands at their sides.

“Good morning, Mr. Hudson Finlay,” said the tall man with the grey fedora. His tall, lean physique was contrasted with his partner’s shorter and bulkier frame.

“My name is Riker, and this is my associate Deltoid.” His soft voice was almost too smooth, with a slight northern European accent.

“I don’t care who you are. What did you do to my wife?”

“I heard about her,” said Riker. “My sincerest condolences on Sophie’s passing. That must have been—”

Hudson stepped within six feet of the men. Deltoid eyed him suspiciously.

“Don’t patronize me! You were there at the hospital. I saw you. What were you doing there?”

“She died of complications due to Covid. I didn’t kill her.”

“I don’t believe you.”

“Mr. Finlay, I never lie.”

“You still haven’t answered my question.” He took a step towards them. “What were you doing at the hospital when she died?”

“I was looking for something that she had which didn’t belong to her."

"Are you talking about the tracker you injected into her?"

"I did not inject her with anything. I am going to ask you one time: give it to me and no one will get hurt." He held out his hand.

"I don't have it." Hudson lied.

Riker pulled out his phone and tapped something on it. "You are *not* telling the truth."

He nodded to Deltoid. "Please search him."

Deltoid stepped towards Hudson. His bulging shoulders appeared to be holding up his head, bypassing the need for a neck. His massive frame appeared on the verge of exploding from his stretched suit.

Hudson shifted his stance with one foot slightly in front of the other and clenched his fist. As soon as Deltoid was within striking range, he swung an overhand right. The man attempted to dodge the punch, but a glancing blow jerked his chin to the left. Hudson followed up with a left jab to the stomach. The blow seemed to have little effect on the big man, who countered with a right hook. Hudson ducked and came back with an uppercut to his nose. Blood sprayed from Deltoid's face and he fell back, stunned.

Riker grabbed at Hudson, who swiped away his hand. He pulled the man two steps to the side before sweeping his right foot. The tall man fell with Hudson immediately straddling him.

"Tell me what happened to Sophie," Hudson barked.

"She snooped where she shouldn't have and got in over her head."

Hudson punched him hard twice – once with each fist.

"What did you do to her?!"

Riker blinked rapidly as if just waking up. "I did nothing to her."

"Liar!"

Just as he was about to lay into him again. Deltoid plowed in from the side charging like a football rusher. He tackled him off Riker, knocking his head on the glossy hardwood. He struggled to remain conscious as Deltoid's heavy body crushed him into the floor. Deltoid punched him twice in the side before Hudson snatched his forearm with both hands. With his legs wrapped around his opponent's arm and elbow, he squeezed his legs and pulled the arms towards him. Using Deltoid's chest as a fulcrum, he pulled the man's wrist to his chest in a classic arm bar. The elbow popped, and Deltoid screamed.

"Enough!" Riker yelled. He stood over both of them, pointing a black pistol at Hudson's head.

"Okay." Hudson let go and held his hands up. "Don't shoot."

Riker held out his free hand. "Give me the tracker and I'll let you live."

Deltoid writhed on the ground in agony.

Hudson stood up slowly. "Okay. I'm reaching into my pocket for it."

Riker stepped back as Hudson retrieved the tin from his pocket.

"Put it on the floor and step back."

Hudson did as he was told. Riker bent down and picked up the tin without taking his eyes or gun off him. He pulled out his phone and clicked on it before nodding.

"Thank you, Mr. Finlay." Then he turned to Deltoid. "Get up, you useless fool."

The two of them walked to the locked door the basketball girls had exited. Deltoid's arm dangled from the elbow, and blood still dripped from his nose. Riker removed the chair from the door and they left.

Hudson noticed the black curtain on the stage moving. "You can come out now!"

Reggie brushed the curtain aside and climbed off the stage. "That was awesome! You broke that guy's nose and arm!"

"It was just a dislocation." Hudson's shoulders slumped. "I also lost the tracker."

"Come on, let's go after them."

Hudson shook his head. "It's over. Go home, Reggie."

"That's it? You're just going to give up?"

"*I'm* not giving up, *you* are. This is way too dangerous for you, kid."

"But I can help," Reggie protested. "You need me."

"What I need is for you to go home and let me handle this."

Reggie crossed his arms. "Do you want to know where they went?"

"How do you know where they went?"

"I'm tracking them." Reggie held up his phone.

"What? How?"

"I used one of the air tags from your wife's bug-out bag."

"You stole my stuff?"

"I borrowed a tag. When I drove to school this morning, I saw the blue SUV with a gimpy tire and stuck a tag under the bumper."

"Oh - that's kind of impressive."

"Thank you," said Reggie with a smile.

Hudson pointed at the phone. "Are you going to tell me where they're going?"

"Are you going to let me come with you?"

"Not a chance."

"Okay, I'm going to follow them by myself." Reggie turned and walked to the door.

"Wait!" Hudson called after him. "I don't want you getting hurt. You can come with me, but you have to do what I say."

Reggie held his head in the air. "I suppose I can let you come with me."

"Don't get cocky."

CHAPTER 12

Reggie sat in the passenger seat with his backpack at his feet. He stared at his phone as they crossed the Wanigas River. "It looks like they're on I-75, going south."

"Why do you think they came after me *now*?" Hudson asked.

"What do you mean? They probably tracked you using the tracker in your pocket."

"But why didn't they find the tracker where Sophie hid it? Instead, they waited until I found it and then came after me?"

Reggie looked up from his phone. "It could be like the air tag I planted in their SUV."

"Isn't it just a GPS tracker? Can't they track it anywhere?"

"Not exactly. The air tag relies on Bluetooth technology. It is short range and needs to connect to nearby devices that have GPS. Where did Sophie hide the tracker again?"

"At the top of the fire training tower."

"Is it close to where people walk?"

"Not really."

"That's it! If nobody was close enough to it with their phone, they wouldn't be able to track it. My guess is that Sophie suspected this and didn't bring her phone when she hid it there."

"What's the range of Bluetooth?"

"Around 30 feet."

"There's a walking trail along the river. People walk it all the time, and it's probably less than 30 feet from the tower."

"Yes, but she also put the tracker in that metal tin. It would have acted as a mini Faraday cage that partially blocked any electromagnetic fields."

"You're a smart kid."

"I told you; you needed me."

They drove for over an hour along the winding interstate through forests the colour of fall, small towns and farmland.

As they approached Motor City, the signal disappeared from Reggie's phone.

"I lost the signal," he said.

"What does that mean?" Hudson asked.

"I don't know. Perhaps they are out of range of any nearby devices, or they drove into an underground parking garage."

"Where was the last place it was tracked?"

"Somewhere on Roberts Av...oh boy."

"What?"

"I know where they went. Take the next exit."

The trees, and the fields on either side of the highway faded behind them as they drove into the city.

Hudson signalled and turned off at the exit. "What's at Roberts Avenue?"

"It's the local executive office for Nanotech."

"Isn't that...?"

"Yes, it's where my dad works." Reggie pointed ahead. "Pull into the gas station up here."

"Why? I still have a quarter tank."

"I'm hungry."

"Already? Didn't you eat breakfast?"

"Yes, I had a hearty meal of poached egg whites and lactose-free probiotic yogurt with blueberries."

Hudson slowed and rolled into the gas station. "And you wonder why you're hungry..."

Once he parked next to a pump, Reggie got out. "I'm going into the store. Did you want me to get you anything?"

"Thanks, but I had a proper breakfast."

After Hudson filled the tank, they got back on the road and drove to the Nanotech offices and parked in the visitor parking lot.

"I expected a locked gate with security." Hudson pointed at the twenty-storey blue-tinted glass facade. "This is just a regular office building."

"These are just the executive offices." Reggie bit into a pretzel.

"I thought you were some sort of health nut. Aren't pretzels full of salt and gluten and stuff?"

"I eat them when I'm stressed."

"If this is too much for you, I can drive you back home. You're the one that wanted to come."

"It's not that." Reggie nibbled at another pretzel. "He's probably here."

"Your father?"

Reggie nodded.

Hudson opened his door and stepped out. "Is his car here?"

After placing his bag of salty goodness on the seat, Reggie joined him outside the truck.

"His car won't be out here. That road around goes around to the rear of the building, to the underground parking.

"That's probably where Riker and Deltoid parked."

"Riker and Deltoid?"

"The two morons that I beat up in the school."

"Their names are Riker and Deltoid?"

Hudson held out his hands. "What's wrong with that?"

"It sounds like a cheesy buddy cop show from the eighties."

"Yeah, well, they're not cops. I think they're your dad's grunts."

Reggie reached into the truck, grabbed his backpack and slipped it over his shoulders. "We should check out their SUV."

Hudson followed him out of the visitor parking lot. "You're bringing your schoolbooks?"

"These aren't books." Reggie pointed a thumb at his backpack. "It's my laptop."

They walked across the weedless grass towards the back of the office building.

Overhead, roiling graphite clouds swam across the sky. A stiff breeze tore the last remaining chartreuse leaves from nearby hackberry trees. The long, ovate leaves fluttered to the ground in a final death spiral, leaving the trees naked and ready for winter.

They paused at the entrance to the underground parking. Nobody manned the small glass booth. A Tesla hummed up to the red and white barrier. The driver lowered his window and swiped a badge across the black reader. Once the barrier lifted, he continued inside.

They waited until the Tesla disappeared into the darkness and before shuffling inside, trying to stay out of view of the security camera.

Overhead fluorescent lights lit up the parking area filled with Teslas, BMWs, Mercedes, Porches and other high-end vehicles. They found the blue SUV five vehicles away from the elevator.

Hudson stopped at the elevator. Instead of a button, a black card reader awaited potential riders. He continued to the SUV with Reggie.

"Now what?" Reggie asked after they checked all the doors. "Are we going to—"

A loud crash followed by a deafening car siren interrupted his question as Hudson kicked in the back window.

"Are you crazy?" Reggie yell-whispered.

"What? They broke into my house. I'm returning the favour."

As the siren alternated between whoops, beeps and mee-moos, Hudson reached inside and unlocked the door.

"What are we looking for?"

Hudson reached across and opened the front door. "An extra swipe card would be nice. Perhaps a journal outlining all their evil plans."

He checked the glove box and under the seats but found nothing.

Reggie bounced from one foot to the other. "Hurry. Someone's going to find us."

"Plan B!" shouted Hudson. He closed the door and beckoned Reggie to follow as he ran towards the elevator.

They stood quietly around the corner from the elevator.

"What are we doing?" Reggie whispered.

"Get ready," Hudson warned.

The elevator binged, and two men in dark suits stepped out. They stalked towards the siren with guns drawn.

"Now!" Hudson whispered and ran around the corner to the elevator. He dove inside, and Reggie followed as the door closed behind them.

Hudson pressed the 2nd floor button. Notices on the elevator walls reminded the occupants of social distancing rules, masking requirements and encouraged them to stay home if they had any symptoms.
"Act like you know where you're going, don't make eye contact with anybody," said Hudson.

"Why are we going to the 2nd floor?"
"The first floor will have security and reception. The less time we're on this elevator the better."
A ding preceded the elevator doors opening. No one greeted them as they stepped out. Long hallways stretched out to the left and right. In front of them was a small open area with potted Ficus plants and a table with masks, sanitizer wipes and boxes of Covid tests. Beyond the table was a vast maze of padded dividers filled with cubicles and desks. A man facing the opposite direction held a phone to his ear.
Hudson dashed to the left, with Reggie tailing close behind. They waited in front of the men's washroom doors and listened. Other than the steady hum of the HVAC system, the only sound was a single voice. Hudson crept down the carpeted hallway and peeked around the corner.
The man still talked on the phone and faced the opposite direction. All the other cubicles appeared empty.
"Where is everybody?" Hudson asked.
"Maybe they're still working from home."
They crouch-walked past the office area to the long hallway on the far side of the elevators. Hudson found the first two rooms off the hallway locked. The next was an empty boardroom. They rushed past two other small offices with employees staring at their computer screens. Hudson led them into a small lunchroom at the end of the hallway.
"Is it break time already?" joked Reggie. "Because I just ate."
"I'm looking for filing cabinets or where they might keep logs."

"This is the 21st century, old timer. Everything is on computers."

"Great! How are we supposed to find evidence of what they're doing?"

Reggie pointed at the pack on his back. "That's why I brought my laptop. I can tap into their network and download their files."

"You can do that?"

"I told you that you needed me." Reggie smiled. "All we need is a computer workstation."

"All the offices are locked. We'll have to go back to the cubicles."

"What about that guy on the phone?"

"Good idea, I'll distract him, while you do whatever it is you do."

They crept down the hallway and peered around the corner at the maze of cubicles.

"How much time do you need?" asked Hudson.

"At least a few minutes. I'll use my new password algorithm to crack into the local workstation. This should give me access to the network mainframe and—"

"Okay, so a few minutes?"

"Sure. What are you going to do?"

"I'm going to distract him."

Before Reggie responded, Hudson strutted forward. The area was almost the size of half a football field. Intersecting passageways connected four rows of cubicles. Five-foot-high partitions broke up the workspaces. Phone guy sat three cubicles in. He clicked off his phone and looked up.

"Can I help you?"

Hudson quickened his pace and disappeared down a passageway. He ducked inside a cubicle and peered over the top. When he was sure the man was following him, he left the cubicle and darted further into the office.

"Hey? Are you supposed to be here?"

Hudson walked briskly towards the far corner and ducked behind a photocopier. When he looked over the edge of the partition, the man stopped and looked around. Hudson entered *one hundred copies* into the copier, pressed start and crouch-walked away. The man took the bait, and Hudson dashed away again. After a few minutes of cat and mouse, the man stopped and pulled out his cell phone. He was too far away for Hudson to hear his exact words, but Hudson was sure he was calling security.

Staying low, Hudson snuck his way back to Reggie, who was sitting at phone guy's desk. A black cord connected two laptops.

"What are you doing here?" asked Hudson. "Couldn't you have tried one of the other three million workstations?"

"I thought he might still be logged in."

Hudson looked out into the office space but couldn't see the man. "Was it?"

"No, but I'm trying to crack his password."

"How long is that going to take?" Hudson tapped his foot and looked back and forth from the elevator doors to the direction of the phone guy.

"This is much harder than the school's firewall."

"What?! You broke into the school's system?"

Reggie looked up and smiled. "That's right. I was able to crack that password in less than one minute."

Hudson glared at him. "Stop bragging and get back to work."

Reggie returned to the laptops. "I'm not sure if I can—"

"Time's up!" Hudson whispered loudly as the elevator dinged. "We have to go *now*!"

Reggie typed furiously. "Just give me a couple of minutes."

"Ahhh!" Hudson grunted. "I can give you about 30 seconds, but then we are going to get arrested."

Phone guy's eyes met his from only a few cubicles away, and the two security men saw him as they stepped out of the elevator.

Hudson charged towards the phone guy. The man was barely five feet tall with a slim build. Ducking low as he approached, Hudson picked the man up in a fireman's carry and ran down the passageway.

"Put me down," the man cried.

The security men spit up and flanked him on either side, one row over.

"Sorry about that," said Hudson as he set the man down and continued running.

He turned the corner at the next intersection and almost ran into one of the security guards. His feet slipped on the carpet as he changed direction mid-slide. As he attempted to stand, he looked up at a pistol pointing at his face.

“Okay. Don’t shoot!”

CHAPTER 13

"What are you doing here?" Lawrence stood beside his stark white desk, looking down at his son.

The spacious office was clean, with minimal decorations. A single framed photo sat on the corner of the glossy desk. Floor-to-ceiling windows extended along the entire length of one wall, offering a panoramic view of Motor City from the 20th storey. Framed abstract art hung on the opposite white wall above a slick black leather couch.

Reggie and Hudson stood in front of the desk, flanked by solemn security guards.

"I wanted to visit you," said Reggie.

Hudson didn't think his acting was very convincing and wondered if the boy was being sarcastic.

"Don't get smart with me," snapped Lawrence.

"We never spend quality time together, so I came to surprise you at work. Surprise!"

Hudson was sure he was being sarcastic.

"It was my idea, sir," he interjected.

"We know you killed his wife with that tracker," Reggie blurted.

Lawrence nodded at the security guards. "Leave us."

The guards turned and left the room.

"Please have a seat." Lawrence pointed at the leather couch. "We need to talk."

"You need to tell the truth!" Reggie remained defiantly standing in front of his father.

"Sit down!" Lawrence barked. His right fist clenched into a ball at his side.

Hudson took a half step forward and glared at him.

"Please." Lawrence's fist unclenched, and he spoke in a softer tone. He walked behind his desk and retrieved his leather office chair and rolled it in front of the couch. "Let's talk about this, like normal people, without losing our cool."

He unbuttoned his suit jacket and sat down.

Hudson and Reggie sank into the couch and looked up at him.

"I don't know what you *think* you know, but I can assure you, I had nothing to do with her death."

"Right." Reggie rolled his eyes.

"How do you two know each other, and why are you breaking into my office? With one call, I could have you arrested for breaking and entering. It's also a little weird that a grown man is skulking around with a young teenage boy."

"Hudson is my friend."

Lawrence's face dropped, and his eyes widened. "You two aren't…I mean…you're not…don't you like girls?"

"No!" yelled Reggie. "It's not like that."

"Sir. I am sorry that I dragged your son into this. I'll understand if you have me arrested, but this was my idea, and…"

Reggie interrupted him. "Why did you send your henchmen after Hudson?"

"My men were retrieving Nanotech property."

"You mean the tracker you injected into my wife's arm?"

Lawrence loosened his navy-blue tie. "You don't know what's going on here."

"I have a *bit* of an idea." Hudson's voice was bordering on anger, but still controlled. "You secretly injected her with a tracker. She developed an infection from it and died. But not before cutting it out of her arm. In order to cover up your crimes, you sent your goons to kill me and take back the tracker."

"You don't have the full story."

"That is exactly why I'm here – to uncover the truth and the full story."

"Nobody was going to hurt you, although I heard you did a number on my men. You broke Deltoid's nose and dislocated his elbow, and Riker has two black eyes and a bruised chin."

Reggie smiled. “That was totally awesome.”

“In my defence, they were trying to rob me,” said Hudson.

“They were asking nicely for the return of Nanotech property.”

“Why didn’t you call the cops and report it stolen?” Hudson asked. “Instead of sending armed men after me?”

Lawrence sighed. “This is way out of your league. You both need to go home and forget about this. Nanotech won’t press charges, and my men won’t bother you anymore.”

“Ha!” cried Reggie. “You want us to be complicit in one of the greatest coverups in the 21st century?”

“That’s not...”

“You’re using the Covid vaccine as a cover for injecting millions of Americans with digital trackers, and you expect us to go home and forget about it?”

“No, Reggie. That’s not at all what’s happened. You don’t have all the facts.”

Hudson held out his arms. “Enlighten us.”

“I cannot disclose confidential company information. What I can tell you is that Sophie died from Covid complications. It had nothing to do with...”

“How do you know that?” yelled Hudson. “Sophie was young, fit, healthy and she had the supposed vaccine.”

“It was probably the vaccine that killed her,” Reggie added. “I heard the vaccines cause myocarditis and blood clots...”

Lawrence pointed a finger at his son. “There is no proof of that.”

Reggie raised his eyebrows. “Not yet...”

“Are you admitting you injected her with a tracker using the vaccine as a cover? Didn’t Nanotech make one of the vaccines?”

“No. There are no trackers in the vaccines.”

“We’re going to the press,” said Reggie. “And we’re going to expose your company.”

“Two things,” said Lawrence. “This isn’t *my* company, and second, you have no proof. You don’t have a tracker and...”

“She cut the tracker out of her arm!” yelled Hudson.

“Yes, but you don’t even have proof of that. Her body was

cremated."

Hudson stood up. His towering frame hovered over the still-seated Lawrence. "Was it *you* that had her cremated against my will?"

"Whoa!" Lawrence wheeled his chair back. "Hurting me will not help your case here. If I call my men back in, they will drag you to the police station."

"You think I care if I'm arrested? I would strangle you with your silk tie and happily walk myself to jail if I thought you had anything to do with her death."

"Things are not what they seem, Mr. Finlay, and hurting me will not get you the answers you seek."

"Possibly, but it would make me feel better." Hudson's anger grew inside him like an inflating balloon.

Lawrence's chair backed up against his desk. "I know what it's like to lose someone you love."

Hudson glared down at him. "Who did *you* lose?"

"Catherine." He reached behind him and plucked the picture frame off the desk. He held it up to Hudson for a moment, before holding it in front of him and staring at it. "She was the love of my life. She was taken in her prime and for no good reason. When she passed, I tried to find someone to blame. Did the doctor do something wrong? Was she given too much anaesthesia? How can someone who is healthy and young go to the hospital for a routine procedure and not come home?"

He looked up at Hudson with glossy eyes.

Hudson's anger deflated. "What happened to her? How did she die?"

"There were complications during her labour. They performed a simple c-section. She lost too much blood and died before she got to hold her baby."

Tears spilled from his eyes, and he held the picture against his face.

"I'm sorry." Hudson didn't know what else to say.

After a few awkward moments, Hudson backed away. "I think we're going to leave now – unless you still want to press charges."

Lawrence shook his head without looking up.

Reggie stood up and looked at Hudson with a distant expression that Hudson couldn't decipher.

As they reached the door to leave, Lawrence looked up and spoke. His tone was sombre but deliberate. "Trust me. I'm on your side."

They said nothing as the guards escorted them down the elevator and out of the building.

"I hope you got something," Hudson said as they drove out of the parking lot.

Reggie opened his backpack and pulled out his backpack. "I don't know."

"What do you mean, *you don't know*? We broke into that building and almost got arrested and you don't know?"

"Breaking past their security was harder than I thought." Reggie tapped on his keyboard. "My algorithm didn't work on the firewall. I even tried installing malware, but the system had a really high-end malware detection system. It was way above my expertise."

"You're not a genius hacker after all..."

"I never said I was a genius hacker...Aha! Got it!"

"What? What did you get?"

"I downloaded some files off the local computer."

"And?"

"I don't know yet. They're encrypted files. This may take some time."

"I'll wait."

"No. I mean it may take a few days."

"Oh, I see." Hudson's words hung heavy with disappointment.

Neither of them talked for a few minutes till they reached the interstate and Reggie asked, "Do you trust my father?"

"No. Do you?"

"No."

CHAPTER 14

Hudson hopped out of his truck and ran through the cold, late October rain towards his trailer. Inside, the rain pelted the mobile home roof like rubber bullets. He dropped the heavy gym bag by the door and removed his wet runners. Slicking his fingers through his dark hair, Hudson moseyed to the kitchen and opened the fridge. The three cold beers seemed to beckon him, but he closed the fridge and filled a tall glass with tap water. Just as he sank into the couch with a deep sigh, someone knocked on the door.

For a moment, he wondered who it was.

"Hudson, I'm getting soaked out here," called Reggie from outside the door.

"It's open!" Hudson yelled from the couch.

Reggie pushed the door, and it creaked open.

"You should get that fixed," he said, pointing at the splintered frame.

"I've been busy," Hudson replied.

Reggie smiled as if he just remembered something.

"You'll never guess what I found – a secret lab!"

He unslung his backpack and walked towards the couch.

"Stop!" Hudson held his hand up. "Take your wet shoes off. I don't want to give the maid more work than she already has."

Reggie slipped off his shoes. "You have a maid?"

Hudson shook his head. "It was a joke."

"Right." Reggie removed his laptop from the backpack and set it on the coffee table in front of the couch. "I finally cracked the code...well not really the code as much as I decrypted the files or at least the html code in the emails..."

"You're still working on that?" asked Hudson. "It's been three weeks since we broke into your dad's office. I thought you had given up by now."

Reggie opened his laptop and powered it on. "I told you at school today that I found something."

Hudson leaned back and put his feet on the table. "I don't care."

"What do you mean you don't care?"

"I've moved on. I'm back at the gym doing some boxing and Jui-Jitsu." He held up his water. "I'm even drinking less beer."

"Don't you want to know what happened?"

"I think it would be best if we left this alone. I should move on with my life, and you should go to school, hang out with your friends at the chess club or do whatever a normal nerdy teen does."

"Are you saying you don't want to know about the secret lab where they are conducting human experiments, making Covid and creating injectable trackers?"

Hudson leaned forward. "Injectable trackers?"

Reggie folded his arms. "Some of it is conjecture, but I did find something."

Hudson eyed him suspiciously. "Tell me what you found."

"I thought you said you wanted to leave this alone."

"You came all this way. I should at least listen to what you have to say."

Reggie continued. "I used a new algorithm I developed to decrypt the—"

"Don't tell me *how* you did it. Tell me *what* you found."

"Right. Although I could only access the files on the local drive, I found the emails for the past two years. Most of it was normal office emails, spam, meetings and stuff, but I found a few strange emails. They referenced research being at their facility in Acor."

"Like the nut?"

"No. *Acor*. It's a small town in northern Michigan. It's not even really a town. More like a few houses."

"I've heard of it. A few years ago, I went hunting near there. I didn't think it was big enough for a research facility."

"It isn't." Reggie pointed at Hudson. "Nanotech doesn't have any official buildings there, and I couldn't find anything that even looked bigger than a house on Google Earth."

"Sounds like a dead end."

"I did find this..." Reggie pointed to his screen. The satellite image showed long, thin roads streaking across vast swaths of green forest. In the centre, a large white triangle contrasted against the surrounding emerald tracts of land.

"What is *that*?" Hudson leaned forward to look closer.

"It is an old army airfield outside of Acor. The US Army officially closed it in 1972. Now it's supposedly used as a winter testing site for vehicles."

"I don't see many buildings."

"I researched a little deeper with some of my buddies on the internet—"

"Buddies?" Hudson raised his eyebrows.

"Yes, they are fellow truth seekers who don't trust the corrupt government, know about the Great Reset and the secret international cabal trying to create a communist world order—"

"Got it!" Hudson interrupted. "What did your crazy buddies say about the Acor site?"

"Rumour has it the army built a network of underground network of tunnels connecting missile silos and a huge bunker in case of nuclear war. Some say there's a secret bio-weapons lab down there now."

"And you think Nanotech Industries has a secret lab down there?"

"Yes!"

Hudson rubbed the back of his neck. "I don't know..."

"Did Sophie ever mention the Acor site?"

"I don't think so."

"What about Rudard, Brimey, Pendal Beach, Ojibwe..."

"Ojibwe! She went there for some training thing during Covid—"

"I found something else. In an email discussing going to Acor, he says the phrase, *on my way to the triangle*. That *must* mean the Acor Army base."

"Hmm." Hudson scratched his chin and reached for the phone. After dialling, he asked for Chief Jones. After talking for a few minutes, he hung up.

"What did he say?" Reggie asked.

"Apparently there was no firefighter training in Ojibwe. The only thing he remembered was Sophie taking a week off to do some hiking up north. This was about 6 months before she ended up in hospital with Covid."

"That's it!" Reggie yelled. "She found out about the Acor Army base and went there to check it out. When she discovered the underground lab, they..."

"They what?" asked Hudson. "How did she end up in a hospital bed with Covid and a tracker in her arm?"

"We have to go up there to find out."

Hudson leaned back. "As I said, I've moved on. These are very nice crazy theories. You should use them for a podcast or conspiracy site or something."

"What is wrong with you?" Reggie yelled the question. "Don't you care...Wait a second...you don't want me to come with you."

"I never said I was going anywhere."

"Fine." Reggie closed his laptop and stood up. "I will go up to Acor Army base by myself."

"You don't even drive."

"I don't have to. I'm rich – remember? I have a credit card with a huge limit. If I wanted, I could hire a limo driver to take me there or hire a private plane." He walked towards the door. "I guess I'll see you there."

"Wait!" called Hudson. "You can come with me, but if anything happens to you—"

"If I go alone, you will feel great guilt that you didn't come along to protect me."

Hudson rolled his eyes. "If anything happens to you, I will deny ever meeting you."

Reggie smiled. "Admit it. You care about me."

"I never said that."

CHAPTER 15

The drive up to Acor Army base was an uneventful, three-and-a-half-hour trip through the endless northern Michigan forests and grassy fields. The late October Saturday was warmer than usual as if Mother Nature was teasing about holding winter back. Traffic on the lonely road was sparse. The only other vehicles were a camper van, a couple of cars and a tour bus.

Rudard was the last town they passed through before they arrived at the small drive into the airfield. A guard shack with a yellow and black barrier arm blocked the entrance.

"This doesn't look high-security." Hudson slowed but did not turn into the drive.

"Ever hear the expression, *hiding in plain sight*?" asked Reggie. "Drive further down the road. There should be a small side road that leads into the back of the compound."

A few minutes later, they found the side road and Hudson turned in. A large *No Trespassing* sign hung on a fencepost, but nothing else prevented them from entering.

The single-lane dirt and gravel road wound through dense evergreen woodlands. Crowds of northern white cedar, red pine and black spruce watched them roll along the serpentine path.

After passing a small clearing and turning down another long road, the view in front opened. Wide pale grey concrete roads stretched right and left and connected to an even wider concrete pad that seemed to stretch out in both directions forever.

"That's the old airstrip," said Reggie.

Hudson turned off his truck, opened his door and got out. Reggie did the same, and they stood in front of the pickup and stared ahead.

"This place is huge!" said Reggie.

"And quiet."

The needled trees stifled the wind's voice, and any road traffic was too far out of audible range. A pair of Canada geese honked overhead. Their wings creaked as they flew across the sky and disappeared behind the trees.

Hudson held up his arms. "What now? Are we supposed to walk around looking for a secret hatch or something?"

"We could—"

The sound of an approaching vehicle behind them broke the silence.

"Someone's coming," said Hudson.

"What do we do?"

"This way." Hudson reached into the truck, grabbed his pack and ran towards the trees. Reggie followed, and as they disappeared into the forest, a brown jeep bounced towards the truck.

Two men in matching black cargo pants and long sleeve combat shirts stepped out. Hudson and Reggie watched from behind a black spruce.

The men talked to each other as they scanned the area. Then the taller man opened the back door of the jeep and pulled out a semi-automatic weapon.

"We need to go." Hudson pulled on Reggie's arm, and they ran into the woods.

They jumped over moss-covered rocks and almost tripped over exposed black spruce roots as they sprinted deeper into the forest. Hudson held his arms up in a defensive boxing stance as he plowed through the dense shrubs. Reggie squealed as he got slapped in the face by a whipping branch.

Their pursuers made no sound.

"Try not to make noise," Hudson scolded.

"Stop smacking me with branches."

Their feet snapped twigs and rustled dead leaves as they continued through the woods. Behind him, Hudson could hear Reggie's heavy breathing.

"Where are we going?" he panted.

"Can you climb?" Hudson asked as he continued jogging.

"Are you kidding?"

"Did you want to keep running?"

"Not really. I think my lungs are bleeding."

"This one." Hudson pointed at a tall red pine.

Reggie stopped, leaned over and put his hands on his legs. "I think I'm done." His body rose and fell with his deep raspy breaths. "Let them take me away…my dad will…"

"You wanted to come," Hudson barked. "The first sign of danger, and you want to run home to Daddy? Get up that tree!"

Reggie looked up at him but said nothing. He grabbed the first branch and began climbing, Hudson followed.

"How far are we going?" Reggie asked. "I'm afraid of heights."

"Look up, and when you don't see any more tree, stop."

As they neared the top of the tree, the pine's dense foliage blocked much of the view to the ground.

"Stop!" Hudson whispered. "Someone's coming. Don't move and don't talk."

He had spent many hours hidden up trees like this, but usually with a hunting rifle. Also, usually, he was the hunter – not the hunted.

They remained motionless listening to footsteps in the dead leaves below. Hudson held his breath as he watched the figure of their pursuer walk up to the tree. He paused, looked around and continued his search.

Almost five silent minutes later, Hudson nodded at Reggie. "Okay, I think he's gone. I'm going to climb down and check."

"Hurry up, my butt hurts."

After descending the tree, he listened intently for any sign of their pursuers. In the distance, he thought he heard a vehicle engine.

"Okay," he called up to Reggie, "You can come down now."

The late afternoon sun dropped closer to the horizon, and the temperature seemed to drop with it.

"Are we safe now?" Reggie asked as he jumped off the bottom branch.

"Safe is a relative term. I think I heard them leave, but we should still be careful. They know we're here and are probably watching the truck."

"What now?"

"Let's get a closer look at this place. If there is really a secret underground facility, then we should see people coming and going and find the entrance. We'll stay in the forest but stay close to the runway. Where is the main building and entrance from here?"

Reggie rubbed the sap on his hands. "We're only on the edge of the base. The triangle airstrip is almost a mile wide."

"We better start walking if we want to get there before dark."

As they traversed the perimeter of the airfield, the sun and the temperature continued their descent. Some of the forest was open, with only a few sparse trees. Other areas were densely congested with trees and shrubbery.

"We should stop for a drink," Hudson said as they approached a gurgling creek.

Reggie recoiled. "I'm not drinking that."

Hudson knelt and pulled a flask and a small pouch from his pack. "Why not? It's gluten-free, fat-free and all-natural!" He filled the flask with water and added a tablet from the pouch.

"That water is contaminated with bacteria, algae and rabbit feces," Reggie complained.

"I'm adding a purification tab. It might taste weird, but it's better than getting dehydrated."

After Hudson had his fill, Reggie acquiesced and took a few tentative gulps. Hudson refilled the flask before replacing it in his pack.

Twenty minutes later, they approached a small clearing. Two foraging cottontails perked up and bounced away. Reggie was the first to spot the rectangular shape in the long, brown grass. The structure was the size of a chest freezer.

"What is that?"

They waded through the swaying foxtail and goldenrod to the strange outcropping. Thick metal encased it on three sides and the top, but the end facing away from the airfield was covered in a steel mesh door. Two hinges held the top, and a metal padlock held the bottom.

As Hudson reached towards the door to check its sturdiness, Reggie yelled, “Wait!”

He pointed to a small, black rectangular object inside the mesh. “That looks like an electronic sensor.”

Hudson pulled his hand back. “The lock looks new.”

A layer of red rust covered the mesh door, hinges and handle, but the lock was shiny and silver.

“This looks like a vent.” Reggie bent over and attempted to look inside.

Hudson nodded. “Yes, and we’re still almost a half mile from the main gate. If there is an underground facility, it must be huge.”

“Let’s keep going,” said Hudson. “We need to find another way inside.”

The sun faded behind the trees., and the sky turned a burnt ember with wisps of crimson clouds as they continued trekking. They passed by concrete pads and foundations – the only remnants of buildings long since destroyed.

As they exited a dense stand of black spruce, they came upon two long buildings. Both metal-clad structures sat parallel to each other and were about 30 feet wide. The longer one stretched over 100 feet. The surrounding area was clear of trees and shrubbery.

Hudson looked around but saw no vehicles or people. The double doors on the side of the buildings were closed. No cameras were mounted on either building.

“They look abandoned,” he said and marched forward.

“This could be the entrance to the underground facility,” said Reggie.

“I doubt it.”

A red-winged blackbird fluttered away as they walked up to the double doors. The lock on these doors was larger but old and rusty. Hudson scanned the area around the doors.

“Do you see any sensors?”

"No, but they may be on the inside," Reggie replied.

They plodded around both buildings but couldn't find an easy way inside. All the doors were locked, and the windows were boarded up with thick plywood.

The sky darkened as evening approached. The only lights visible were from other buildings about a quarter mile away.

"There's nothing here," said Hudson. "Let's keep going."

They hiked towards the buildings. A large open area with a circular track sat between them and the cluster of buildings. They stuck to the edge of the forest and took the long route around it.

Ten minutes later, they crouched in the grass at the edge of the tree line. They looked across a small clearing. A long, paved road ran from right to left, servicing seven buildings. At the far left, it turned towards the main gate. A bulbous halogen light mounted on the side of the largest building cast an eerie pale-yellow glow. Above it, a tiny red light on a security camera blinked.

Suddenly, they heard a vehicle approaching and dropped into the grass. From their prone position, they watched as a brown jeep drove slowly by. At the end of the road, to the right, it made a wide circle before returning and disappearing again to the left.

"We should wait here and watch."

"Cool!" said Reggie. "A stakeout."

"Probably not as cool as you think. You should get comfortable."

The jeep drove by twice over the next two hours as they lay in the cool grass.

"I'm hungry," said Reggie.

"Me too," said Hudson as he searched his pack. "Unfortunately, all I have are MREs. Let's wait a while longer. We can eat later."

Reggie fell asleep in the grass, but Hudson remained alert. Twenty minutes later, Hudson nudged Reggie awake. A tour bus rumbled towards them from the direction of the gate. The brakes squealed as the bus slowed to a stop under the halogen light.

The far side door on the bus hissed open. Although they couldn't see the side of the bus with the door, Reggie and Hudson heard people exiting the vehicle amidst a flurry of conversations. The bus creaked as men removed luggage from the lower compartments. Everything fell silent for a while until another group emerged from the building. The bus creaked again as the men heaved luggage back into the compartments, and people climbed aboard. The door hissed closed, and the diesel engine roared as the bus moved forward. It drove to the end of the road on the right, took a big circle and drove back towards the gate and disappeared.

Hudson and Reggie waited for another twenty minutes, but the only other vehicle that passed was the brown jeep.

"Let's go," said Hudson finally.

Reggie got up and started towards the building with the halogen light.

"Not that way!" Hudson beckoned him back towards the forest.

"Don't we want to break into that building? That's probably the entrance to the underground facility."

"The door is locked, they have a security camera above the door and there are probably guards inside. We need to find another way."

Reggie sighed and followed Hudson. It was too dark to hike through the woods, so Hudson led them along the outskirts of the tree line.

"Where are we going?" asked Reggie.

"Back to those two long buildings. If we can find a way inside, we can sleep there for the night."

"And then what?"

"I don't know yet. I'm too tired and hungry to think."

When they returned to the buildings, it was almost pitch black. Dark clouds passed by the thin sliver of a moon overhead. Reggie pulled out his phone and turned on the light.

"Save your battery," said Hudson, "I have a flashlight."

Hudson pulled out a flashlight from his pack and turned it on. He found a suitable rock and handed the flashlight to Reggie. After four hard hits with his rock, the rusted lock broke and fell to the ground.

The door creaked open, and they stepped inside. Reggie panned the flashlight across the room. Two long tables extended down the length of the building, shrinking in the distance like railroad tracks in a high school art project. A thick film of dust, dead flies and dirt covered the tables. Broken, rotting benches lined either side. They warily walked forward. Between the tables, three rusting cast iron woodstoves sat evenly spaced in the centre of the room. One of them was still connected to the ceiling with its black chimney pipe. Something scratched and shuffled on the floor under a table. Reggie's light swung towards the noise. A black rat stared back at them with dark, beady eyes before skittering away.

A loud screeching noise behind him caused Reggie to let out a scream. When he turned around, Hudson stood in front of the now closed double doors.

"You could have warned me!"

Hudson set his pack on the table and sat on the bench. As he opened his pack, the wooden seat beneath him disintegrated and he tumbled to the floor.

Reggie laughed as he held up his phone and clicked a photo.

Hudson stood up and brushed himself off. "You should save your phone battery."

"Trust me, this is worth it."

Hudson rolled his eyes. "We can use some of this wood to start a small fire in the woodstove."

"Won't someone see the smoke?" asked Reggie as he put his phone away.

"We'll keep the fire small and make sure it's out before the sun rises. I'll start the fire. You go see if you can find any blankets."

Reggie found some tattered, dusty wool blankets. Hudson gathered non-rotten wood for a fire. Using a lighter from his pack, he started a small fire in the wood stove. The long rusty chimney pipe carried the smoke outside. They huddled near the stove staring through the open iron door. Warm, lemony light flickered on their faces.

Hudson pulled out two MREs and handed one to Reggie.

"What is *this*?" Reggie held the grey pack up to the light.

"Food." Hudson handed him a long flat pack. "Add a bit of water to this, wrap it around your meal and wait ten minutes."

"What is that supposed to do?"

"It's a self-heating MRE," Hudson answered.

Five minutes later, they opened steaming MREs. The powerful aroma reminded Hudson how hungry he was. He grabbed two forks and handed one to Reggie. "Dig in!"

Reggie peered inside his pouch and winced. As he opened his mouth to say something, Hudson cut him off.

"If you dare ask if it's gluten-free, fat-free, salt-free or contains lemon grass, couscous or a tofu meat alternative, I will throw you into that fire and eat your scrawny body for dessert."

"Huh..." Reggie pushed his fork slowly into the pouch. "It actually smells good."

"It *is* good."

"How did you know we might need this food?" Reggie asked as they ate.

Hudson pointed to the black backpack beside him. "This is... was Sophie's bug-out bag. In case of World War three, alien invasion, zombie apocalypse or viral outbreak, she wanted to be prepared."

They ate in silence for a few moments till he continued. "I told her she was crazy. The world wouldn't end in our lifetime. Little did I know that our world *did* end. She died, some of her crazy conspiracies may be true and I'm left alone to figure out what happened."

"You're not alone."

"You know what I mean."

"That pack is sure helping us now. It's like *she's* helping us."

"Yeah."

They finished their meals and huddled in their musty wool blankets by the stove. Hudson added a few more pieces of wooden bench to the fire and shut the door to the stove. The room quickly darkened. Other than small, tiny flickers from the cracks in the stove, the inky darkness closed in.

"Can you keep it open?" asked Reggie.

"The fire won't last long if we keep it open. The fire will burn slow and all night if we keep it closed."

"Can you at least wait till I'm asleep?"

Hudson opened the door with a loud creak. Golden light spilled back into the room.

They both stared at the dancing flames for a long time.

"I don't even like lemon grass," said Reggie.

"I don't even know what lemon grass is."

"My father is the health freak, you know."

"Oh, yeah?"

"He is overprotective of me. I think he's afraid to lose me, like he lost my mother."

"That's good. That means he loves you."

"He has a strange way of showing it sometimes."

"I'd say something meaningful and inspirational about the inseparable bond of parent and child, but I don't have any kids."

"That's okay. As long as you don't throw me in the fire and eat me for dessert."

Reggie giggled. Hudson snickered. Then they both erupted into a full-on laughing fit.

Once they settled down, Reggie lay his head down and, a few minutes later, fell asleep.

Hudson closed the door to the stove, lay back and stared into the blackness. The muffled crackle of fire in the stove and the skittering of a small creature on the wood floor were the only sounds.

A faint spectre of Sophie's anguished visage materialized in his vision before he willed it away. He thought about the injectable tracker, the underground facility, the guards, the bus, the people...

"That's it!" he yelled.

Reggie woke with a startled look and sat up. "Who's there? What's going on?"

"I know how we can get into the underground facility!"

"Great," said Reggie unenthusiastically and lay back down. "Tell me in the morning. I'm busy dreaming of being burned alive."

CHAPTER 16

Early the next morning, they ate more MREs, packed up and returned to their previous stakeout position. The grey sky, thick with heavy clouds, delayed the rising sun's effect, but the subtle daylight provided an unobscured view of the road and buildings. Behind them, a red-bellied woodpecker machine-gunned a tall spruce tree. The rat-a-tat echoed through the cool forest. A thin layer of frost covered the grass and the building roofs.

"Tell me what we're doing here again?" A thin vapour puffed out of Reggie's mouth as he talked.

Hudson rubbed his hands together. "Last night I was thinking about the bus and all those people. I think they replace the crew that works underground every few days, weeks or every month."

"You mean they live down there?"

"Exactly. That's why they have luggage. The bus ferries them here every week or whatever. This eliminates all the traffic that might make the locals suspicious, something is going on here. The workers live and work down there for an extended period."

"So we might be here for a month, waiting for the next shift change?"

"That's not what we're waiting for."

"Good, because I can't eat MREs for another month and I want my nice soft bed back."

Hudson blew warm breath into his cupped hands. "All those workers down there need to eat. The company must make regular shipments of food and other supplies. This would involve a big truck, a forklift, pallets, buckets and stuff. There must be a big delivery entrance somewhere around here."

They looked towards the buildings as the morning light

triggered a sensor, and the halogen light flickered off. The brown jeep drove by, turned around and rumbled away again.

Hudson stood up.

"I only see one security camera on the big building where the bus stopped last night. Let's get a closer look at the other buildings. Look for a delivery door with a security camera. We'll stick to the tree line as much as possible. The jeep just left, so we should have a bit of time before they return."

He led them to the right, away from the direction of the security gate. They trampled through the frosted grass with the forest to the right and the road and buildings to the left. The first smaller building beside the bus stop contained only a steel door. A curved road led to the rear of the building. Further along, the next pair of buildings had a man door and a large garage door but no security camera.

A tiny building sat where the road ended and where the jeep made a U-turn. A single man door with no camera above it was the only entrance.

Hudson led them around to the rear of the buildings, sticking close to the safety of the tree line. They walked through the grass to look at the back of each of the buildings. One had a rear man door exit, and two others had nothing.

"Found it!" shouted Reggie. He pointed at the curved road coming from the front of one building, winding behind another and down a ramp to a large loading dock. The door was about four feet from the ground with large black bumpers at the bottom and side. Beside it was a short set of stairs leading to a steel man door. Above the man door, a camera pointed at the loading area.

"That's our way inside," exclaimed Hudson.

"How do we get past the locked doors and security camera?"

"I'm not sure yet, but I think we have to wait."

"Wait for what?"

"The next delivery."

"We could wait a month!" Reggie protested.

"I don't think so. If the facility is as big as we think, they need food, lab supplies, cleaning supplies, office supplies and a bunch of other stuff. We haven't seen a big truck since we got here. My bet is they'll make a delivery soon. When they do, we can sneak in."

"Soon? How long is soon? Hours, days, weeks, months?"

Hudson pointed to the forest. "Let's find a comfortable spot in the bush and wait for at least a day. They probably towed my truck away. We don't even have a way out of here."

"Fine." Reggie's shoulders slumped, and he followed Hudson to the trees.

It was difficult to find a spot that wasn't wet, so Reggie returned to the mess hall to retrieve some blankets while Hudson waited. No truck came by while Reggie was gone. They made themselves somewhat comfortable on the blankets and waited a few more hours, but still no truck. By the middle of the day, they got hungry and ate more MREs. There were only two more left, and Hudson wondered what they would do when they ran out.

While Reggie was napping early in the afternoon, a white-tailed deer loped by, and Hudson longed for his hunting rifle. The obscured sun didn't warm the day, and Hudson wondered if it was getting colder. They watched the brown jeep do its rounds, but it never drove around the back of the buildings. It was mid-afternoon when the distinctive growl of a diesel engine roared.

"Yes!" Reggie pumped his fists.

The transport truck slowly turned around the building before backing up to the loading dock.

"Here's the plan," said Hudson. "We wait till the driver leaves the cab then we shimmy along the side of the building to the stairs and get in through the man door. Hopefully, it will be unlocked."

"What about the camera?"

"It's pointing away from the building, and I don't think it will see us if we stay against the wall."

The truck bumped against the rubber guards before stopping. After a minute, the driver hopped out of the cab and plodded towards the stairs and disappeared.

"Okay," said Hudson. "Go!"

They crouch-walked quickly to the corner of the building.

"What if we get caught?" whispered Reggie.

"We probably *will* get caught. It's just a question of when. I'm hoping we can confirm this underground lab first."

"I don't want to go to jail!"

"Your father will bail you out of trouble. This is his company. He'll ground you for a month while *I* go to jail."

They reached the building and pressed their back against the wall. As they shuffled forward, they heard the jeep driving on the other side of the building. It stopped, and they heard voices coming closer.

"Are they coming here?" Reggie panic-whispered.

"I think so," Hudson replied. "Shuffle faster!"

The guards' voices got louder as the pair crouch-shuffle-ran along the wall towards the truck. Hudson beckoned Reggie as he dashed under the truck.

The guards exclaimed something as they rounded the corner.

Hudson and Reggie huddled behind the truck between the back tire and the side of the concrete stairwell.

Reggie mouthed the words, "Did they see us?"

Hudson shrugged his shoulders.

Although they couldn't see them, they heard the guard walking towards them.

Other voices emanated from inside the building as well as the whining sound of a forklift.

Hudson pointed at the door at the top of the stairs, then hoisted himself up. Reggie watched nervously as Hudson tried the door. He tried the handle, then shook his head.

Then he looked up and realized the camera was pointing in his direction. Quickly, he lowered himself back down.

The truck was backed against the rubber pads leaving no space between them. There didn't appear to be any way inside. Hudson looked at Reggie and pointed up.

Reggie gave his best mime of, *what the heck are you pointing at?*

The guards sounded like they were on the other side of the truck. As they walked towards the front, Hudson ran back under the truck, with a confused Reggie close behind. The guards rounded the front of the truck. Hudson and Reggie popped out the far side. A scraping sound inside the truck startled both of them.

The guards continued their walk on the opposite side of the truck as Hudson ran to the space between the cab and the trailer. He climbed onto the hitch and up the back of the cab and helped Reggie follow him onto the roof. They slowly walked across the roof towards the back of the truck. The thin metal beneath cried, threatening to give away their position. Slowly they crept towards the building. As Hudson hoped, a small gap between the back of the truck and the loading door was about a foot wide. They peered through the gap, watching the forklift removing pallets below. After a few minutes, everything went quiet.

“Where did they go?” Reggie whispered.

“I don’t know. Maybe they’re signing paperwork or something. Now’s our chance.”

It was a tight fit, but Hudson lowered himself and squeezed through the opening. As he dropped to the floor, he quickly scanned the area but saw no one. Reggie fell/jumped to the floor with a yelp.

“Shhhhh!” whispered Hudson.

“I almost broke my ankle,” Reggie moaned quietly.

The room in front of them contained stacks of crates, pails and boxes. A hand cart and forklift sat in front of a large freight elevator. Muffled voices came from behind a door to the right. As Hudson moved towards the elevator, the voices got louder and the door opened. The neatly stacked boxes, crates and shelving provided few obvious hiding spots, so Hudson grabbed Reggie and dove into the back of the truck. They crouched behind a large white object the size of a small chest freezer strapped to a wooden crate near the back of the trailer.

Hudson peered around it and saw the driver arguing with a woman.

“I know what your computer says,” said the driver.

“I can’t take delivery of any item unless it’s on the approved receiving manifest,” said the woman.

"That's nice, but I have another pickup today. I don't have room for it."

"What do you want me to do?"

"Can't we just unload and leave it here? Otherwise, I'm going to dump it outside."

"I don't know what to tell you."

He folded his arms. "Your choice. I either dump it outside your door or we unload it in this room. I'm back next week. If the issue isn't resolved by then, I will take it back."

"Whatever." The woman turned and walked back to the office. "Put it somewhere out of the way, please."

Hudson looked at the white object in front of him. It was, in fact, a chest freezer. With the jackknife in his pocket, he cut the straps and opened it. He pointed inside, but Reggie shook his head vigorously.

The driver started the forklift.

Hudson nodded his head just as vigorously and climbed inside. Reggie squished in beside him. After significant readjusting, they scrunched low enough to allow the door to close above them.

The truck dropped slightly as the forklift rolled onto the trailer. It stopped before reaching the freezer. The driver walked towards the freezer and cursed. They didn't hear him again for several minutes. When he returned, they heard the sound of packing tape above them. A moment later, the forklift pushed its forks beneath the crate and lifted. The forklift drove off the truck and set them down before parking and shutting off the forklift. After the bay door rattled closed, Hudson waited till the sound of the truck faded before pushing up against the freezer door above them.

"We're going to suffocate and die in here," muttered Reggie. "And you're squishing my arm."

"Stop whining and help me push."

Hudson braced his back against the underside of the door and pressed hard with his leg. The tape snapped, and the door burst open. They unfurled themselves and scrambled out of the freezer and huddled behind it.

“I think she’s back in her office,” whispered Hudson.

He crouch-walked out with Reggie close behind. The area in front of the elevator was slightly inset and out of view of the door to the office. A *B1* glowed from the LED screen above the elevator.

“Where’s the button?” Hudson scanned the walls beside the elevator doors.

Reggie pointed to a small, circular black disc attached to the wall. “Its keycard activated only.”

Hudson looked towards the office. “We need to get into her office and find that card.”

“What if she keeps it around her neck?”

“We have to hope not.”

“You could knock her out,” Reggie suggested.

“I’m not hitting a woman.”

“But you’d hit her if she was a man? That’s sexist.”

“No, that’s being a gentleman. Besides, I’m not hitting anybody. We’re not here to hurt innocent people.”

“They’re not innocent if they are involved in implanting microchips in unsuspecting citizens.”

“I’m still not hitting her.”

“How are we going to get the card?”

“Can’t you use your hacking skills to bypass the card reader?”

“I might be able to if I had a card reader and my laptop.”

The *B1* on the LED changed to *G*.

“Hide!” Hudson whisper-yelled, and they ran back to the freezer as the elevator dinged open behind them.

A short, balding man in a lab coat and a serious expression exited the elevator.

“Jaden?” he called out.

The woman exited her office with a half-eaten chocolate sprinkle donut in her hand.

She greeted him with a wide smile. “Bob. What’s up?” she mumbled through a mouthful of pastry.

“Where are my lab supplies? I was told they would be here by this morning."

"They just arrived. Did you want a donut?"

Hudson noticed that although Bob kept his key card around his neck, Jaden's was not visible.

"No, I don't want a donut. Why haven't my supplies been taken down yet?" Bob asked with his hands on his hips. "I need them, *now*!"

Jaden held her hands up. "Okay, Bob. No need to get so angry. They're right over there."

She pointed to a collection of boxes shrink-wrapped and sitting on a wooden pallet.

"Let's go, then." Bob cycled his hands.

Rolling her eyes, she stuffed the rest of her donut in her mouth and wheeled a manual pallet jack out of the corner.

Hudson and Reggie shuffled around the side of the freezer, barely out of view.

She pumped the pallet jack and wheeled it to the elevator doors. As she approached the doors, she grabbed a lanyard with her key card hanging from a nail on the wall.

Bob, Jaden and the crates crammed into the elevator, and the doors closed.

"Her keycard was right there the whole time!" exclaimed Reggie.

"I think we need to work on our situational awareness," said Hudson. "Let's search her office before they return."

The *G* on the LED screen above the elevator changed to a *B1* and then a *B2*.

"You wait here and watch the elevator," said Hudson. "Tell me when she's coming back."

"What are you looking for?"

"I don't know."

Jaden's office was larger than Hudson expected. It was a cross between a tiny. messy kitchen, a lounge and an office. It reminded him of the lounge at the fire hall where Sophie worked. Papers and folders lay scattered across a wide, laminate desk. A toaster oven, microwave and a coffee maker sat on a short counter littered with cups, plates and a half box of donuts. A tall fridge sat between the counter and a round table with two well-used chairs. Beside the dining area was a worn leather couch and a mismatched green chair facing a large flatscreen television mounted to the wall. Four grey lockers lined the far wall.

Hudson rifled through the papers and the desk drawers but found nothing useful.

"Hurry," Reggie called.

Hudson poked his head out the door. "Are they coming?"

"Not yet."

Hudson returned to the office and continued his search. When he looked inside the lockers, he found two blue lab-style overcoats.

"They're coming!" yelled Reggie.

Hudson dashed out of the office with the lab coats in one hand and a Boston cream donut in the other. He followed Reggie back to their hiding spot behind the freezer seconds before the elevator dinged open.

Jaden emerged with the empty pallet jack.

After hanging her key card on the nail, she returned the pallet jack to its corner and went back into her office.

"You stole a donut?" Reggie asked.

Hudson offered him the last half. "Do you want the rest?"

"That deep-fried, sugar-laced, carb-heavy, over-processed poison will clog your arteries and shave at least three years off your life."

Hudson shrugged and popped the rest into his mouth. He handed Reggie a blue lab coat. They donned their new disguises and grabbed the lanyard with the key card from the nail. The card reader beeped when Reggie tapped the card, and the elevator doors opened.

"What floor?" Reggie asked.

There were five buttons, *G, B1, B2, B3 and B4* with another round card reader beside them. The G was lit up.

Hudson pressed *B4* and swiped the reader, but nothing happened. When he tried *B1*, the reader beeped, and the elevator moved down.

"Act like you know where you're going." Hudson wiped the chocolate icing from his mouth and straightened the lab coat lapel. "Also, don't look anyone in the eye. Keep your head down and keep walking."

CHAPTER 17

The elevator doors slid open to a wide hallway with blank off-white walls. A man in a blue suit carrying a black leather briefcase glanced in their direction as he walked past and disappeared down the hallway to the left.

Hudson buttoned up his blue lab coat, stepped out of the elevator and turned right. Reggie paused and looked in both directions.

"Keep moving!" Hudson hissed. "Act like you're on an important mission."

Reggie had to jog to catch up. "This *is* an important mission."

A woman in dress pants and a collared blouse nodded at Hudson as she passed. A bearded man in pleated pants and a navy buttoned shirt carrying a laptop appeared from a doorway and rushed by.

Hudson and Reggie passed offices, boardrooms, conference rooms and more men and women in business attire.

"We aren't blending in very well with these disguises," Reggie whispered as they turned down a random hallway.

"Hey!" a woman yelled from behind them.

"Don't turn around," Hudson whispered and continued walking.

"What are you doing here?" the woman jogged to catch up. "You're not supposed to be up here."

Hudson stopped and smiled at her. "We're from IT. Mike from accounting had an issue with his printer."

"Accounting is *that* way." She pointed down the hallway behind them.

Hudson turned to Reggie and shook his head. "I told you we were going the wrong way."

The woman looked at Reggie. “Aren’t you a little young to work here?”

“He’s an intern,” said Hudson, smiling again. “Anyway, we should get going.”

“That’s right,” added Reggie. “Mike from accounting will wonder where we are.”

“Wait!” she said as they turned to leave. “While I have you, can you take a quick look at my computer? I’m having trouble connecting to the network.”

“We should—” Hudson began.

Reggie interrupted. “We can help you with that.”

Hudson gave a subtle shake of his head, but Reggie ignored him. “Where’s your office ma’am?”

“My name is Iris, and my office is this way.”

She led them through another smaller hallway to a large open office containing a dozen workspaces. Her desk was a mess of papers, folders, pens, sticky notes and a dirty coffee cup.

Reggie sat down and moved the mouse. The ocean beach screensaver disappeared and was replaced by a login screen.

“What’s your login?” he asked.

Iris looked around nervously. “There are strict policies about giving that out to anybody.”

“You’re right,” said Reggie. “But if you want me to fix your computer, I need to log in.”

“Don’t you have an IT administrator password?”

“Yes, but this issue may be related to your profile settings. It’s easier to fix if I can log in under your profile. I could access it from my computer in the IT office tomorrow morning…”

“I need this fixed now.” Iris grabbed a pen and wrote her information on a sticky note and handed it to Reggie.

“Thanks,” said Reggie and logged in. “What exactly is the issue?”

“I don’t have access to the network,” Iris replied. “Most of my files are on the network, but when I go to the file explorer, the network isn’t there.”

“Hmm…” said Reggie.

“Shouldn’t you be doing this?” Iris asked Hudson. “He’s just an intern."

"It's good practice for him," Hudson replied.

He and Iris watched while Reggie dove deep into the operating system with a flurry of keystrokes, clicks and mouse movements.

Almost a full minute later, the window went black.

"What happened?" asked Iris.

"I installed the newest network driver and updated the network configuration settings. After a fresh reboot, the settings will be configured and the network will be back online."

When the computer completed its reboot sequence, Reggie stood up and smiled at Iris. "Try it now."

She sat down and logged in. After a few clicks, she smiled. "Wow, you did it! Thanks!"

"You're welcome," said Reggie.

"We need to get going to accounting to help Mike," said Hudson, and he and Reggie quickly left.

"That was impressive," said Hudson as they walked back towards the elevator. "You really know what you're doing."

"I didn't *do* anything," said Reggie with a smile.

"What are you talking about? You installed the configuration network and fixed her computer."

"I pretended to do stuff. The only thing that fixed her network connection was the reboot."

"Yes, but you knew that would fix it."

"Nope. That was just a guess. With computer issues, most of them can be fixed with a fresh reboot."

"What happened if the reboot didn't work?"

"I didn't plan that far ahead." Reggie held up the sticky note with Iris' login and password. "It doesn't matter, because now we've got this!"

Hudson smirked. "Good work, kid. Let's get back to the elevator and go down a level."

"This is awesome," said Reggie as they descended to *B2.* "We're like spies on a secret mission!"

"Get Smart or Austin Powers?" Hudson asked.

“More like Tom Cruise in Mission Impossible.”

“Right.” Hudson rolled his eyes.

“I told you there was a secret, underground facility here. Now we have proof.”

“We still don’t know what they are doing here,” Hudson said as the elevator doors swished open.

A woman sat behind a large reception desk. She was looking at something behind her when the elevator doors opened. Before she turned around, Hudson pulled Reggie out of view.

“What are you doing?” Reggie whispered.

Hudson pressed his finger against his mouth and pushed the *B3* button behind him.

After the doors closed, he said, “There’s a woman behind a reception desk. She’s probably going to ask for ID.”

“Where are we going now?” asked Reggie.

“We’ll try B3.”

When the elevator reached B3, the doors opened, revealing a wide corridor that was empty except for two signs on the far wall. The first read, “Dorms 1-50, Fitness Room, Entertainment,” and pointed left. The other read, “Dorms 61-100, Commons and Cafeteria”, and pointed right.

Reggie pointed right. “Let’s go this way.”

“Why?”

“Because I’m hungry.”

“We’re here to gather intel, not steal food.”

“It’s hard to spy on an empty stomach.”

A group of two women and one man laughed as they passed by. All of them wore casual clothes. One of them turned to look at Reggie and Hudson and creased his brow.

“For super spies, we aren’t very good at blending in.” Hudson unbuttoned and removed his blue lab coat, and Reggie did the same. Hudson hooked a thumb in the collar and hung it over his shoulder while Reggie rolled his into a ball and held it at his hip.

“Try to look older,” said Hudson as they turned the corner and entered another hallway.

“How am I supposed to do that?”

"I don't know, use your hoodie."

Reggie flicked his hoodie on. "Now I look like a shady gangster."

The wide hallways branched off in every direction. Instead of offices and workspaces like on B1, this level contained mostly living quarters. Everyone wore casual clothes.

It took them 15 minutes to navigate the maze of hallways to find the cafeteria.

A few small groups of diners sat scattered amongst the many rows of tables and chairs. A long serving counter lined the near wall.

Reggie ran to the stack of trays and grabbed one. Before Hudson could catch up, he was already ordering food from the servers behind the counter.

The woman behind the counter served them without question. They took their trayfuls of food and drink to a sparsely populated area of the cafeteria and sat down.

"What are you eating?" Hudson looked repulsively at Reggie's food.

"Can you believe it? They offer vegan *and* gluten-free options."

"When you're finished your *food* – if you can call it that – we need to get another keycard so we can get past security on B2."

"I say we break down one of those dorm rooms and demand they hand over their keycards," said Reggie. "When they say no, you start busting skulls!"

"We are not busting anyone's skulls. This is a low-key undercover operation."

"Now you sound like a super spy," Reggie said, smiling.

They discussed a violence-free plan while Reggie finished his cauliflower and lentils, and Hudson devoured his spaghetti and meatballs.

Hudson got up and walked toward an older man in a sweater vest, eating and reading by himself. Besides the book, splayed out next to his tray was a lanyard with a keycard. It was a different color than Jaden's card.

"Excuse me, sir," Hudson said to the man. "Can I ask what you're reading?"

"Pardon me?" the man looked up at Hudson.

Hudson smiled. "I was wondering what you were reading. I'm a big fan of books and am always interested in what other people are reading."

"Usually, I read more academic books." He held up the book to show Hudson the front. "But today I'm deep into a purely entertaining read. It's an apocalyptic adventure called Black Flag – Surviving the Scourge."

As he talked, Reggie crept up to him on the opposite side and reached for the lanyard.

"Wow!" Hudson said with an exaggerated flare. "What's it about?"

"A deadly virus spreads and kills everyone. A small group struggle to survive amidst a crumbling society." He held up his hand. "I know what you're thinking – it's a little morbid to read about a pandemic after we just had one – especially when we work here!"

"Sounds interesting," said Hudson, still smiling. "I'll have to check it out. See you around."

Hudson returned his tray to the counter and met Reggie at the cafeteria exit.

Reggie gave him the *thumbs up*. "Mission accomplished!"

"That was incredible," said Reggie as they rushed back to the elevator. "We make an awesome team!"

"Maybe they'll give us adjoining cells," said Hudson, motioning to the two men walking in their direction.

Both men wore dark suits and carried radios. Hudson looked around for a place to hide, but all the dorm room doors were closed and locked.

"Turn around," he whispered.

They pivoted and walked in the opposite direction.

"Are they following us?" Reggie whispered.

"I don't know. Keep walking."

After a few minutes of speed walking down various hallways, Hudson snuck a look behind them. The men were no longer behind them.

"That was close," said Hudson. "Let's get back to the elevator."

"Which way?"

"I'm not sure."

After wandering the hallways for almost twenty minutes, they eventually found the elevators. This time, two women joined them inside.

"You guys going up?"

"Yeah," replied Hudson.

The elevator dinged and Hudson motioned for the two women to go first.

"What now?" whispered Reggie.

"Do whatever they do," Hudson responded.

They followed behind the two women, who walked up to the counter and swiped their cards on a black reader on the counter. The woman behind the reception desk looked down at her monitor and smiled.

Hudson and Reggie swiped their cards, but as they walked away, the woman behind the desk called after them.

"Excuse me, Mr. Rekaf and Ms. Sugob?"

Hudson turned. "Ummm…yes that's us. Is there a problem?"

The woman stood up. "Yes. Can you please wait a moment?"

Hudson smiled nervously, while Reggie's eyes widened.

"What seems to be the issue?" asked Hudson.

The woman held up a finger and picked up the phone. "Yes, can I get someone down here? We have an issue that needs to be resolved."

She looked up at Hudson. "Your friend does not look like Ms Sugob. I know her - she works up top in shipping. It's probably an IT issue with the system. Please wait there against the wall."

"Go!" Hudson said in a quiet but stern voice to Reggie.

They ran through the corridor with the security woman's voice yelling behind them. After they rounded the first corner, they slowed down. A man in a blue lab coat, carrying a blue plastic box with a biohazard symbol, nodded at them before opening a door and entering a room.

All the others around also wore blue lab coats.

"Put your lab coat on."

"At least we're fitting in a little better on this level," said Reggie.

"Too bad, security will chase us down shortly. Keep moving. Walk fast, but not too fast to attract attention."

They speed walked deeper into the level. Most of the rooms on this level appeared to be labs. Hazards symbols adorned many of the doors, including biohazard, flammable and toxic.

"What are we looking for?" asked Reggie. "I don't see any signs that say secret *injectable tracker lab*."

"Do you still have that login and password from Iris?" Hudson asked.

Reggie held it up. "Yes, but they probably have a sandboxed system."

"Meaning?"

"Meaning, if we want to access their system using this login, we have to do it from in here."

"This way." Hudson pointed to a door to a darkened room.

The warning symbols on the door included biohazard, toxic, poison and many other ominous pictograms.

The door clicked open when Hudson swiped Mr. Rekaf's card, and they quickly shuffled inside.

Reggie reached for the light switch, but Hudson stopped him. "Leave it off."

Loud footsteps and serious voices outside made both of them step away from the door. After a few seconds, their pursuers moved on.

They walked cautiously into the darkened lab. The only light shone through the small rectangular window in the door.

A long, stainless-steel island counter stretched into the darkness. Microscopes, sinks, beakers, test tubes and various lab equipment sat on the counter along the far wall.

A strange squeaking sound emanated from the back of the room.

"What's that noise?" asked Reggie.

Hudson shrugged.

More squeaks and scratching joined the squeaking as they tread cautiously deeper into the dark lab.

"I found some needles," said Reggie.

"Touch nothing," Hudson scolded.

He found a doorway leading into a small office at the back and turned the light on. Hundreds of medical books sat neatly on a five-tier bookshelf along one wall. Filing cabinets and more medical equipment sat on the other. Between them, a small wooden desk contained a lamp, file folders and a thin LED monitor.

"In here," Hudson called out. "I found a computer."

When Reggie didn't answer, Hudson left the office to look for him.

He found him staring at something.

"Reggie? Is everything okay? I found a computer to. . ."

Hudson's words petered out as he saw what Reggie was staring at. A hairless rat stared through the tiny steel bars of a cage. The flashlight beam gave his eyes a silver glow. Reggie panned the light across multiple cages filled with more hairless rats.

"They're just rats," said Hudson. "Come on. We need to log in to the computer before they find us."

"They are living, breathing animals with feelings and emotions," said Reggie, reaching towards the cage.

"Don't touch them!" said Hudson. "They probably have diseases."

"Only because the cruel, evil scientists gave them diseases.

Hudson grabbed Reggie's arm and led him away. "Which is why we need to expose this place for what it is. And we can do that by logging in to their computer..."

Reggie reluctantly followed and sat down at the desk in the office. He turned the monitor and computer on.

"Don't you feel bad for those innocent creatures?" he asked as they waited for the computer to boot.

"It's better to test animals than humans."

"There are better ways to do science than sacrificing rats."

"Rats are disgusting, disease-spreading ugly rodents that operate solely on instinct."

Reggie pulled out the sticky note and logged in. "I have a friend that keeps a rat as a pet. They are smart, friendly animals."

"Good for him. I prefer my rats stuck in a trap rather than eating the insulation in my trailer or leaving contaminated feces on my counter."

"I almost forgot – you're a *hunter*." He said the last word with exaggerated revulsion.

Before Hudson could respond, Reggie said, "I found the list of directories and files on the main server. What am I looking for?"

"Are there any specific project descriptions?"

Reggie scrolled to a folder labelled Projects. The folders within were labelled with codenames and he had to open each one to find a description. It was a time-consuming process. The projects included drug testing, immune responses, rare disease research, medical equipment testing and pandemic protocols. None of the projects contained the words *Covid* or *injectable tracker*.

Reggie skipped down to the bottom of the list to a folder labelled *MITA*, but when he clicked on it, a window appeared, asking for a password. He inputted Iris's login credentials, but they didn't give him access.

"That's it!" yelled Reggie. "That is the top-secret project they are working on."

"But you can't open it..."

"No, but at least we know it exists."

"Can you copy it to a USB and crack it later?"

Reggie rifled through the drawers in the desk. "I don't see any here. But they might not work, anyway."

"Why not?"

"A high-security facility like this won't allow their computers to read USB's."

He returned to the computer, clicking and typing. "I have another idea. If I search for the MITA as a keyword...maybe, we can...aha!"

"What did you find?"

"It's a report from the accounting department talking about financing for Project MITA. The report tracks where the funds for the project are coming from."

"And?" Hudson looked nervously back at the door, expecting security to come charging in. "Where are they coming from?"

"A bunch of places. This file is like over a hundred pages, and I'm not an accountant. There are a bunch of numbered companies from the Cayman Islands and—"

The rectangular window in the door to the lab went dark. Someone was standing outside the lab.

"Turn the computer off now!"

As Reggie fiddled with the mouse, Hudson pulled the plug from the power bar. The office darkened, and Hudson and Reggie ducked behind the desk.

Someone opened the door to the lab and turned on the light. Footsteps clacked across the lab towards the office.

"You can come out now," said a man's voice.

"Hi!" said Hudson, standing up. "I was working late, lost track of time and fell asleep—"

"Cut the crap and stand against the wall. And your little buddy, too!"

"You can take him out," Reggie whispered to Hudson.

The security guard pointed a pistol at them.

Hudson looked at Reggie and shook his head.

"Not this time."

CHAPTER 18

"What were you hoping to achieve?" asked Julian Terces.

Julian introduced himself as director of operations at the Nanotech Acor Facility. He may have been a good-looking muscular man in his youth, but the decade after middle age was not kind. Copious portions of gel kept his thinning hair in place. His suit jacket covered his oversized gut, and the button strained to keep it in place. Dark pouches under his eyes distracted from what used to be striking brown irises. He leaned against his desk and held his hands in front. His shiny, silver oversized watch glittered on his wrist, and his middle and index fingers were stained the colour of rust.

Hudson and Reggie sat in front of him on metal chairs. Their hands were bound with zip ties behind their back.

The two security men who brought them to Julian's office stood with their arms crossed at the door behind them.

"We uncovered your secret underground facility where you make trackers to put in the Covid vaccine." Reggie held his head up in defiance.

"There is only one portion of that sentence that is true."

"You admit it?"

"This *is* Nanotech's underground facility. We conduct research into vaccines and other pharmaceuticals."

"If everything you do here is lawful, then why keep it a secret?"

Julian laughed. The smoke-infused phlegm caught in his throat, and the chuckle morphed into a hacking cough.

"This isn't a secret, you idiots!" Julian said once he recovered. "It may not be common, public knowledge, but the government knows about the place."

“The government is in on it as well!” shouted Reggie. “I knew it!”

“We keep it underground for safety reasons.”

“Are the elites at IEC involved in this?” asked Reggie.

“No!” Julian snapped, then quickly recovered when he realized his tone. “They have nothing to do with this.”

“Why bus all the employees in?” asked Hudson.

“Although this isn’t a super secret facility, it is better for public relations for some groups not to know about our location.”

“By *groups*, you mean the general public?”

“I mean certain animal rights activists.”

“We found your cages of defenceless rats. What you do to those rats is despicable!”

“You have the right to your opinion, but Nanotech abides by all standards and regulations regarding animal testing. There are no illegal activities here unless you count you two breaking and entering.”

Julian unclasped his fingers and tapped on the desk.

“What happens on B4?” asked Hudson.

Julian stepped away from the desk. “The basement level? That’s just storage. Anyway, I don’t need to explain what we do here or give you a guided tour. The police have been called, and the two of you are going—”

Before he finished his sentence, his phone rang. “Give me a sec,” he said after looking at the screen.

He left the room for a few minutes before returning in a huff.

“Apparently, the bigwigs at head office want to send you away with just a warning. The two gentlemen that brought you here will escort you back to your truck. If you return, we will press charges. If you go to the press and tell them about this facility, we will press charges. If you write a blog post or rant about us on social media, we will deny it and press charges. We have indisputable video footage, and breaking and entering is a felony in Michigan and is punishable by up to 10 years in prison.”

He nodded to the security guards at the door. “Take them away. I need a smoke.”

CHAPTER 19

Hudson hissed as he punched the heavy vinyl bag.

Jab. Jab Uppercut. Hook. Jab. Cross.

Sweat dribbled down his face, neck and back, making his black tank top stick to his skin. He ducked and weaved around an invisible opponent and continued his rampage against the punching bag.

Moe's MMA and Boxing Gym was not as drab, murky or dimly lit as Mickey's Gym in the Rocky films. However, when Hudson trained, the rest of the world became as dark as Mickey's Gym at 3 am.

His thoughts projected images of people onto the punching bag.

Jab. Rear hook. Jab. Jab. Lead hook.

A flash of Sophie crying out from the tablet appeared. With a steak knife, she screamed and cut the tracker from her shoulder. Blood sprayed out, and the tracker clinked on the floor.

Duck. Weave. Weave.

Mr Schmidth from Schmidth Funeral Home told him with a soft, quivering voice that he burned her body and there was nothing left.

Jab. Jab. Uppercut. Hook. Cross.

At the Wanigas Diner, Reggie ordered a garden salad with low-fat raspberry vinaigrette.

Jab. Jab. Weave. Parry.

Sophie pulled off her red firefighter's helmet in slow motion. A gust of hot summer wind ruffled her blond shimmering hair. Her honey-coloured eyes glinted when she smiled at him.

Block. Parry. Roll. Duck.

Lawrence Hargreaves punched his son Reggie square in the chin.

Jab. Cross. Parry, Rear hook.

In the high school gym, Riker sneered from behind the brim of his grey Fedora. Beside him, neckless Deltoid smiled.

Jab. Jab. Jab. Cross. Jap. Uppercut.

Just as the punching bag morphed into a sharp-dressed Julian Terces, someone yelled.

“You’re not kicking!” Coach Benny’s high-pitched voice broke Hudson from his flashbacks.

Benny was not officially Hudson’s coach, but everyone at the gym called him Coach Benny. Although in his late sixties, he still maintained a muscular physique. His round head was as hairless as a lab rat.

“If you want to be an MMA fighter, you have to kick more,” said Coach Benny.

“Who said I want to be an MMA fighter?”

“I did! Your punches are impressively powerful, but mix it up with some side kicks, front kicks or even a roundhouse.”

“I’m just blowing off some steam here, coach.”

“I don’t care! You have potential. Don’t squander it.”

Coach Benny rubbed his shiny scalp as he sauntered away to find another victim to harass.

Hudson wiped his brow with the back of his hand.

“There you are!” Reggie poked his head from behind the punching bag and smiled.

“What are you doing here?” asked Hudson. “And how did you find me?”

Reggie picked up a pair of boxing gloves hanging on a post and pushed them on. “Maybe I’m here to learn to fight.”

He posed in an awkward fighting stance and held up his gloves. “Whoa! These are heavy!”

Coach Benny appeared behind him and kicked Reggie’s feet apart.

“I’m not actually—” Reggie struggled to remain standing.

“Feet, shoulder-width apart. Bend your legs. Raise your rear heel with the weight on the ball of your foot.”

Coach Benny configured Reggie as if he were a bendable action figure.

"Hey, don't—"

"Keep your pelvis under your shoulders, your core tight."

He tightened the straps on the gloves and continued. "Put your right elbow close to your body to protect your ribs and put your left arm up here."

Reggie looked at Hudson for help, but Hudson smiled and stepped back.

Coach Benny took a step back and placed both hands behind his back. "Okay, now hit me."

"What? No…I'm not…"

"Hit me! Hit me as hard as you can."

Reggie looked back at Hudson again, who nodded. "You heard the bald old man. Punch him!"

Reggie swiped his fist at Coach Benny, who took the mild punch without moving.

"Really? That's all you got? Come on, Kirk Cameron."

"Who's Kirk—"

"If you don't punch me as hard as you can, I will pants you and spank your lily-white—"

Whoosh! Reggie's fist flew at Coach Benny's head but passed by when Benny leaned back.

"Awww." Coach Benny mocked. "You missed! Try again, pansy."

Reggie punched with his left, but Coach Benny ducked.

"Oops! You missed again! I'd say you punch like a girl, but Amata there could punch better than most guys in this gym."

He nodded at a fierce-looking, muscular girl strutting by. She smiled through her yellow mouthguard.

Coach Benny reached out and slapped Reggie across the face.

"Hey, that hurt!"

"Does that make you angry? You must exact revenge on the evil old fart that taunts you a second time!"

Benny gritted his teeth and attacked with a flurry of punches. None of them connected with the weaving, ducking, and swaying coach.

Reggie stopped and leaned over, gasping for breath.

Coach Benny stood behind him and smacked him on the back. "Good try kid but you better stick to bowling or golf."

He walked away, shaking his head before yelling at another unsuspecting victim.

"That man is crazy," said Reggie, still panting.

"He's a fighting genius," said Hudson. "*You're* the one who came into his gym and put boxing gloves on."

Reggie struggled awkwardly, trying to remove the gloves. "How do you get these stupid things off?"

"With help." Hudson grabbed his arm and unclasped the Velcro. "What *are* you doing here? Other than passing you by at school, I haven't talked to you in months."

"That was some crazy stuff at the airbase, wasn't it?" Reggie slipped out of his gloves. "Do you fight? I'd love to see you knock the life out of someone again."

Hudson removed his gloves, grabbed a towel and wiped his head and arms.

"I don't fight competitively anymore."

"Why not? I bet you're really good."

"My time for fighting competitions has come and gone. This is just recreational to keep in shape."

"You're not that old."

"I'm thirty-five. Technically, I can still fight, but most of these guys are younger and stronger. But you didn't come here to talk about my fight career. Shouldn't you be in school?"

"Christmas break started yesterday. Also, I have new breaking developments in the case."

Hudson sighed. "I don't know how you escaped your father's wrath with your life from our last adventure, but I think we should drop this."

"Have *you* given up?" asked Reggie.

"I didn't say that."

"Neither have I. According to my contacts, the secret cabal at the IEC is about to make another major move in their goal of creating a new world—"

"Keep your voice down." Hudson looked around at the nearby

fighters.

"I also discovered something about Project MITA."

Hudson eyed him suspiciously. "Do you know what it stands for?"

"Not exactly."

"What *did* you find out?"

"You're still here!" yelled Coach Benny as he sauntered towards them. "Did you want to work on your ground game?"

"Can we talk somewhere else?" asked Reggie.

"Let me get changed." Hudson threw his damp towel over his shoulder. "I'll meet you out front in fifteen."

Outside, snowflakes wafted down like tiny feathers. Some disappeared as they landed on the wet, salted pavement. Others collided with the warm hoods of passing cars. The rest collected on Christmas shoppers' parked cars, streetlights and garland decorations. The temperature hovered just below freezing and the overcast sky diffused the early winter sunlight. Garbled Christmas music pushed through an old outdoor speaker of a chocolatier and bakery. Hudson and Reggie splashed through the slushy, wet sidewalk as they talked.

"What do you think Project MITA stand for?" asked Hudson.

"I don't know for sure…yet. But we *do* know is that it's a secret Nanotech project at the secret Acor underground facility."

"That's a lot of secrets. You said you discovered something else."

"Yes! The top-secret international cabal known as IEC—"

"What is the IEC? Julian reacted strangely when you mentioned that."

Reggie smiled. "You noticed that too. The IEC is the International Economics Congress. They meet in Sovad, Switzerland every year. They created the idea for the Great Reset, a New World Order, digital IDs, the destruction of capitalism and are using vaccines to control the population by altering the DNA of—"

"Pause! You're going off the rails again. What did you find out about MITA?"

"A reliable source told me that there is a secret meeting between a top executive from Nanotech and a high-ranking member of the IEC. The top executive is supposedly giving a report about Project MITA with the IEC guy. If we can find out who the IEC guy is, we will be one step closer to the top of this conspiracy."

"A reliable source? Are you talking about one of your online conspiracy friends?"

"Remember how I told you about a guy that told me about the facility at the Acor Army Base?"

"Yes..."

"This is the same guy. He was right about the secret underground lab, and I *know* he's right about this."

"Does this *source* say where the mysterious meeting is supposed to happen?"

"The Sentinel says—"

"Wait! The *Sentinel*? He calls himself the *Sentinel*?"

"I know, right? It's *such* a cool name!"

"Right..."

Reggie continued. "The Sentinel says the meeting will happen at the Empire City Christmas Gala."

Hudson shook his head and held up his hands. "Why would they have a secret meeting at a public Christmas party? Why not two guys in trench coasts under a bridge at 2 am?"

"First, the Gala is not a public party. It is by invitation only. Select top executives and other rich and powerful people are there. Besides, I doubt they'll have a PowerPoint presentation or a USB handoff. More like rich drunk guys bragging to each other about their exploits in creating a new world order."

"Even if that's all true, how are we going to get an invitation to this hoity-toity gala?"

"That has all been taken care of. Do you own a tuxedo?"

CHAPTER 20

Hudson felt like the first kid to walk into the gym at a school dance. However, this wasn't homecoming. It was the snowy tarmac of the Motor City Airport. Ahead of him was a shiny, sleek Learjet 60. He pulled up his hood and pushed through the brisk gale towards the stairs.

When he reached the top, he stepped inside. As he suspected, there was no one else aboard, except one stewardess.

"You're early," she said with a smile.

Hudson brushed the snow off his parka and stuffed it in the overhead compartment. "I thought security would have taken longer," he said sheepishly.

"First time on a private jet?" she asked.

"How can you tell?"

"Please have a seat anywhere. I'm sure the other passengers will arrive shortly."

Hudson had only been to Empire City twice, and both times he and Sophie drove the ten hours across the country. He walked to the rear of the plane and picked a seat by the window.

"Excuse me?" he called to the stewardess. "How long is the flight?"

"About an hour and a half, sir."

That was the same time it took him to drive from Wanigas to the Motor City Airport. Now here he was, the first eager kid at the dance. When he and Sophie went to Bermuda for their honeymoon, they arrived at the airport three hours early and still almost missed their flight. Today, he showed up three hours early and made it to the plane in less than a half hour. He waited an hour inside the terminal for the plane to arrive, and now he was on board with almost two hours till takeoff.

After reclining the soft leather seat all the way back, Hudson fell asleep.

Over an hour later, he awoke to the sound of passengers boarding the plane. He rubbed his eyes and sat up.

"Hudson!" Reggie shuffled between the seats and sat beside him. "You here already! How long have you been waiting?"

"Not long."

"This is going to be awesome!"

"What is this gala that we're going to?"

"Dad!" Reggie called out. "What's the full name of the gala?"

Lawrence Hargreaves handed his overcoat to the stewardess and joined them at the rear of the plane. "It's the Empire City Christmas Environmental Gala and Fundraiser."

He held out his hand to Hudson. "Mr. Finlay, I'm glad you came. This will be good for both you and my sister."

Hudson shook his hand. "Again, I'm sorry for all the trouble I've caused you and your son. It is more than gracious of you to invite me."

Lawrence waved him off. "Don't worry about it. I'm so busy at work, I don't get to spend as much time as I'd like with my son. You seem like a good, upstanding young man. I'd rather he got into trouble with someone like yourself than with drunken teenagers. Besides, you're also doing me a favour."

Hudson didn't know what that meant.

After everyone found their seats, the pilot's voice came over the intercom.

"Welcome aboard. After a quick de-icing, we will get this show on the road. The weather is a little blustery, and we may experience some turbulence. On the bright side, we're getting a boost from a decent tailwind, and our trip to the city that never sleeps should only take about an hour and twenty minutes. Please make yourself comfortable and enjoy the ride."

Twenty minutes later, they were cruising over southern Ontario.

"What did your father say about his sister, and how am I doing him a favour?" asked Hudson.

"Don't worry about Aunt Sera–she's nice." Reggie opened his laptop. "This is going to be great. This is like Phase II of our secret spy mission. Or is it Phase III, if you count recovering the tracker..."

"We're *not*..." Hudson looked around and lowered his voice. "We're *not* doing anything illegal. We go to the gala, drink champagne, clap at the speeches or whatever they do at these things and listen to some conversations. That's all!"

Reggie typed something into his computer. "Yes! Raven has agreed to meet."

"Who's Raven?"

"An old friend from grade school. I haven't seen her in like five years. We sort of met up virtually during Covid and shared hacking tips. You're going to love her."

"I have *so* many questions. How did you get me an invitation to this gala? Why doesn't your dad hate me? Who is Aunt Sera? Who is Raven? Why are you meeting her? Also, when they say black tie event, is it *literally* a black tie?"

Reggie closed his laptop. "Don't worry, we'll get the concierge to arrange a tux rental from the Konrad."

"We're staying at the Konrad? I can't afford a fancy hotel..."

"Don't worry, my dad's paying." Reggie reclined his chair and closed his eyes. "I need a nap. You should get some sleep too. We can talk more at the hotel."

"I'm not tired."

As Reggie drifted into dreamland, Hudson stared out the window. Clouds below obscured most of the view, but intermittent gaps in the cumulus provided brief glimpses of Lake Erie below. It looked like an endless sea.

Sophie would have loved this. Flying on a private jet to Empire City. Staying at a fancy hotel. Dressing up and going to the gala. Add in the possibility of uncovering a secretive plot by an international cabal of global elites and she'd be living her dream. Add in a trip to the zoo to see the elephants, and *then* all her dreams would come true in just one weekend.

But Sophie would never get a chance to travel to Empire City. She would never go to a fancy hotel or gala, and the only secretive plot she almost uncovered got her killed.

Hudson swallowed the growing lump in his throat.

CHAPTER 21

Whoever was knocking on the hotel door was relentless. Hudson rolled over and buried his head in the soft down-filled pillow. The bed was the most comfortable bed he had ever slept on, and he didn't want to get up. Compared to his thin mattress in the trailer home, it was like heaven - except Sophie was not next to him. The knocking continued.

He slid out of bed and stretched. The knocking got louder.

"I'm coming!"

After stubbing his toe on the rolling tray with the remnants of last night's dinner, he hop-limped to the door. As he reached it, he realized he was only wearing boxers.

"Hudson, time to get up!" said Reggie from outside the door.

Hudson unlocked and opened the door.

"It's about time!" said Reggie, bursting into the room, but then turned away. "Dude! Put some clothes on. Nobody wants to see that."

"You've never seen a man in boxers?"

"I'm a skinny teenager with low self-esteem. Seeing a big guy like you with your bulging muscles is making me feel...inadequate."

"You're the one waking me up."

"It's almost nine in the morning. I thought you were an early riser."

Hudson shimmied into his jeans. "I had a rough night."

"This is supposed to be fun. You should have come out with us for dinner."

"I know. I'm sorry. Doing all this without...Is your father mad?"

"Nah, he's fine. Just get dressed, because we are going out."

"Are we looking for a tux for me for tonight?"

"No, the concierge is looking after that."

"Don't they have to measure me or something?"

"He can size you just by looking at you. We have a more important mission for today."

Reggie held up a small paper bag. "I brought you some breakfast."

Hudson finished dressing and grabbed the bag.

"One bagel…" he said, looking inside.

"Empire City is famous for its bagels with cream cheese and lox."

"What is lox?" Hudson pulled it out of the bag and took a bite.

"It's brined salmon. Now get your boots on, we're leaving."

"Not bad," he said, swallowing and taking another bite.

Hudson dressed and slipped on his boots before grabbing his coat off the rack. "Where are we going?"

"We're meeting my friend Raven."

"Can we get a couple more of these bagels on the way? That was fantastic."

"Did you eat it already?"

"Pouting all night makes this big man hungry."

"You're an animal," said Reggie, rolling his eyes.

They made a quick pit stop in the hotel restaurant to grab two more bagels before calling a cab.

The sun shone brightly outside, and the snow from the previous night had finally stopped. The taxi swerved in and out of the noisy traffic along the busy Empire City streets.

"Are you sure you have the right address?" asked the driver. "It's not exactly the nicest part of town."

"Yes, I know. I have a friend that lives there," said Reggie.

"Excuse me," Hudson said to the driver. "You have a zoo here, right?"

"Yeah. It's only five minutes from here. Is that where you want to go now?"

"Do they have elephants?"

"One, but a lot people are trying to get it out of there. It's inhumane the way they keep that poor elephant alone. She's not happy. The Empire Times called her the loneliest elephant."

"You want to go to the zoo?" asked Reggie.

"Not anymore."

Ten minutes later, they reached their destination. Reggie paid the driver, and they got out.

"Thank you and Merry Christmas," said the driver and rolled away.

Unlike the skyscrapers, shiny cars, and rushing business people of downtown, this neighbourhood was different. Tall, skinny houses with high-pitched roofs lined one side of the street. A pawn shop, an old stone church and a run-down bar sat on the other. A small gang of sketchy teens leered at them from further down the narrow street.

"This is where Raven lives?"

"Somewhere around here," said Reggie, crossing the street.

"You don't know where she lives?"

"We're not going to her house. Raven is part of a hacktivist collective. They got some cool gear that they're going to lend us."

"A hacktivist collective?"

Reggie looked at his phone before climbing the stone steps of the old church. "It's a group of hacker activists."

"Yeah, I figured. If this is something illegal, I will personally call your father..."

"They do nothing illegal...usually."

Before Hudson could argue further, Reggie opened the creaky wooden door of the church and stepped inside.

A tall, smiling man greeted them. "Are you here for the AA meeting?"

"No, I'm looking for the Dungeons and Dragons club," answered Reggie.

"They meet in the basement." He pointed to a narrow hallway to the right. "The stairs are at the end of the hall, on the left."

The hundred-year-old stairs creaked as they descended. Reggie knocked on the tiny wooden door at the bottom.

"Raven?" Reggie called.

The door opened, and a girl stood in the doorway.

Her thick ebony hair flowed out of a tight ponytail on top of her head like a black fountain. Various studs, rings, chains, barbells, plugs, screws, retainers and bars pierced her ears, lips, nose and eyebrows. Tattoos covered her shoulder, neck and one arm, and thick makeup darkened her already dark eyes. She wore a black mesh top, a black-checkered mini-skirt and heavy charcoal army boots.

"Pretzel six, sixty-six?" she said through smiling black licorice lips.

Reggie's eyes widened. He looked as if he was trying to talk, but his heart was holding his tongue.

"It's been a long time!" She looked him up and down. "You've grown up."

She held her arms out to receive a hug, but his teenage brain was in full-blown panic mode. Every muscle froze, and his body refused to respond.

Hudson shoved him from behind, and he tripped into her waiting arms.

"I'm *so* glad you came."

"Me too," he squeaked.

She released him and looked at Hudson. "This is your friend? He's huge!"

"Nice to meet you. I'm Hudson."

Reggie shook his head, blinked, and adjusted his glasses. "Uh... yes...this is my friend Hudson...but he already said that...I mean, he's Elephant zero-five-eleven's husband."

"This is quite the setup you got here," said Hudson, giving Reggie more time to recover.

The fluorescent lights fixtures on the low ceiling above sat empty, and D&D posters covered the black walls. Glowing neon blue and pink emanated from the many desktop towers on the five computer desks facing each other in the centre of the room. Countless flatscreen monitors covered the desks, and LED light strips glowed along the ceiling line. Cables, wires and cords serpentined around the computers and monitors. More monitors covered an entire wall on one side and stacked shelving filled with various techno-gadgets sat on the opposite side.

"Welcome to the Dungeons and Dragons Hacktivist Collective," she said, motioning to the room like a gothic model on the Price is Right.

"Where is everybody else?" Reggie appeared to regain a modicum of composure.

"They're a little skittish with outsiders, so they took the day off. But please, have a seat anywhere."

Hudson sat on a chair that looked like it was a pilot's seat from an interstellar spaceship. "What do you do here? Play games?"

"We *do* play lots of games, my new muscular friend, but we also use our computer skills to create social change, promote free speech, and expose nefarious plots."

"Do you break the law?" asked Hudson.

"Think of it more like civil disobedience."

"Right."

"This is some righteous gear!" Reggie picked up a drone from the shelf.

"Thanks. Wait till I show you what you're getting."

Raven held up a pen.

"Wow, is that a real pen?" asked Hudson.

"It *is* a real pen," said Raven, handing it to Hudson.

"Wow, that's a very nice gift," Hudson said in a monotone and clicked the pen. "I can finally write my memoirs."

"It's also an audio recorder. And do you see the little round lens at the top of the clip?"

Hudson leaned close to look. "No..."

"Good. That means no one else will either. That's a hidden camera which takes 1080p resolution video."

"I don't know what 1080p is, but it sounds impressive."

"It is," Reggie interjected.

She held out her hand, and Hudson gave her the pen back. After clicking the pen, she unscrewed it, and it came apart in the middle. Her many bracelets jangled as she removed a tiny SD card. She inserted the card into something resembling a chunky USB drive, then pushed the drive into her computer.

"Check this out," she said, pointing to her screen.

Reggie and Hudson huddled behind her and watched Hudson's face fill the screen and say in a sarcastic tone, "I can finally write my memoirs."

"Whoa!" yelled Reggie. "This is so awesome! This is like in the Bond movies where he goes to Q and gets a bunch of cool gadgets."

"Except we're not trained spies, and this isn't a movie. Isn't recording someone without their permission illegal?"

Raven held up a finger with shiny black nail polish. "I looked it up. Empire State is a one party consent state, meaning recording someone is legal as long as one party consents."

"I'm assuming you want us to take that pen into the gala tonight?"

"No, we want *you* to take it to the gala tonight," said Reggie. "Adults don't talk about adult stuff when kids are around."

"How am I supposed to get it past security?"

"If it sets off the metal detectors, you can show them it's just a pen."

"What if they have one of those bug detectors?"

"The pen does not differ from a phone," answered Raven. "Also, as long as you don't click the pen, it won't be on."

"What are we hoping to record?" asked Hudson. "Do you really think they're going to discuss their evil plans with a stranger at a Christmas gala?"

"Pretzel...I mean Reggie will have the SD card reader on him. If you pass him the card, he can upload the data to his phone and send it to me. I'll plug the pictures into facial recognition software. If I find some people that are on our watchlist, I'll relay that information, so you can buddy up to those people."

"And then what? Am I supposed to slip some truth serum into their drink and ask if they're part of a conspiracy?"

Raven pointed at Hudson. "Truth serum is an excellent idea, but we don't have any. But we do have this."

She held up a brown device that looked like a USB drive, except the USB plug was a USB-C plug.

"If you plug this into someone's phone for fifteen seconds, it will install an undetectable tracking app on their phone. We can see their emails, phone calls, texts and GPS location."

"I'm sure that is illegal in *every* state."

"They put tracking devices in thousands of Americans' arms without consent – including Elephant0511."

"Her name was Sophie," said Hudson.

"And if Sophie was here, do you think she would have hesitated at a chance to track some of the most powerful people involved in a worldwide cabal attempting to create a new world order?"

"She's not here!" yelled Hudson. "She died because she got involved with these people."

Raven took a step back and looked at Reggie.

"You don't have to do this if you don't want to," Reggie said in a soft voice.

"That's not it," Hudson said in a calmer tone. "If anything happened to either of you, I—"

"If anything happened to us, it would *not* be your fault. We will still do this even if *you* don't. If anything, having you involved makes it safer for us."

Hudson leaned back and folded his arms. "Where did you get that watchlist you mentioned?"

"It is a collection of powerful individuals that we believe may be involved in the Great Reset, the New World Order initiative and Project MITA," Raven answered.

"Right, but where did you get the list?"

"Years of research, online tips, and more recently from the Sentinel."

"Who *is* this Sentinel?"

"We don't know for sure, but we suspect that because of his knowledge of inside information, he's someone within the organization."

"What if he's deliberately feeding you bad intel?" Hudson asked.

"It's possible, but so far his info has been rock-solid."

Hudson nodded.

"So, you'll do it, right?" asked Reggie.

"Yes, I'll do it."

Raven handed him the pen and the spyware installer. "Have fun at the gala."

Hudson stood up and thanked Raven. After a few awkward goodbyes between the two teenagers, Hudson and Reggie left.

"You still haven't told me how I'm doing your father a favour," said Hudson as they climbed the church stairs.

"Umm..." Reggie hesitated. "You won't be going to the gala alone..."

"No, because I'm going with *you*."

"Everyone at the gala has to either be invited or is a *plus one* of someone who's invited."

"I'm my father's plus one, and you are Aunt Sera's plus one."

"I have a date?!"

CHAPTER 22

"Hudson, hurry up! The car is waiting," said Reggie from outside Hudson's hotel room door.

"I'm coming, hang on." Hudson would have been ready for the gala on time, but he had trouble getting dressed. For almost an hour, he sat on the edge of the bed beside his neatly laid out tuxedo. The knot firmly tied at the bottom of his gut, holding him down. He hated dressing up. He hated fancy events. He hated being without Sophie.

Eventually, he slipped into the trousers, dress shirt, vest and tuxedo jacket. As he picked up the unravelled bowtie, Reggie banged on the door. He flung the bowtie onto the bed and went to the door.

"We have to go," said Reggie when the door opened. He looked Hudson up and down. "Why aren't you ready?"

"I'm almost ready."

"No, you're not. First, change your socks."

"What's wrong with my socks?"

"They're white."

"I'm going for the Michael Jackson look."

"You look like a guy from a trailer park who's never worn a tux."

"I *am* a guy from a trailer park who's never worn a tux."

"Where's your bowtie, cuff links and the handkerchief? And put some gel in that wild nest on your head."

Reggie snatched the bowtie from the bed and wrapped it around Hudson's neck. "Remember, pull your cuffs out so the whites are showing."

"I feel like you've done this before," said Hudson.

Reggie's hands swiftly manoeuvered the bow tie with a practiced flourish. "Many times. Have you never been to a black tie event?"

"Sophie and I went to her cousin's art show once."

"Did you dress in a tux?"

"It was a dark suit with an already tied bowtie."

"That doesn't count."

"We talked to her cousin for five minutes, grabbed some fancy sandwiches and bubbly wine, and left."

Reggie folded the handkerchief and slid it into the pocket. "Sounds like a wonderful night on the town."

"It was. Later, we stopped at the Arby's drive-thru before skinny dipping under the bridge."

Reggie shook his head. "Tonight, there will be no cheap, pre-tied bow ties, massive meat sandwiches or doing *anything* naked. Go gel your hair and don't forget your spy pen."

Once Reggie finished dressing Hudson properly, they hurried down to the waiting car in front of the hotel. A man in a black suit opened the rear door of the stretch limousine. A stiff gust of snowy wind swirled, and he held on to his chauffeur cap.

"I should have brought my coat," said Hudson.

"We're not walking to this gala," said Reggie. "Besides, I've seen your winter coat. You are not wearing that camouflage monstrosity to a high-society gala.

"It's not a monstrosity, it's a windproof fleece jacket."

"Yes, but the gala is in a heated building, not a forest."

Hudson and Reggie pushed through the wind and stepped inside the car. The driver slammed the door, shutting out the wind, snow and cold. Hudson settled into one of two tanned leather bench seats and brushed the snow off his tuxedo jacket and pants. Reggie sat beside him. Two other occupants sat in the other bench seat. One of them was Lawrence Hargreaves. The other was a woman in a bulky winter coat.

"Hudson, so glad you could make it," said Lawrence as the driver drove them away from the hotel.

"Thanks again for inviting me," Hudson replied, shaking his hand.

"This is my sister, Seraphina. Seraphina, this is Hudson Finlay."

The dim interior lights of the limo barely illuminated the woman in the puffy coat. She brushed aside the long curly dark hair from her face, revealing a pretty, smiling face with delicate features, smooth, mocha skin and chocolate eyes.

She held out her down-turned hand. Hudson took her hand and shook it. He gave a brief smile before looking away.

"Sera," she said, smiling. Her voice was smooth and sweet.

"Sera is an Engineer and—" Lawrence began.

"I would rather not use up all the small talk for the ride there," she said. "I need something to talk about when we're listening to boring speeches or as a backup for awkward silences."

"Are you going to give a speech, Aunt Sera?" Reggie asked.

"Not tonight, Reg. I'm just here for the free food."

Her phone chimed. She reached into her jacket pocket and looked at the screen on her cell.

"It's him again, isn't it?" said Lawrence, shaking his head. "Why don't you get a new number?"

"It wouldn't help. He would find other ways of harassing me. Also, I have a job where customers need my number. I can't just keep changing it."

"Hudson can beat him up for you," Reggie chimed in. "He's a boxer, and I've seen him fight."

"That won't be necessary," said Lawrence. "There is a lot of security at this event. Adrian won't get past the front door."

Before Hudson could ask questions, the car stopped.

Lawrence looked at Sera with a stern face. "Leave the coat in the car."

"No way! I like this coat. If I leave it in the car, I'll never see it again."

"Promise you'll take it off as soon as we get in there."

She held her hands up. "Yes, I'll give it to the coat check people. I wouldn't want to offend any of your rich friends with a warm coat in the middle of winter."

The driver opened the door, and an unimpressed Lawrence stepped out. The rest followed.

A tall concrete building with long Corinthian columns loomed over them. Concrete relief sculptures and a Roman numeral clock bedecked the pediment high above. A red carpet led up to two twenty-foot-high doors with massive gothic lanterns on either side. A thin layer of trampled snow covered the carpet.

"Arm!" Sera shouted at Hudson.

"What?"

"Hold out your arm," whispered Reggie. "Pretend you're a gentleman, and she's your date."

"I *am* a gentleman," he whispered back.

"And you *are* on a date."

Hudson held out his arm, and she grabbed it.

"Catch me when I slip in these stupid heels."

Lawrence turned around and smiled. "Are we ready?"

"Lead the way, big brother," Sera answered.

Her heel slipped on their way up the stairs, but she held on to his steady arm. They stepped inside the massive doors, and Hudson looked up at the ornate coved ceiling sixty-five feet above them.

"Wow!"

Sera released his arm and handed off her coat to the coat check. When Hudson's gaze returned from admiring the massive lobby, he saw her for the first time without her coat. His eyes widened, and he stepped back.

Her long black dress accentuated her figure and the lobby lights illuminated her face. She reminded him of a young Janet Jackson.

"Are you okay?" she asked.

"Yes...sorry, I—"

"Welcome," said a woman with a tablet in her hands. "You are...?"

"Hudson Finlay..."

"...and Sera Hargreaves," she said.

The woman looked down at her tablet and creased her brow. "The only Sera I have is a Seraphine Oxborough."

"Sorry, yes."

"Can I see your IDs, please?"

Once they proved their identification and passed through the metal detector, they walked through a wide hallway. She grabbed his arm, and he stiffened.

"Are you okay?" she asked.

Hudson nodded. "Mmm hmm."

Their shoes clacked on the marble floors as they followed the signs for the gala. Marble columns and beige padded walls lined the hallway on both sides, and gold inlay panels covered the ceiling.

The lobby and hallway were impressive, but the ballroom was spectacular. Emerald green and cobalt blue lights shot up sixty-foot columns. Stylishly dressed men and women sat or mingled around dozens of elegantly set round tables. Decorative moulding and intricate designs covered sixty-five-foot-high walls and the coved ceiling. More green and blue lights emanated from corners, behind moulding and along the ceiling. A video montage of jungles, forests and oceans glowed from a screen on the far wall. An instrumental version of *O Come All Ye Faithful* reverberated from hidden speakers. The massive room looked part nightclub, part theatre and part Roman coliseum.

Hudson sucked in a breath.

"It's not as scary as it looks," said Sera. "Just smile and nod at everybody."

Reggie turned around and smirked at Hudson. "Pretend like you're supposed to be here."

A man with a tablet led Reggie and his father to their table, while he directed Hudson and his date to a different one.

"We're not with them?" Hudson asked.

"My brother wanted to give us some privacy," Sera said with an apologetic smile as they sat down.

Hudson looked at the other six empty chairs at their table.

"Are we supposed to mingle or network or something?"

"We can do whatever we want," Sera answered. "Why don't you tell me something about yourself?"

Hudson fiddled with his wedding ring. "Not much to tell. I work as a janitor at a high school in Wanigas."

Sera tilted her head. "How long has it been?"

"I got off for Christmas break a few days ago."

She pointed at his ring. "How long ago did your wife pass?"

He paused for a moment before answering. "Over a year."

"How did she—?"

He looked away. "I don't want to talk about it."

"Fair enough." She held her hand up. "Why don't you ask me a question? Ask me anything."

"Why are you alone?"

"I'm not alone. I'm here with you."

"I mean, why don't you have a boyfriend? A nice woman like you rarely stays single very long."

"A nice woman? Is that your idea of a compliment?"

He scratched his forehead and looked down at the plates and cutlery. "An attractive woman?"

"That's a little better. To answer your question, I was married to a very bad man. Technically, we're still married...separated till the divorce goes through."

"Oh."

"Hudson, look at me."

With his head still tilted down, he looked up at her.

She placed a finger under his chin and tilted his head up. "I'm guessing you feel guilty about going on a date with an attractive woman?"

He looked at her but didn't respond, and she continued. "It feels like you're cheating on your wife. Don't think of this as a date. If I know my brother, I'm guessing that you owe him for something, and that's how he convinced you to come here tonight. Pretend this isn't a date but a job you're doing for him. Act civil and respectful – although I don't think that will be a problem for you. Relax and enjoy the free food and boring speeches for a few hours. At the end of the night, we'll say our goodbyes without hugs, kisses or an exchange of phone numbers. But *please*, try to relax and enjoy a night out. Can you do that?"

"Okay." He stopped fiddling with his ring and put his hands on his lap.

"Welcome, everybody." The voice boomed across the room.

"Please take your seat, and we can get this party started."

The crowd shuffled noisily as people found their assigned place settings. Charles and Lena were the first couple to join Hudson and Sera at their table. Both appeared to be in their eighties, and Charles looked vaguely familiar. Lena smiled graciously and shook their hands, with her husband Charles making introductions. A moment later, two men in their thirties pulled out their chairs beside the elderly couple and sat down. Scott and Christopher introduced themselves. Hudson assumed they were a couple, and this was confirmed by the awkward smiles of Charles and Lena.

"Hello, friends!" said the latest addition to the table. "My name is Patrick, and this is my partner, Savannah."

His voice was as confident as Charles's but much louder. They were the youngest pair at the table, both in their late twenties. Patrick smiled through his neatly trimmed beard, and Savannah puffed out her chest and held her chin high as if everyone were admiring her astonishing beauty.

A few moments later, servers delivered the first course, and the conversations began.

Hudson looked at the two upturned shells on his plate, and his eyes widened. Inside the shells, strange alien blobs floated in a slimy soup. Hudson had gutted and cleaned many animals including pheasants, rabbits and deer. This looked like the entrails that were removed and discarded before butchering the meat.

"It's oyster," Sera whispered.

Lena placed her hand on his shoulder and leaned close. "It tastes better than it looks," she whispered.

Patrick held his hands back as if the oyster was about to explode. "I clearly stated that we are vegetarians," he exclaimed with a mixture of anger and disgust.

"Sorry, sir," said the server. He snatched the plates away from Patrick and Savannah.

Charles was the first to raise his oyster shell to his lips and down the contents in one slurp. The others did the same, with Patrick and Savannah averting their gaze in contempt.

"That is absolutely disgusting!" said Patrick.

"Don't knock it till you try it," said Charles.

"I agree," said Scott. "The flavour is intense and sophisticated."

Beside him, Christopher nodded.

"You can request the vegetarian option," Sera whispered to Hudson.

The server returned with Patrick and Savannah's vegetarian option, which looked like a pile of recently plucked weeds.

Hudson shook his head. "I'll stick with the seafood. How bad can it be?"

Sera shrugged and slurped her second oyster. Trying not to spill the soupy guts, Hudson lifted the shell to his mouth. As if downing a shot of tequila, he poured the contents into his mouth and swallowed.

Although the texture was like mucous, it tasted slightly fishy with a smoky, buttery, salty mineral flavour.

"What do you think?" asked Sera.

He looked at her with a creased brow. "I think I like it."

"I don't know how you can call yourselves friends of the environment when you insist on eating murdered animals," said Patrick.

Hudson restrained himself from replying and instead slurped his second oyster.

"Oysters are hardly animals," said Charles. "They don't even have the capacity to know they are being killed."

"I hope not," said Savannah. "Because you're eating them alive."

Hudson looked to Sera with a questioning look. She smirked and nodded.

"Those plants you're eating are alive too," said Charles, pointing at the salad. "Everything we eat was alive at some point."

"Yes, but plants don't have brains, feelings or emotions," Patrick replied. "Those oysters are living, thinking beings. Also, plants are a more sustainable source of food. An acre of animal-based agriculture produces around 800 pounds of food while an acre of vegan agriculture produces over 30,000 pounds of food!"

Scott spoke up for the first time. "I think we can reduce the amount of meat products we consume, but there is nothing wrong with including a small portion of protein-rich meat in our diets."

Christopher rested his hand on Scott's arm and gave him an approving smile.

"There is more than enough protein in legumes and beans to keep you healthy," said Patrick. He turned to Hudson and Sera. "What about you two? What is your opinion on murdering animals for their meat?"

"I don't think you're interested in my opinion," said Hudson.

Patrick leaned back and folded his arms. "No, I really want to hear your thoughts about this subject."

"Death happens all the time," said Hudson. "Farmers kill their cattle, lions kill gazelles, hawks kill mice, people kill mosquitoes."

"That doesn't make it right," Patrick interjected.

"When you eat those plants on your plate, you are killing them," Sera added. "After you swallow, your digestive enzymes attack and break down the plants into smaller molecules. When a virus enters your body, white blood cells attack and kill it. Your body is a brutal and effective killing machine."

"I doubt anyone here is ignorant enough to believe that digesting kale is equivalent to slaughtering a mother deer."

"Why don't we talk about something we can all agree on," suggested Lena. "We are all here because we are friends of the environment. What are some innovative ideas to stop climate change."

Nobody spoke for a few moments as the server delivered the next course, which thankfully was vegetarian canape.

"I think Covid has given us all a moment to reflect on our priorities," said Scott. "Zoom meetings are an environmentally friendly alternative to driving or flying to other states or countries."

The tone of the conversation mellowed somewhat as they discussed the benefits of renewable energy and reducing food waste.

Hudson finished his tiny canape and was wondering when the actual food would arrive when Reggie tapped him on the shoulder.

"Can I talk with you for a second?"

"Now?"

"Just for a second before the main course arrives."

"I'll be right back," Hudson said to Sera and stood up.

He followed Reggie out of the room and down a short hallway, but stopped outside the washroom.

When Reggie saw Hudson was no longer following him, he said, "Are you coming?"

"I am not going to the washroom with you," said Hudson. "If you need to powder your nose and gossip, you'll have to do it alone."

Reggie looked around. "They might be listening. I wanted to talk in private."

"I don't know who *they* are, but they might also have cameras in the two-way mirrors in the washroom," said Hudson. "Why did you pull me away from my riveting conversation?"

"Have you found out anything yet?"

"Sure. Patrick and Savannah are hipster vegetarians, Scott and Christopher are gay, and Charles and Lena are a nice older couple who like oysters."

"Do you suspect any of them might be connected to the New World Order?"

"It's weird, but that hasn't come up in the conversation yet."

"Try asking them their opinions on the Great Reset and see who responds."

"Really? You want me to inquire about everyone's involvement in a secret conspiracy to instate a communist world order?"

"No, but you could ask if anyone has read the book."

"There's a book about the Great Reset? I thought it was a covert scheme."

"It is, but they hide it in plain sight. The Great Reset is the topic of books, conferences and media reports, but only a few know the real endgame."

"And you're one of those people?"

Reggie held out his hands. "Keep your voice down."

He pointed at Hudson's chest pocket. "Did you record anything yet?"

Hudson looked at the end of the pen peeking from his pocket. "I forgot all about that thing."

Reggie rolled his eyes. "Click your pen on to record. Go back to your table and ask what everyone thinks about the Great Reset. If someone seems really interested in the subject, come see me again, and I'll take the SIM card from your pen and I'll send the video to Raven. She can let us know if that person is on the watchlist."

Reggie pulled out the tracking device from his pocket and handed it to Hudson. "Then you can steal his or her phone and plug this into it for fifteen seconds."

Hudson pulled out his pen, clicked it with his thumb and returned it to his chest pocket.

"This won't work."

CHAPTER 23

"If we all do our part, we can stop and even reverse climate change," said Patrick. "Savannah and I share one car, and it's a Tesla."

"We don't own a car." Scott pointed to himself and Christopher. "We use public transportation or cycle everywhere. I think *that's* the way to go."

"Our cars are *not* electric," said Charles. "But we donate more than our share to carbon offset projects."

Hudson dug into his Japanese Wagyu tenderloin as he tried to find an opportune moment to insert *the Great Reset* into the conversation. It was hard to concentrate while eating the most delicious steak he had ever consumed. He remembered splurging on 2-inch-thick steaks, which he grilled to a juicy mouth-watering, medium-rare perfection. However, this was a level above that.

"You should all give yourselves a pat on the back!"

Sera was silent for most of the conversation so far, so when she interrupted the flow of self-congratulatory dialogue, everyone turned to listen.

"Do you really think any of this makes a difference?" she continued. "China, Russia and India account for over 40 percent of the world's emissions. Without their commitment, nothing is going to change."

"That is why we must convince them stop polluting, to stop building and using coal and oil," said Patrick.

"Why should they?" she asked.

"Because it's the right thing to do," said Scott.

"At what price?"

"At any price," Patrick answered.

"All of you sit here eating your fancy food while ten percent of the world is starving. You drive your Teslas while 80 percent of the world does not own a car. All of you have one or more bathrooms in your homes, while sixty percent of the world's population does not have a toilet in their home. Seven percent of Indians own a car. You have the choice to buy a gas-powered car, an electric car or public transportation. But a typical family in India does not have that choice. If they can afford a gas-guzzling, CO2-emitting car, they would snatch it up in a second. Those of you with children would do anything to help your kids secure a successful future, and so would a mother in India. She doesn't have the luxury to think about how much pollution her fire is emitting into the atmosphere as she tries to keep her children warm at night. Instead, she is worried about her eight-year-old working at a garment factory sewing the clothes you're wearing to a gala that could feed her family for life."

Hudson tried not to smile while others stared in stunned silence.

"That doesn't mean we shouldn't do what we can," said Patrick, "Before the climate crisis turns into an extinction event and everyone dies. The global temperature rose over one and a half percent last year. This is a crisis we can't ignore."

"And what do you think is the cause of that temperature rise?" Sera asked.

"Carbon dioxide emissions obviously, have you not seen the graph?" asked Patrick.

"I've seen the zoomed in graph for the last couple hundred years," Sera answered. "However, I've seen zoomed-*out* graphs showing the past 400,000 years. CO2 does not precede temperature rises but lags behind the temperature by 200 to 1000 years. Hotter worldwide temperatures appear to be a driving factor *causing* the increase in CO2 concentration rather than the other way around."

"That's absurd." Patrick waved her off. "You don't know what you're talking about."

"Are you saying we shouldn't reduce our emissions or take steps to stop polluting our environment? Why are you here at this Environmental Gala, anyway?"

"I agree, we should all do our part. However, being among the richest people in the world, I also think it's hypocritical to drive your son to school in an electric car and say that the Indian family should sleep in a cold house instead of lighting a carbon-emitting fire."

"We all do what we can with what we have," said Charles. "One of my charity organizations provides safe, fuel-efficient biomass stoves for heating and cooking to numerous third world countries. They reduce the effect on the environment and save lives from fires and toxic fumes."

A server approached the table and tapped Sera on the shoulder. Hudson couldn't hear what she whispered in Sera's ear, but the look on her face was unsettled.

"Who is it?" she asked the server.

"He said he was an old friend, ma'am. He was very insistent and said it was an emergency."

Sera looked across the room at two shadowed figures near the ballroom entrance.

"You let him in?!" Her unsettled look morphed into one of fear and anger.

"Is everything okay?" Hudson asked. "Who is it?"

"Someone who shouldn't be here."

The man stepped into the green glow of decorative LED lights. He unbuttoned his brown oversized suit jacket and squinted as he scanned the room. His pant legs accordioned at his ankles, almost covering his scuffed leather loafers. The mismatched blue tie sat loosely around his neck, and too much grease held his slicked back hair in place.

Behind him, a man in a tuxedo held his arm.

Sera pointed at the server. "Call security, now!"

"That man holding his arm is part of our security team," said the server. "I can tell him to escort the man out."

"Please do!"

The man's wild eyes suddenly locked onto Sera, and he smiled.

Not a *happy, I'm-so-glad-I-found-you* smile, but a *hunter's, I've-got-you-now* sneer. He squirmed away from the security guard and speed walked towards Sera.

Hudson pushed his chair back and stood up shortly before Sera did. She held up her hand. "I've got this."

"Sera! There you are!" The man careened around the table towards them with the guard running to catch up.

"Adrian, you're not allowed to be near me, and how did you find me?"

The din of conversations in the room died away, and everyone stared at the interloper.

"There is no limit to the lengths I will go for the one I love." Adrian slurred some of his words as the guard grabbed his arm from behind.

Hudson stepped forward, but Sera pushed him back. "This isn't your fight. Let someone else take care of this."

Adrian whirled around and punched the guard in the face. He took the blow and stepped back before pulling a pistol from beneath his jacket.

"I've got one of those, too." Adrian drew a six-shooter revolver from his pocket and pointed it at the guard.

Guests nearby let out a chorus of gasps.

The guard pointed his gun at the floor and held the other hand in the air. "Let's not do anything rash, sir."

"Put your gun on the floor!" Adrian yelled.

"Don't do it," Hudson whispered to himself. "Don't give up your gun."

The guard bent over, placed his gun on the floor, and stepped back. Adrian picked the gun up and shoved it in his pocket before turning back to Sera.

"What are you doing?" she yelled.

"You forgot to invite me to your party."

Lawrence Hargreaves appeared. "Adrian don't do this. Don't hurt my sister."

Adrian pointed the gun at Lawrence. "You should shut up. You're the reason she left me. I should kill you now."

"No!" yelled Sera. "Look at me! I'm the reason you're here."

"What are you doing?" Hudson whispered.

"He won't shoot me. He still loves me."

"That's right." Adrian turned back to Sera and pointed the gun at her. "I came for you, but if you no longer want me, then you are of no use to me."

Sera stepped forward. The gun was only a foot from her face. "You don't want to shoot me. You love me too much."

Hudson stared fiercely at the man. Every muscle twitched with murderous anger. "Leave Soph — I mean leave Sera alone."

"Is this your date?" Adrian leered at Hudson.

"Don't worry about him." Sera stepped between the gun and Hudson. "This is between you and me."

Three more security guards with guns drawn slowly closed in.

With a backhand that surprised everyone, including Hudson, Adrian slapped Sera across the cheek. She remained standing and stared back at him with hateful eyes.

Hudson moved out from behind his date. "She's wrong. You should be worried about me."

"What are you going to do, tough guy?" He pointed the gun two feet from Hudson's face.

"Before you shoot me, answer one question." Hudson's arms hung loosely at his side as he stared back at Adrian. "Are you afraid of dying?"

"Am *I* afraid of dying? Are you?" He waved the gun to stress his question.

"I have few family or close friends anymore," continued Hudson. "My wife died recently in the hospital, and they didn't allow me to be by her side as she choked to death on her own mucous. Like you, I am an angry, sad man with nothing left to lose. However, you're holding that gun too far from my head. Also, you are inebriated. When you pull the trigger, the kickback and your drunken impairment will cause the bullet to only hit a glancing blow off my skull, or perhaps my ear. If it is not a perfect shot, and I am still standing, I will return your bad shot with a stepping overhand punch so hard, your tiny little brain will rattle in your skull. So, I suggest that if you shoot me, do it from a closer range."

Adrian stepped closer and pressed the muzzle to the centre of Hudson's forehead.

"Don't tempt—"

Before he could finish his threat, Hudson made a series of rapid, simultaneous movements. He shifted his head to the right while swiping at the gun with his left hand. His right arm reared back and returned with the speed and force of a fighter jet.

Adrian's feet left the floor as he flew backwards, soaring for a moment before crash-landing in front of a wide-eyed security guard. The revolver tumbled across the carpet.

More guards converged around Adrian.

"Is he dead?" Sera stared down at him as they rolled him over and cuffed him.

"He's just unconscious — I think. I'd say there might be some brain damage, but I don't think he had much to damage."

Sera slapped him on the arm. "Why did you do that?"

Hudson shrugged. "I figured he deserved it."

"I mean, why did you step in front of the gun? He could have shot you."

"The gun wasn't loaded."

"How do you know?"

"All the chambers were empty."

"Oh."

"That was incredible!" said Charles, slapping him on the back. "Remind me never to get on your bad side."

As the guards carried a bleary-eyed Adrian out of the room, a voice boomed from the speaker. "Friends! Everything is under control. We are so sorry for this incident. The proper authorities are taking care of this, and we can continue with our gala. Please return to your seats. Dessert is on its way, and we will start the presentations shortly."

With excited murmurs and discussions, the crowd regained their composures and sat back in their places.

Lawrence and Reggie rushed over as Sera stared at the floor and breathed in and out heavily.

"Are you okay?" Hudson asked.

"That was incredible!" exclaimed Reggie.

"Sera, I'm so sorry," said Lawrence. "I don't know how he found you, I—"

"Please!" Sera shouted as she squeezed her eyes shut. Tears flowed down her cheeks, leaving a trail of makeup. "Everyone, just leave me alone."

"Let's go get you cleaned up." Lena pulled Sera away. She turned to the others. "She'll be fine. I'll take care of her. Go back to your table. We'll be back shortly."

They returned to their seats as Lena led Sera out of the room. A security guard followed them.

"Come on Reggie," said Lawrence, and led his son back to their table.

"Sir?" The security guard that dropped his gun tried to get Hudson's attention without touching him. "Sir, the police would like a word."

"*After* the gala," Charles said in a stern voice. "If you want to keep your job, you'll tell the police they can speak to him *after* the gala."

The guard nodded. "Of course, sir."

Hudson looked behind him where Sera had left, then back at Charles.

"I don't know what you do for a living, but if you ever need a job, I could use you on my security detail on my next trip to Switzerland."

Hudson didn't reply. Instead, he looked behind him again.

Charles followed his gaze. "She's in excellent hands. If you want to make sure she's okay, go to her, but say nothing until she asks."

Hudson pushed back his chair and stood up.

Charles pointed at him. "Stand outside of the woman's bathroom and wait. Remember, say nothing. Just be there."

Hudson joined a security guard standing against the wall opposite the women's bathroom door. The guard nodded at Hudson.

After about five minutes, Sera and Lena emerged. Sera gave Hudson a pained smile. He smiled back but said nothing.

Lena held Sera's arm. "Remember, if you need it, we always have a place for you at the shelter."

"Thank you," she said, but remained in place.

Lena looked at her, then at Hudson and the guard. "Let's give them a moment," she said to the guard.

The guard took five steps down the hallway and faced the opposite direction with his arms crossed in front of him.

"I am so sorry you had to do that," said Sera, fighting back her tears. "I am embarrassed, angry, upset, grateful — I don't know what I feel."

Hudson desperately wanted to give her words of encouragement. He wanted to wrap her in his arms and tell her she was going to be okay, and he wouldn't let anything happen to her. But he stood there, silently.

"You are a big idiot, you know?"

Hudson raised his eyebrows but didn't respond.

"I don't know a lot about guns, but I'm pretty sure that if there was a bullet in the chamber, you wouldn't be able to tell. But you risked your life to save someone you just met. I'm no one to you. You don't even want to be here. You'd rather be on a date with your wife."

Hudson swallowed hard and looked into her eyes. It reminded her of the pain she saw in Sophie's eyes as she clung to life – fear and hopelessness. However, Sera was not dying on a tablet. She was standing in front of him. He clenched his fists and resisted the urge to pull her into his arms.

"What's wrong?" She reached up and wiped a tear he didn't realize was on his cheek.

He shook his head.

"It's okay," she said. You did good, and I'm okay. Can I hug—?" she asked. Before she finished, his arms wrapped around her.

"We're okay," she said.

Tears streamed down his cheek. "I couldn't save her."

They embraced in the hallway, sobbing on each other's shoulders for a long time.

CHAPTER 24

"You should have seen him!" Reggie shouted. "When that scumbag put the gun against his head, he swiped it away and punched so hard the man flew ten feet into the air!"

Hudson stood and listened to Reggie exaggerate the previous night's events to Raven in the Dungeons and Dragons clubhouse. This time, two other hacktivists joined them in the church basement.

"We can see for ourselves," said Raven. "If you give me back my pen."

Hudson held out the pen. "I need you to delete the ending."

She shook her head. "I'm not deleting anything."

"Okay, then I'll destroy it."

Hudson held the pen in both hands, threatening to snap it in half.

Raven shouted, "Wait! I'll delete the ending. Don't be so dramatic. Chill."

He glared at her, but held the pen out of her reach.

Raven grabbed her lacy black top by the shoulder and pulled it back, revealing an intricate tattoo of roses amidst a thicket of thorns. The rose vine wrapped around a large word in an elegant serif.

Reggie's eye's widened at the sight of her bare skin.

"You see what that says?" she asked.

"Yes, I can read, it says *integrity*."

"Integrity means that I'll do what I say and say what—"

"I know what integrity means. Put your shirt back on before Reggie starts drooling."

"What? I didn't...what are you..." Reggie turned his head, but his eyes remained locked on her naked shoulder.

Raven smirked and covered the tattoo with her top. "I don't lie. I said I'll delete the end, and I will."

Still glaring at her, Hudson handed her the pen.

A moment later, the view of Hudson walking through the ballroom at the gala appeared on the large monitor. The screen bounced up and down as he walked to his table and sat down.

"Whoa!" said Raven. "Who's the hottie? Is that your date?"

"She's my aunt Sera," said Reggie.

Raven gave Hudson a playful nudge. "You lucked out, big guy. She looks like a young Janet Jackson."

He tried not to react. "What are we looking for? I told you; I didn't have an opportunity to ask anyone about the Great Reset, vaccine trackers or Project MITA. Besides, this was just a fancy dinner for rich people."

"The Sentinel said that there were many people at this gala from the IEC and some involved in MITA," said Reggie, "and probably the New World Order, enslaving the world's population with vaccines—"

"I didn't see anyone at the gala with a copy of the book *Taking over the World for Dummies* or—"

"I know that guy!" Raven shouted, pointing at the screen.

"That's Patrick," said Hudson. "A *vegetarian*." He spat out the word as if tasted bad in his mouth. "He thought he was better than everyone because he didn't eat meat."

"What *did* you think of the food?" asked Reggie.

"It was amazing! The oyster was weird and looked like snot, but it tasted pretty good. The tenderloin was the best steak I have ever had!"

"Those were five-hundred-dollar wagyu tenderloins."

"I can see why. Not that I would ever waste that much money on —"

"No, that guy." Raven shook her finger at the screen again. "Him!"

"Oh, you mean Charles," said Hudson. "He was a nice older gentleman, and his wife was a pleasant woman too."

"That is Charles Porter!" shouted Raven. "He's a multi-billionaire who owns media companies, technology conglomerates and a bunch of pharmaceuticals."

"I thought I recognized him," said Hudson.

Reggie shook his finger in the air as if pumping the starter for his memory motor. "Isn't he the man who wants to control the world with vaccines?"

"Yes! The pandemic was his idea," said Raven. "He uses his Porter Foundation *charity* as a smoke screen for his socialist agenda."

"I thought the Porter foundation provided third world countries with free vaccines," said Hudson.

"Is it so hard to believe?" Raven flicked back her shiny black hair. "He has amassed billions and controls many of the world's most powerful companies. With all his free time and more money that he knows what to do with, he wants to mould the world into his idea of an idyllic society. He is a puppet master, and the world is his castle."

"Watch this part!" Reggie looked at the screen.

Adrian stormed into the gala with his gun. Everything darkened for a moment as the pen slid to the side of his pocket. It fell back again and recorded the encounter with Adrian. Although the picture bounced around, they could see Hudson smash Adrian's face.

"That was incredible," said Raven. "Your like Jason Bourne or something."

"Okay, stop it now," said Hudson when the video showed him getting up from the table to find Sera in the washroom.

"STOP!"

Raven and Reggie jumped.

Although there was no echo in the small room, it felt like they could still hear the word.

The trio stood silently for an awkward moment, as if his angry outburst still hung in the air like a dark cloud.

She pressed a button on the keyboard, and the playback paused.

Except for the hum of computer cooling fans, the room was silent.

Raven broke the silence, but her voice was soft and almost

apologetic. "I'm assuming you want me to delete the rest?"

Hudson nodded.

"Did you two get it on? After the hero saves the damsel in distress, she repays him with some..."

Raven gave up her attempt at lightening the mood with humour when she saw Hudson's face.

"Yes," Hudson said in a monotone. "Delete the rest."

"I said I would, and I will."

She pointed at the prompt on the screen.

Are you sure you want to delete it?

She clicked the *okay* button.

"Happy?"

Hudson nodded.

Reggie attempted to clear the dark, awkward cloud. "Do we think Charles is the guy from the IEC who was having the secret meeting with the top executive from Nanotech?"

"I don't know," said Raven. She rewound the video to show them discussing the virtues of a meatless diet. "Was there anyone at the table from Nanotech?"

Reggie leaned forward to scan the faces on the screen. A waft of Raven's perfume reminded him Raven was close. His gaze moved to her like a dog seeing a squirrel.

She smiled. "The screen is that way."

"What? Yes...I know. Sorry, you smell nice and..."

"Is there anyone at the table you recognize is from Nanotech?"

He shook his head as if trying to awaken from a dream. "Right... um, I don't recognize anyone."

"I could run their faces through my facial recognition software."

"There were a few people at the gala from Nanotech...including my father. Any of them could have the secret meeting with Charles."

"I don't see how any of this gets us any closer to knowing who might be involved in Project MITA."

"He's right." Raven nodded. "We missed our chance at this gala, but we may get another one."

"How?" asked Reggie.

"The International Economics Congress meets every year to discuss their plans for world domination, solving overpopulation and enslaving humanity with vaccines."

Hudson rolled his eyes. "We could buy a ticket and listen to lectures about their evil plans for creating a world communism order."

"That isn't a thing," said Raven. "It's not just what they say publicly, but the many backroom deals and behind-the-scenes planning."

"And I don't think you can just buy a ticket," said Reggie.

"If only there was a way to infiltrate the organization to listen in on these backroom discussions..."

"Does Charles go to this Congress meeting thing?" asked Hudson.

"Yes, of course, Charles Porter goes to the WEC." Raven fiddled with the barbell piercing in her left eyebrow. "He is one of the few people we suspect is part of the secret elites that attend the annual Congress in Switzerland."

"What if I knew of a way to go to that Congress?" Hudson stared at the wall, trying to organize the plan formulating in his mind.

"Anyone can go listen to the lectures," said Raven, "but we need to get closer to the elites."

"What are you thinking?" Reggie asked.

Hudson clasped his hands behind his head. "I've never been to Switzerland before. What do you think the weather is like?"

"How are you going to get close to the elites?" asked Reggie.

"I'm going to be on Charles Porter's security detail when he attends the WEC congress."

CHAPTER 25

Drip.

Drip.

Drip.

Hudson lay in bed, staring at the trailer ceiling, listening to the incessant dripping. Snow had fallen for the past three days with the temperature hovering around freezing. Overnight, however, the mercury in the thermometer rose. The thick snow on the trailer roof began melting, and the water found a path into his home.

Drip.

Drip.

Drip.

For the past hour, he lay in bed contemplating his plans for the day while water continued to remind him of the liquid intrusion somewhere in the kitchen.

Drip.

Drip.

Drip.

It sounded like a ticking clock. As if reminding him that time kept moving while he wasted the morning laying in bed.

Eventually, he sat up and rubbed his eyes. When he ambled into the living room, half-dressed he found the source of his irritation. The ceiling tiles above the kitchen counter sagged with water. Large droplets formed before falling to the counter with a splash. He cleaned up the small pool of water on the floor and counter before searching the cupboards for something to catch the water. Most of his cups and jugs were too small and would be full in minutes. In the back of the cupboard over the fridge, he found what he needed. The large glass beverage dispenser could hold over a gallon of water. A small brass tap jutted out from the bottom. He set it under the drip and watched the water ping into the empty glass pitcher.

Ping.

Ping.

Ping.

The sound was a little less irritating than the previous drip. Mostly because he knew it wasn't falling onto the counter, spilling onto the tiles and seeping into his floor.

He stared at the pitcher. This was *not* the intended use for the pitcher. It had never held just water before. A memory of the pitcher filled with a tangerine-colored liquid with large ice cubes floating amongst orange slices flashed in his mind.

His phone rang, and he jumped, breaking him from the flashback. Since Sophie died, he rarely used his phone. Sophie was always the outgoing person in their relationship. She kept in touch with family and friends, organized parties and get-togethers and filled their social calendar. The Covid lockdowns stifled much of their social interactions, and when the lockdowns were over, Sophie was gone. As the government removed the lockdowns, he devolved into a depressive funk and never revived his relationships. Almost nobody called, messaged or emailed him. He found his phone on the side table and picked it up.

"Hello?"

"Did you get it?" someone asked.

"Who is this?"

"Dude, I programmed your phone with my number. It says right on your phone who this is."

Hudson held his phone out and looked at the screen.

The Great and Powerful Reggie.

"Seriously? The great and powerful?"

"You should be more careful who you give your phone to, Hudson."

"Why are you calling me?"

"I wanted to know if you got it?"

"Got what?"

"Got the job, knucklehead."

"I don't know."

"Did you go for the interview?"

"Yes. I sat down with three executives from the Porter Foundation last week."

"Aaaaaand?" Reggie's voice went from normal to high as he stretched out the word.

"And I answered their questions. They said they like what they heard, but still had to do a thorough background check.

"When will you know?"

"They said they would try to get an answer before Christmas."

"That's tomorrow, so you should know sometime today, right?"

"I guess, but I don't think I'm going to take it."

"Why not? This is our big break. If we go to the Economic Congress in Switzerland, we can find the masterminds behind Project MITA, evidence of the New World Order and prove the elites knew the vaccines cause myocarditis and blood clots and —"

"Don't be naïve, Reggie. Even if I worked security for some rich guy at a conference, how am I going to find out anything? We aren't super spies or genius detectives. You're a nerdy teen, and I'm a school janitor. What did you think we were really going to do? Besides, Sophie is dead, and nothing will bring her back."

"What about justice? This isn't just some crazy conspiracy theory. She was healthy and had the useless vaccine and still died. Even if the tracker didn't cause her death, the vaccine may have. A lot of otherwise healthy people have died after taking the vaccine. I'm telling you, someone out there knows why she died."

"Perhaps."

After a long pause, Reggie asked, "Are you sure you don't want to come over here tomorrow?"

"I'm not barging in on your family Christmas."

"You wouldn't be barging in. My father likes you; I think you're okay, and Sera will be here too."

"I think I'd rather be alone."

"Okay, but don't give up on me. This thing with Charles Porter could be huge."

"Right. I have to go. I have a busy day."

He pressed the red phone icon and set down his cell.

Ploink.

Ploink.

Ploink.

The dripping water filled the pitcher with a half-inch of water and the sound changed from pinging to a steady ploink.

After eating a light breakfast while listening to a ploinking water soundtrack, he packed his gym bag and got into his pickup.

The truck splashed through growing puddles as he drove into town. The ploinking sound still echoed in his head. As he pulled into Moe's MMA and Boxing Gym, his phone rang again. Two calls in one morning were the busiest his phone had been in years. This time, he looked at the screen before answering.

Seraphina Hargreaves.

For a moment, he debated answering. They hadn't spoken since the night of the gala. His hand hovered over the green phone icon.

"Hi."

"Hi." Her voice was calm and sweet. "I'm sorry."

"Why are you sorry?"

"During the night of the gala, I said we would say our goodbyes without hugs, kisses or an exchange of phone numbers. We did hug, and now I'm calling you."

Hudson took a deep breath. He didn't want to talk to her, but a niggling in the back of his mind was glad to hear her voice.

"Are you still there?" she asked.

"I'm here."

"Are you okay?"

"I'm fine."

"Do you have plans for Christmas?"

"Sure."

"This must be a hard time for you."

"Is there a reason you're calling?"

"I just wanted to check in with you. It's Christmas. Your wife's gone and—"

"You think I don't know that?" he asked with more anger than he intended.

"Sorry. You're welcome to come to the Hargreaves family Christmas tomorrow. We don't always have a perfect family Christmas, but..."

"Reggie already invited me and I already declined."

"Yes, but this is *me* inviting you—"

"I'm sorry, but I have to go. I have a really busy day."

He hung up before she could respond.

Hudson splashed through the puddles to the gym. He opened the doors and ran into Coach Benny. The man punched him hard in the solar plexus.

Hudson's stomach instinctively flexed, but a moment too late. He gasped for air.

"You should *always* be ready, Hudson." Benny's voice sounded extra shrill today.

"What are you doing here?" Hudson asked as he tried to suck in air.

"This is my gym. I could ask you the same question. It's Christmas. Shouldn't you be home with family or something?"

"I came to work off some steam."

"I'm leaving," said Benny. "I just came in to do some cleaning, but I'm off to see my bratty little grandkids. Lock the door on your way out."

"Thanks, coach," he said, still bent over, trying to regain his breath.

As Benny reached the door, he stopped and turned around. "Are you okay? Did you want—"

"I'm fine!" Hudson yelled. "And if you invite me over for Christmas, I will return your sucker punch with an uppercut to your wrinkly old chin!"

"Merry Christmas to you too, Scrooge!" Benny walked outside, leaving Hudson alone.

He turned his phone on silent and wrapped his hands before donning his training gloves. Each punch echoed across the empty gym as he pummelled the heavy bag into submission. Muscle memory guided his fists, and his mind was free to wander.

Like drifting seaweed in a tidal ocean, his thoughts drifted away from the empty gym. The last time he used the glass pitcher was before Covid.

Before the lockdowns.

Before the masks.

Before social distancing.

Before the government banned Christmas parties.

Before Sophie's death.

Orange slices floated in tangerine rum punch as Hudson pushed the brass spigot at the bottom of the pitcher. He filled his glass mug with the festive nectar and took a sip.

Over the stereo, Springsteen's rugged voice belted out the best version of *Santa Claus is Coming to Town.* In the living room, Sophie sat with their friends, Vic and Holly next to a large easel with crude stick drawings. His brother, Jeffery, leaned over-the-counter eating chicken wings while his wife Janice used the bathroom.

"Don't drink too much!" yelled Sophie from the living room. "We already lost the first two rounds of Pictionary."

"Your artistic skills may *improve* with more rum punch!" laughed Vic.

Beside him, Holly simultaneously laughed and hiccupped, almost spilling her punch.

"Your wife makes the best wings!" Jeffery said from the kitchen, his hands and mouth plastered in barbecue sauce.

Janice danced her way out of the bathroom, down the hallway and into the kitchen. "Clean your hands, you slob," she scolded her husband. "We're next, and this year we *will* be Christmas Pictionary champions!"

Hudson took another swig of the best punch ever and sauntered into the living room. Games were not really his idea of a good time, but he played them because Sophie and their friends enjoyed them.

"I think we'll concede defeat," said Sophie. "We'll let Jeffery and Janice play the next round."

"We're coming!" yelled Janice as she dragged her husband away from the wings.

Sophie took Hudson's hand and smiled. "Let's take a walk."

Her smile and the touch of her hand were enough to make him follow her into the depths of hell. Like an eager puppy, he gladly followed her down the hall to their bedroom.

"Some might say this isn't an appropriate time for this, but screw the guests," said Hudson. "I'm getting lucky!"

She shut the door and shook her head. "No, you're not. Sit down. We need to talk."

His face dropped as he sat on the bed. The expression *we need to talk* usually meant he was in trouble. Their marriage wasn't perfect, but he was pretty sure he hadn't screwed up lately.

"No, you're not in trouble," she said, reading his mind.

Hudson's heart resumed its normal rhythm.

Sophie sat beside him, clutching an elephant pillow. "Remember last week when I was really sick?"

"Yeah, you said it was something you ate."

"I lied. I had a miscarriage."

"What?!" His mouth dropped, and he almost spilled his drink. Instead, he set in on the side table and took his wife's hand. "You didn't tell me you were pregnant. What happened?"

She held up a placating hand. "Don't get hysterical. I was only a few days or perhaps a week pregnant. It's not a big deal."

"It seems like a big deal. Are you alright?"

"I didn't want to tell you until I was sure, but I missed my period by only a few days and was about to get a pregnancy test when I lost it."

Hudson's heart felt like it was breaking. "I'm *so* sorry."

"Stop!" she said. "I told you, it's not a big deal, but it got me thinking."

Hudson smiled. "You want to have a baby?"

"This wasn't planned, but maybe we should try…"

"Yes!"

"We both have good jobs. We have a great house in a friendly neighbourhood. Both of us are young and healthy. This could be the perfect time."

"Yes! I already said yes!"

She held out both hands. "Not so fast, Hudson. Let's get through Christmas first, but I think we should start trying after New Year's."

"I can turn the spare room into a baby room. We should look for cribs and baby seats and other baby stuff."

"Slow down," she laughed. "I'm not pregnant yet."

"I can help with that!"

She looked at him sternly. "You can't tell anyone yet."

"No, of course not."

Sophie wrapped her arms around him.

"Merry Christmas, Hudson. I love you."

"I love you too, Sophie."

Hudson stopped beating the heavy bag and wiped sweat and tears from his face with the back of his glove. His brows creased as he remembered bumping into the woman outside the funeral home. The nurse recognized him and said she looked after Sophie. However, something else she said that made little sense at the time was making sense now.

Without showering, he left the gym. The spinning pickup tires sprayed dirty slush as he flew out of the gym parking lot towards the hospital.

CHAPTER 26

Reggie lay in bed, staring at the Tomb Raider poster taped to his ceiling. Lara Croft held her bowstring back, ready for her arrow to pierce someone's heart.

Christmas morning at the Hargreaves residence was nothing like the ones in the movies. It was a dull, drab affair that was tolerated rather than enjoyed. Before Covid, Aunt Sera and Uncle Adrian would come for Christmas Dinner. Uncle Adrian was a jerk, but his loud, obnoxious personality was at least entertaining. His father was always quiet and glum during holidays, as if it were a chore to make it until January. Aunt Sera was the only cheery part of Christmas. She always tried to make the holidays happy and fun. However, during Covid, Reggie was stuck inside the big house with just his father. They were the worst two Christmases ever.

Now that the pandemic was over, this year might be different.

With a glimmer of festive optimism, Reggie jumped out of bed and dressed.

He walked down the stairs and stepped into the living room.

The lights on the tall fake Christmas tree in the corner were not on. Every year the maid Maria would put the tree up and decorate it before she took her time off for Christmas.

He reached under the tree and flicked the button on the power bar. Red, green, blue and white lights glowed brightly from the tree.

His father sat on the big chair, staring at the in one hand and holding a coffee in the other. He didn't look up when he spoke. "Morning."

"Do you mean Merry Christmas?"

"Right...of course. Merry Christmas, Reggie."

"Is Aunt Sera coming over for Christmas?"

"Yeah."

"I see your festive spirit is as gleeful as ever," Reggie mumbled.

"I got you something." His father pointed with his coffee cup to a present under the tree. Amongst other identically green foil-wrapped gifts was a larger box that wasn't there yesterday.

"Can I open it now?" Reggie asked with cautious optimism. His father's previous record of Christmas gifts was not good. It included a little kid's bicycle with a bell when he was twelve, a business management book at thirteen and a Monopoly game during Covid. He didn't care too much since his almost unlimited allowance allowed him to buy almost whatever he wanted.

"Sure. You can open one now, but we'll wait for Aunt Sera to open the others."

"Cool." Reggie tore at the wrapping paper as his father watched. Inside was an X-Box. "Wow...thanks," he said with muted enthusiasm.

"That's the newest and latest X-Box," his father said proudly. "I hope you like it."

Reggie sighed. "Thanks."

"What's the problem? Do you know much that cost?"

"Yeah, Dad, I do. I bought this same one, last year."

"How was I supposed to know that?"

"Because I told you. Remember last summer? When I brought it home, I asked if you wanted to play."

"I'm much too busy to play children's games." He gulped the last of his coffee.

"Of course you are."

"Don't give me that attitude." He stood up, still holding his empty cup.

Reggie stood up and turned to leave. "I'm going to my room to play on my *other* X-Box."

"Hey!" his father yelled. "I thought it was the thought that counted. Be a little grateful."

"Grateful?" he spat the word out. "For what? Enduring another stupid Christmas?"

"Give me a break. At least I try to give you a nice Christmas."

"Do you? You can't be bothered to decorate the tree – instead, you have Maria do it. You're working on your phone or in your office every Christmas, and instead of asking me what I want for Christmas, you just buy something stupid."

Lawrence whipped the coffee cup towards Reggie, who ducked at the last moment. It smashed against the wall, sending ceramic shards spraying across the floor. Reggie moved to leave the room, but his father grabbed his arm and pulled him back.

"Where do you think you're going, you ungrateful little brat?"

"Leave me alone." Reggie tried to squirm away, but his father's grip was too strong.

"I'm sorry, okay?" yelled his father. "Your mother is gone, and sometimes I'm lost without her."

His eyes welled up, and his face reddened in a confused mix of grief and anger.

"But I'm not gone!" Reggie yelled back. "I'm still here. Don't take out your anger on me. I didn't kill her."

"If you weren't born, she would still be alive today."

The words stung like acid. He wanted to retort with *sorry for being born* or *I wish you were dead,* but all the fight left his body. He sagged and pulled away from his father, who let him go.

"I'm sorry, Reggie...I didn't mean to...you make me so angry sometimes and..."

Reggie ran out of the room as his father mumbled an incoherent jumble of excuses and apologies.

He threw his door open and then slammed it behind him. With hot tears streaming down his cheeks, he flopped onto his bed.

Twenty minutes later, someone knocked on his door.

"Go away!" Reggie yelled.

"It's me, Aunt Sera."

He wiped the tears from his face, got up and opened the door.

"Sorry," he said. "I thought you were my idiot father."

"Are you okay?"

"Why does he hate me so much?" He tried desperately to hold back the tears.

"He doesn't hate you. Christmas is a difficult time for him, that's all."

"Now you're on his side?"

She leaned close and studied his face. "Did he hit you, again? We talked about this. If he hurts you—"

"No, he didn't hit me. This was worse."

She pulled him in for a hug. "I'm so sorry you have to go through this."

He cried on her shoulder till he felt drained of his tears.

"You should ask your friend, Hudson over for Christmas dinner," she suggested as they walked down the hallway from his room.

"I tried. Y*ou* should invite him."

"I tried too. I think he's mad at me."

Reggie's phone rang in his pocket. He looked at the screen. It was Hudson.

CHAPTER 27

The automatic doors to the Wanigas General Hospital didn't open fast enough, and Hudson ran into them. When they finally opened, he burst inside.

"Please take a mask, sir," said the nurse sitting behind a small table protected with plexiglass.

"I'm looking for…" He struggled to remember her name.

With a deep breath, he calmed his mind and tried to recall the nurse from outside the funeral home.

"Ursala…Vanwick…I think?"

The nurse pointed to the box of masks.

"I thought the pandemic was over," he yelled.

"There is still the ongoing risk of Covid, sir."

"I'm willing to take my chances. Can you please page Ursala?"

"There are many vulnerable people here, sir. Please don a mask, or I will have to call security."

He snatched a mask and looped the elastics over his ears.

"Happy?" he asked in a loud but muffled voice.

She nodded. "Is there something I can help you with?"

"Yes, I'm looking for a nurse that works here. Her name is Ursala something. Capwick?" The mask muffled his voice.

"Pardon me?" she asked.

He pulled down his mask and repeated the question.

"Sorry, but I am not at liberty to divulge any information about employees at the hospital."

"I'm not asking about her personal information. Can you ask the head nurse or something if she is working today?"

"That's not possible."

Hudson took another deep breath. Since anger or violence

wouldn't help in this situation, he tried another tactic.

He leaned down to her level and lowered his voice to a calmer tone.

"My wife died, and we are having a funeral in two days. I was hoping the nurse who looked after her in her dying days might say something at the service. Can you please page her and tell her that Hudson Finlay wants to talk to her? If she says she doesn't want to see me, I will leave."

The nurse stared at him for a moment.

"What did you say her name was?"

"Ursala Tanwick, I think."

"Wait here," she said and walked to the reception desk.

After a hushed conversation, she returned.

"I'm sorry, sir. Ursala Janwick is not working today."

"Can you give me her phone number?"

"We can't give out personal information."

Hudson rolled his eyes. He ripped off the mask, tossed it in the garbage can and stormed out.

Back in his truck, he pulled out his phone and opened his contacts app. He tapped on *The Great and Powerful Reggie*.

"Merry Christmas, Hudson," Reggie answered in a melancholic tone.

"Same to you."

"Did you get the job?"

"I don't know yet," answered Hudson. "But I need a favour."

"Okay..."

"I need someone's phone number."

"Can this wait till after Christmas?"

"No! It can't."

"Fine. Hang on. Let me get my laptop..."

After a few moments, Reggie came back on the phone.

"Okay, what's the name?"

"Ursala."

"Last name?"

"Vanwick...Janwick...Lapwick...or something like that."

"What city does Ursala live?"

"I'm assuming Wanigas, but I'm not sure."

"Hmmm...nothing is coming up. Who is she? Did you get another lead? Is she an elite at the Economics Congress, a lead scientist with Project Mita or part of the New World Order initiative? Did the Sentinel contact you?"

"No. Nothing like that."

"Come on, man. Tell me something. Aren't we a team?"

"Please!" Light tones of anger tinted his voice. "I need her number. She was a nurse that was with Sophie when she died."

"Do you think she knows something?"

"Yeah."

"What?"

"Can you find her number or not?"

"I'm looking. Why don't you go to the hospital and ask them?"

"That's where I am! They won't tell me anything."

"It's difficult without a last name. Also, everyone has cell phones, and those numbers aren't listed."

"Aren't you a hacker or something? Can't you hack into the cell phone listings or the hospital network or something?"

"I could try, but this may be beyond my skills."

"Reggie, this is important. Are you sure—"

"We might know someone who can find what you're looking for."

"Who?"

"Raven."

"Excellent. Call your girlfriend."

"She is not my girlfriend, and you *do* realize it's Christmas, right?"

"I know, but I need to find Ursala as soon as possible."

After hanging up, Hudson stared out the pickup truck window. A light rain fell from the slate grey sky, melting the last bit of slushy snow. Twinkling Christmas lights wrapped around the branches of the large pine tree outside the emergency entrance. For the next hour and a half, he watched people walk through the puddles, past the tree, into and out of the hospital. His mind swirled with anger, impatience, grief, frustration and confusion.

Suddenly, the passenger door opened, and Reggie climbed in.

"Did you miss me?" he asked.

"What are you doing here?"

"I have an address for you. Raven couldn't find her number, but she got into the hospital's system and—"

"Why didn't you call me? Why are you here?"

"I *know* this has something to do with our investigation, and I want to be part of it. Also, you smell gross. Did you just run a marathon?"

Hudson shook his head. "You shouldn't be here. I need to do this alone."

"No way. We're partners and—"

"No, we're not!" yelled Hudson. His tone was now fully coloured with dark anger. "We're not partners, friends, buddies or anything else!"

Reggie tapped at his phone and then opened his door. "I texted you Ursala's address," he said before stepping out of the car and slamming the door.

Hudson watched him saunter away through the rain and puddles. The late afternoon drizzle pattered loudly on the truck. He sighed and muttered to himself before starting the truck and pulling up to Reggie. After leaning across the seat and rolling down the window, he called out.

"Hey!"

Reggie ignored him and continued walking.

Hudson rolled the truck forward to keep pace. "You're getting wet."

Without a response, Reggie continued slogging through the parking lot.

"Sorry," Hudson mumbled.

Reggie stopped and poked his head in the window. "Pardon?"

"Sorry," he said, louder this time.

Reggie crossed his arms and glared. "For what?"

"That's all you're getting," said Hudson. "Either get in the truck or walk home in the rain."

"Are we friends again?" Reggie hopped into the passenger seat.

"I didn't say that."

"Partners?"

"No. Where are we going?"

Reggie gave directions as they drove across town.

"Shouldn't you be home, opening presents, drinking eggnog and watching Christmas movies with your family on Christmas?" Hudson asked.

"If I spend one more Christmas with my father, someone is going to die."

"That bad?"

"Yeah."

"Want to talk about it?"

"No."

They drove down the wet, snowy road in silence for a few minutes until Reggie asked, "Are you going to tell me why we're going to Ursala Janwick's house?"

"Janwick – that was her name."

"What do you think she knows?" Reggie pointed to a white two-storey house on the far side of the cul-de-sac. "It's that house."

Hudson parked against the curb next to the red brick bungalow. Strings of blue, red and green lights lined the eaves troughs and windows. A spotlight lit up a manger scene in the front yard. The melted remnants of a snowman puddled next to the front deck. A brightly lit Christmas tree glowed from inside the front bay window. A young girl danced in the arms of a man while a young boy sat amongst opened boxes, crumpled wrapping paper and a pile of toys near the Christmas tree.

"I need to do this alone," said Hudson. "Wait here."

Without waiting for a response, he exited the truck and walked up the laneway. As he neared the front door, he heard the muted tones of Christmas music. He pressed the doorbell and waited.

A moment later, a middle-aged man with a neatly trimmed beard opened the door. The young girl in his arms smiled.

"Hello, may I help you?"

"My name is Hudson Finlay. I'm looking for Ursala Janwick."

"May I ask what this is about?"

"I need to discuss a personal matter with her."

The man raised his eyebrows. "Oh, really?"

"It's okay, Henry. I know him." Ursala appeared behind him and smiled. "This is Hudson. I worked with his wife at the hospital. Please, both of you, come in."

Hudson turned and found Reggie standing behind him. "I thought I told you—"

"Is everything okay?" asked Ursala. "Come in out of the rain. We have hot apple cider and eggnog."

"No thank you, ma'am. We don't want to impose. I have a quick question, and we'll leave you to your family Christmas celebrations."

"What is it?"

"What did you mean when you said *sorry for your losses*?"

She shook her head in confusion, and he continued. "Outside the funeral home, you said it wasn't right that they wouldn't let me see her and you were sorry for my losses. Why did you say *losses*?"

Ursala bit her lip. "You didn't know?"

"Know what?" said Henry.

"Yeah, know what?" echoed Reggie.

She looked at her husband. "Henry, take Jenna into the living room, please."

"Why, what's—?"

"Please," she implored.

After he left, Ursala looked up at Hudson with pitying eyes. "I thought you knew. I'm sorry."

"Say it," he said. "I need to hear you say it."

Ursala swallowed hard. "Sophie was six weeks pregnant. The fetus died when she did."

"You mean her *baby* died."

"Yes."

"Why didn't anyone tell me!?" His face reddened, and he looked like he was about to explode.

"We thought you knew. After your violent outburst, the doctor was probably scared to tell you."

Hudson stepped towards her, his face darkening with rage. "Tell me the truth. What killed my family?"

Her eyes widened in fear. "She died of Covid, Mr Finlay."

"We both know that's not true. Did the vaccine kill my wife and daughter?"

His fists clenched tightly at his sides.

"There may be evidence that the vaccine has side effects on certain individuals, but I don't know if that's what killed her. I swear." Her voice trembled.

Reggie jumped between them. "Thank you for your time, Mrs. Janwick. We are sorry to bother you on Christmas Eve. We'll be leaving now."

He pushed at Hudson, who wouldn't budge. He quivered with rage and pulled back his clenched fist as Reggie still stood between him and Ursala.

"Get out of my way before I—"

"Before you what? Are you going to hit me?"

Hudson's rage eased somewhat, and Reggie persisted. "She did not kill Sophie. *They* did."

Hudson stepped back from the door. Grief and anger mixed like toxins in his bloodstream.

He stumbled into the puddle that used to be a snowman. The world spun in dark grief. Blurry blue, red and green Christmas bulbs glimmered through his tears.

"Is he going to be okay?" Ursala looked on from the porch with a look of concern on her face.

"I've got him." Reggie hooked an arm under Hudson's and led him towards the car. "Come on, big guy."

"Get off me!" Hudson yelled and stumbled into the truck like a drunken pirate.

As they drove away, Reggie sat in silence, afraid to speak and unsure what to say.

Hudson leered through the swaying wipers as he pushed away the heartache and embraced the rage. The trip across town was silent until they reached Reggie's house.

As Hudson pulled into the driveway, his phone rang. Reggie looked up expectantly.

"Are you getting out?" asked Hudson.

"Not till you answer that."

Hudson rolled his eyes and picked up the phone. After a brief conversation filled with *yes's, uh-hu's, right's* and an *I'll be there*, he hung up.

With a look of newly acquired determination, Hudson glared at Reggie.

"I'm going to Switzerland, and I'm going to find who's responsible."

CHAPTER 28

Hudson woke from his late afternoon nap and sat up. After splashing cold water on his face, he opened the hotel curtain and looked out. The mid-February weather in Sovad, Switzerland, was not unlike Michigan. A fresh layer of cotton candy snow blanketed the parked cars, buildings and evergreens. In the distance, white, rolling mountains loomed at the edge of the city, like a protective wall. He rubbed his eyes and stretched. The six-hour time difference was strange, but his jet lag symptoms were minimal.

He grabbed his suit from a hook in the armoire and pulled on his freshly pressed pants, shirt and bulletproof vest. After donning the shoulder holster, he picked up his Glock 20 and slipped it into the holster. His suit jacket fit nicely over it, and he looked in the mirror to see if the bulge was noticeable.

Walking through the northern Michigan forests with a bolt-action Remington 700 in his hands felt natural, but having a pistol hidden under his jacket still felt odd.

The phone on the nightstand vibrated, and he picked it up.

"Are you ready?" asked Reggie.

"You shouldn't be calling me," said Hudson.

"Soon, I won't have to. I'm in Sovad too. Are you staying at the Luxury Grand Hotel?"

"I thought we discussed this. You were supposed to stay home and—"

"This is too exciting to miss. It's our first international mission."

"How did you get here, and how are you at the same hotel?"

"I asked my dad if I could come with him to the IEC conference. I told him I wanted to go skiing. There aren't that many fancy hotels in Sovad, so most of the rich and famous people at the conference stay here."

"I have to go to work. I'll talk to you later."

"Remember to listen to Charles' conversations. The chat rooms are going crazy with talk about secret meetings and backroom deals at this conference."

"I know what I'm doing, Reggie."

"Try to steal his phone and install the tracking app. Did you remember the tracking installer that Raven gave us?"

"Goodbye, Reggie," he replied and hung up.

As he finished dressing and slipping into his shoes, someone knocked on the door.

"Hudson, are you ready? We're leaving in five."

John's low monotone voice matched his equally unreadable personality. Charles Porter's security detail comprised three teams of two. Each pair took an eight-hour shift for around-the-clock protection. Another team was currently standing outside Charles' hotel room, amd Hudson and John were about to start their afternoon shift.

Hudson tied his shoes and joined John in the hotel hallway.

"Is Charles going anywhere today?" he asked.

"We don't use his name," John answered without expression.

"Right, sorry." Hudson spent six weeks of training but had little experience in the field. Most of his job so far was standing outside Charles's house or sitting in the back of his private jet. He was looking forward to some real action.

"We're heading to the IEC conference for the opening session," said John.

The fifteen-minute drive from the hotel to the convention centre was uneventful. The small town was alive with conference attendees. Hudson sat in the passenger seat of the black sedan while John drove. The window behind them blocked their view of Charles Porter in the back seat. It also muffled the conversations he had on his cell.

John handed Hudson an earpiece and put a matching one in his ear.

"It's going to be loud in there. We'll use these to communicate."

At the conference centre, a valet took their car, and Hudson and John followed Charles inside.

Hundreds of men and women from around the world milled about, talking, laughing and discussing the future of the world. Charles stopped to smile, shake hands and talk with dozens of people before finding a seat near the front of the main auditorium. Hudson sat in the row behind Charles, while John stood against a wall to the right.

Soon, the chairs filled with eager attendees. John's head turned slowly as he scanned the room for potential threats, and Hudson did the same.

"Good afternoon," said a man on the stage with a heavy German accent. His voice boomed from large speakers facing the audience. "Guten tag. Bon apres-midi. Buon pomeriggio. Buna saira. My name is Kraus Smawbe."

The din of conversations quieted, and the man continued.

"Welcome to the International Economics Congress. We are so pleased that you could all come."

As he talked, Hudson watched the surrounding people. Although he was here to spy on Charles Porter and attempt to uncover any links to Sophie's death, MITA or the trackers, he still wanted to do his job. Since he was a teenager, he always had a good work ethic. Whether it was sweeping floors at the auto shop, stocking shelves at the outdoors store or working on the assembly line, he always worked hard at every job. Even his employers at the school commented on how clean everything at Wanigas Private Academy looked. Despite his ulterior motives, Hudson still wanted to keep Charles Porter safe.

On his left, a man with long curly hair and a patchy beard meandered down the aisle. His gaze kept moving to Charles, then looking away.

"Suspicious person at my ten o'clock," Hudson whispered into his mic. "Curly hair, mid-twenties."

The man looked again at Charles before sitting on a chair across the aisle.

John's all-business voice came through the earpiece. "Got him. He looks okay for now, but I'll keep an eye on him."

The conference host introduced the opening speaker, who ran on to stage to thunderous applause. Hudson recognized him as a young social media entrepreneur that was worth billions.

"Friends!" the man shouted. "We have a lot of exciting new ideas to talk about."

Hudson only half-listened as he rambled about the 15-minute city, climate change and the green revolution. When he talked about how the pandemic was an opportunity to reimagine a better future, Hudson resisted the compulsion to pull out his Glock and fire a round into his kneecaps.

For the next three and a half hours, Hudson and John followed Charles Porter to various symposiums, talks, and mingling. After the opening speech, the man with curly hair and a patchy beard disappeared, and they never saw him again.

After sipping cocktails with some German executives, Charles whispered something into John's ear. A moment later, John spoke into his earpiece.

"Hope you're okay working late tonight. The boss is going out for dinner."

A half hour later, Hudson sat at a table in a dimly lit dining area of Ristorante Roma. Except for the occasional passing server or patron, his view of Charles Porter and his two guests was unobstructed. John stood near the doors to the kitchen with his hands clasped in front. Hudson wondered how the man could stand in one place for so long.

For the next hour, he watched Charles laugh, talk, eat and drink with the two Germans. Hudson was too far to hear any of their conversations and wondered if this entire trip was a waste of time. As he pushed the ice cubes in his water around with a mushy paper straw, a waitress tripped on her way to Charles's table. The platter of desserts flew off the tray as she tumbled across the carpet. In a flash, John seemed to appear at the table. He inserted himself between the downed waitress and Charles. The restaurant quieted, and all eyes turned to the commotion.

John helped the waitress up as other waiters came to assist. The conversations resumed as the waiter quickly cleaned the mess. Once the commotion died down, John spoke into his earpiece.

"All clear. I'm going to the men's room to clean the tiramisu off my pants. Keep watch. I'll be back in five."

A moment after he left, Hudson saw a figure walk into the dining area. Behind him, the host called out, "Sir, do you have a reservation?"

It was the curly-haired man with the patchy beard from the convention. A bulging, burlap crossbody pouch hung over his shoulder as he strode across the room towards Charles' table.

Hudson flew out of his chair.

"We know what you're doing!" the man yelled. "You can't solve overpopulation by killing people with vaccines!"

In a few quick strides, Hudson caught up with the man just as he pulled something out of his pouch and wound up to throw.

Hudson grabbed the man's reared back arm and threw him to the floor. The man hit the carpet with enough force that he bounced. A tomato rolled out of his hand as he looked up at Hudson with wide eyes. Hudson put a foot on his chest and grabbed the pouch. Inside, he found three more tomatoes.

"You can't—" the man protested, but Hudson's foot pushed harder on his chest and he cried out in pain.

John ran to the scene. "What's going on? Is everyone okay?"

"It appears Hudson has everything under control," said Charles with raised eyebrows.

"Please call the police," said Hudson to the gathering servers.

A woman in a suit stepped forward. "I am the manager of this establishment." She bowed slightly to Charles and his guests. "I apologize for this intrusion and will speak to my front staff."

The manager smiled at Hudson. "Please take this trespasser through the kitchen and out the back. The police are on route."

Hudson threw the pouch of tomatoes over his shoulder and lifted the protestor to his feet. He shoved the man's arm behind his back, and he winced in pain.

"If you say one word, I will break your arm," Hudson whispered in his ear.

The man opened his mouth but reconsidered when Hudson pushed his arm up further. As they exited the dining room, the man struggled. Hudson slammed his head on the doorway to the kitchen and pushed through the swinging doors.

He dragged the stunned man through the kitchen and out the door into an alley.

"Sit down!" Hudson commanded.

"I can't, it's wet."

Several inches of snow covered most of the alley. A trodden pathway through the snow led from the door to the garbage bin. Flattened wet snow surrounded a large coffee can filled with sand and cigarette butts. To the right, the alley ended at a chain-link fence. Fifty yards to the left was a small cobblestone side street.

Hudson kicked out the man's legs, and he fell into the snow by the garbage bin.

"Stay!"

"This is unlawful confinement," the man complained.

"No, it's a citizen's arrest."

He pulled his knees to his chest and looked up at Hudson.

"How can you work for a man like Charles Porter?"

When he realized he was not getting a response, he continued. "That man is responsible for killing what he calls *non-performing* people in third world countries by introducing free vaccines."

John opened the door into the alley and peeked out. "Everything okay?"

Hudson gave him the thumbs up. "All good."

After he left, the shivering man sitting in the snow continued talking while Hudson leaned against the brick wall.

"The Porter Foundation is a front for his New World Order agenda. The Covid pandemic was just the beginning."

In the distance, a siren wailed.

"Did you know that there are trackers in all the vaccines? The global elites at the IEC conference in 2019 developed the idea for MITA to enslave the population. We are living in an Orwellian society—"

Hudson perked up. "What did you say?"

"You know...George Orwell...1984...big brother is watching."

"No, you said MITA."

The man leaned back and smiled. "I knew it! I told them Porter was involved. You've heard of MITA, haven't you?"

Hudson bent down and grabbed him by his coat collars. He hoisted the man to his feet and shoved him against the garbage bin.

A car on the side street screeched to a stop next to the alley.

"What is MITA?" Hudson growled. "I will smash your head against this bin till you have permanent brain damage unless you tell me."

The man looked behind Hudson. "The cops are coming."

"A moment ago, you wouldn't stop talking. Now you're the one with the secrets."

"Okay...chill."

"This way," said a voice from the street.

Hudson glared at the man.

"Microscopic Injectable Tracking Apparatus," he said, staring back.

"What?"

"M...I...T...A. It stands for Microscopic Injectable Tracking Apparatus."

"Is this the guy?" said the policeman behind him.

Hudson turned and looked at the two policemen. He shoved the man in their direction.

They cuffed him and asked Hudson a few questions.

As the police escorted the tomato thrower to their cruiser, he yelled back. "We could use someone like you for our cause!"

Hudson returned to the restaurant where Charles and John were waiting. His German dinner guests were no longer at the table.

"Good job, Hudson," said Charles, shaking his hand. "I knew I could count on you."

"Just doing my job, sir," he replied.

John nodded at him.

"That was an eventful day," said Charles. "John will take me back to the hotel. Feel free to stay here and have a free meal on me for a job well done. The chef here is amazing. The veal Milanese is incredible!"

Hudson thought for a moment. "Thank you. I think I will."

Charles cuffed him on the shoulder. "Excellent. Enjoy your meal."

He motioned towards the manager, who speed walked to the table.

"Please give this man anything he wants and put it on my bill."

"Of course, sir. It would be our pleasure."

As Charles turned to leave, Hudson asked, "Have you ever heard of MITA?"

He adjusted his tie and smiled. "Is that an Italian dish or something?"

"No. Nevermind. Enjoy your night, sir. I'll see you in the morning."

"Very good," said Charles and left, with John following close behind.

"Have a seat," said the manager. "A server will be with you shortly."

His phone vibrated, and he read the text message from Reggie.

How did it go today? Can we meet up?

Hudson texted back: *I'm busy right now with something VERY important. I'll be back at the hotel in an hour and a half.*

CHAPTER 29

"What was *very* important?" Reggie burst into Hudson's hotel room. "Did you install the tracker on Charles Porter's phone? Did you uncover a plot to instate a new world order?"

Hudson patted his stomach. "Food."

"What?"

"Free food. Charles was right, the veal Milanese was incredible."

"Where did you eat veal Milanese?"

Hudson pressed his thumb against his fingers and said in a bad Italian accent, "Ristorante Roma!"

"What are you talking about?"

Hudson removed his suit jacket and hung it in the armoire.

"Whoa!" yelled Reggie, pointing at Hudson's gun and shoulder holster. "They gave you a gun! That is so cool. Can I hold it?"

"No."

"How did you get free food at an Italian restaurant?"

Hudson ignored the question. "I found out what MITA stands for."

"Microscopic Injectable Tracking Apparatus," said Reggie.

Hudson held up his hands. "How did you know?"

"Raven told me a couple of days ago. I guess I forgot to tell you."

"I thought we were a team?" Hudson yelled. "That means we share new information with each other."

Reggie folded his arms and smirked. "Are you mad because I didn't tell you or because you thought you discovered something before I did?"

Hudson untied and removed his shoes. "How did Raven find out?"

"She heard it from the Sentinel. Did you just say we were a

team?"

"That's not what I said. Did you want to hear my story about how I saved Charles Porter from a tomato-throwing protestor and had an incredible free meal of sturgeon caviar, veal Milanese and espresso cannoli?"

"Did you shoot somebody?"

"Shut up and listen."

Hudson told him everything that happened at the IEC conference and the Italian restaurant.

"Did you think Charles would admit he knew about MITA?" asked Reggie.

"No, but I wanted to see how he reacted, and when he answered, it seemed like the question made him a little uncomfortable."

"I told you he's part of this! And it's all making sense now. Raven also found out that Charles Porter's offshore companies own a majority number of shares in Nanotech Industries. I don't think he's on the board, but he pretty much owns my father's company."

"That is very interesting."

"Now what?"

"I'm going to install that tracking software onto his phone."

CHAPTER 30

Later that week, on a Saturday afternoon, Hudson sat next to John in the black sedan. Charles Porter talked on his phone in the back seat.

For the past five days, Hudson looked for an opportunity to steal Charles' cell phone. The man kept his phone in his hand almost every minute of the day. For the rare times he wasn't looking at or talking on his phone, he still had it in his hand or his inside pocket. Hudson was not a skilled pickpocket and never found a chance to swipe it. He considered sneaking into the hotel room and grabbing it while Charles slept, but it seemed too risky. Besides, John watched Charles' every move like a hawk. It may have been Hudson's imagination, but John appeared to be watching him too.

They were scheduled to return to the States in two days, and his opportunities to install a tracker on his boss's phone were slipping away.

None of the talks, conversations or lectures at the conference suggested anything nefarious. Although some ideas for reducing climate change and making the world a better place seemed preposterous.

"Where are we going?" he asked, as they drove away from the hotel and out of downtown Sovad.

"The IEC conference," John answered.

"I thought it was over."

"That was the *open* conference. The one today is the original IEC conference."

"What's the difference?"

"This is the conference where we make real plans to secure a better future," said Charles from the back seat.

"Oh," said Hudson. "I didn't realize you were listening."

"The original annual conference of the IEC was held behind closed doors. However, when the media and crazy conspiracy theorists found out, they all went nuts. In order to assuage their fears, the IEC started another forum that was open to the public. However, they still hold a one day conference for invitees behind closed doors. It's held at the end of the open forum in a secure location. Normally, personal security isn't necessary at this event because of the high-security protocols already in place. However, because you've done such an exemplary job this week, I thought you might find this interesting."

"Thank you, sir."

John drove out of the city down a long snowy road towards the mountains. They turned right into a short drive before stopping in front of a tall chain-link gate blocking the road. John pulled a card from his jacket and drove to the card reader. He opened his window and tapped the card. A motor on the gate whirred to life, and the gate slid open. They drove through as the gate closed behind them.

After driving down a winding road for another ten minutes, they stopped. The road ended at a massive steel door set into the side of a mountain. Four men wearing military uniforms and wielding SIG SG 550 assault rifles guarded the door.

A guard strolled to John's window and asked for their identification and Charles' official invite.

Eventually, the guards let them through. The steel door opened with a loud groan, and they drove inside. Caged lights on the tunnel ceiling lit the road like spotlights. The rumble of the car's engine echoed off the walls as they travelled deep into the mountain.

At the end of the tunnel, John pulled up to what looked like a strange underground parking area.

"Leave your phone and any other electronics in the car," said John, placing his phone in the centre console.

Hudson pulled out his phone and put it in the glove box. He

waited till John stepped out of the car before removing the tracker installer from his pants pocket and shoving it in the glove box with his phone. Raven's recorder pen remained in his breast pocket.

A valet took the car, and Hudson followed Charles and John to a set of large doors on the side of the tunnel. They joined a small group waiting in line. Four armed guards stood outside the door, checking credentials. At the front of the line, two men in traditional white robes and checkered ghutras draped over their heads waited their turn. Hudson was sure he recognized one of them from the news. Behind them, three Japanese men and one woman patiently waited their turn.

Hudson watched as the Arab and Japanese groups walked through the metal detector.

Charles pointed to his leg. "They stop me every time for my titanium leg."

Hudson took a breath and considered how to get the pen through. If the guards were distracted, he could throw it over the detector. Or if he pretended to tie his shoe, he could slide it along the floor. It felt like all the guards were staring at him.

As Charles' group stepped up, a guard held out a bin. "Last chance to hand over any electronics. Also, place any firearms in the bin. You will get them back on your way out."

John placed his pistol in the bin and walked through the detector without incident. However, when Charles stepped through the detector, it beeped. While he discussed his titanium leg with the guard on the far side, Hudson stepped forward and placed his Glock in the bin. The guard motioned him to walk through. He held his breath and moved through the detector. The beeping was immediate, and Hudson's heart skipped a beat.

"Spread your arms and legs," the guard commanded.

"Is it my belt?" he asked as the man waved a detector wand over his legs and arms.

"What's in there?" he asked, pointing at Hudson's breast pocket.

He pulled out the pen and smiled. "Sorry. This is my lucky pen."

"Nothing goes inside."

Hudson leaned forward and whispered. "This is my first time here. I was hoping to get a few autographs."

The guard shook his head, grabbed a plastic bin filled with an impressive collection of pens and held it out for Hudson.

"What's going on?" Charles called.

The guard turned when he spoke, and Hudson saw his chance. He dropped his pen in his pant pocket as the guard turned. Then he reached into the bin and grabbed a different pen. When the guard turned back, Hudson's hand was in the bin holding a pen. With an exaggerated sigh, Hudson dropped the pen back in the bin.

"Thank you," said the guard.

Hudson nodded and joined Charles and John. They stepped onto a subway platform similar to the ones in Empire City. A group of about fifty men and women chatted while they waited on the platform. Some groups were security contingents, but most were high-ranking dignitaries from around the world. The platform overlooked a tunnel with tracks that led in only one direction.

Soft humming reverberated across the platform, getting louder as a five-car electric train rolled down the track. It stopped in front of the waiting crowd and double doors slid open. Unlike the subway cars in Empire City, these were flat black and windowless.

The interior of the train reminded Hudson of the fancy Konrad Hotel in Empire, except at a smaller scale. He walked across the thickly carpeted floor to large, upholstered chairs lining one side of the car. He chose one with a view of Charles, who bellied up to a bar beside two Japanese dignitaries.

The smooth, quiet ride gave him a chance to think. If only Sophie was here. She would be living out her dream. Instead, *he* was on a covert operation travelling on a secret train inside a mountain in Switzerland to uncover a secret plot by the global elites. She might have been proud of him.

Twenty minutes later, the train reached its destination. They disembarked at a carpeted platform. The group funnelled into a long hallway with offices and corridors on either side. At the end, two large corridors went to the right and left. Ahead, two massive double doors opened into a large boardroom with a round table with about forty chairs.

“This is as far as we go,” said John.

“Wait!” Hudson called to Charles. He reached into his pocket and clicked the pen.

“Sorry,” said Charles. “You’ll have to wait out here. I hear they have an excellent cafeteria and lounge area.”

Hudson pointed to his tie. “Let me fix this first.”

He tightened Charles’ Windsor knot while dropping the pen in his side jacket pocket. “You need to look your best for all the other world leaders.”

“Okay…” said Charles with a confused look.

John placed his hand on Hudson’s shoulder. “Let’s go.”

Hudson stepped back and nodded while Charles turned and walked into the boardroom.

“We don’t touch the boss unless we’re protecting him,” said John in his signature monotone.

“Not even if we’re protecting him from a fashion faux pas?”

“Just do your job.”

“Right, sorry.”

John glared at him. Hudson didn’t know if it was his paranoid imagination or if John looked at him with suspicious eyes.

He wondered if John saw his sleight of hand or heard a quiver in his voice. His heartbeat was so fast he imagined John staring at the pulsing artery in his neck.

“I’m going to find that famous cafeteria,” said Hudson and hurried away, trying not to look back.

The movies made this seem easier than it was. He and Sophie watched all the Bourne, Mission Impossible and Bond movies multiple times. This was different. Every moment felt like he was standing on the edge of a precipice. One mistake and he would slip over the edge.

His nerves calmed when he found the cafeteria and scarfed down a plate of double-smoked salmon with horseradish cream and glazed carrots. His nerves rattled again as he formulated a plan to retrieve the pen.

Three hours later, John walked up to his table. "They're out in five."

Hudson nodded and grabbed his cup of water. If he tripped and spilled water on Charles' suit, he could offer to dry it off and get the pen back.

Confident with his plan, he followed John out of the cafeteria.

"No drinks on the job," said John. "You should know that."

"Right."

Hudson downed the rest of the water and tossed the cup in a nearby trash bin.

In his mind, Hudson activated Plan B: trip and fall into Charles while slipping a hand into his pocket with the pen.

They arrived at the large double doors just as Charles exited the boardroom. He was having an animated discussion with a man in a colourful African dashiki. As Hudson stepped forward, John held his hand out to stop him.

"Hang back. Everyone here is a high-level dignitary, government official or influential billionaire. There are no threats."

Hudson tried to think of Plan C as they exited the hallway back to the train platform. He might have another chance to trip into Charles, but the more he thought the plan through, the less he liked it. Too many things could go wrong. He still wasn't an experienced pickpocket, and he was probably just really lucky with his successful pen drop.

On the return train ride, he replayed different scenarios in his head, but none of them ended well. He was *so* close. Whatever was discussed in the secret meeting with the most influential people in the world was on that pen. The proof of the global elite's plans was almost within his grasp. However, if he misstepped now, it would be gone forever, and he would be in jail or dropped in the Atlantic with concrete shoes.

When the train stopped, they got off and retrieved their guns. After a valet brought their car, Hudson opened the rear door for Charles. Inside, he saw Charles' cell phone on the seat.

“Hey, is that the Prime Minister of Canada?” he asked, pointing behind them at a group exiting the platform. As soon as Charles turned to look, Hudson reached inside the car and flicked the phone off the seat. As planned, it slid under the front passenger seat.

“Yes, it is,” said Charles. “Do you follow politics? Because there were a lot of famous politicians here.”

“Not really, but I recognized a few of them.”

John stood outside the driver’s side door and leered at him.

Charles climbed into the car and, with a deep breath to calm his nerves, Hudson got into the passenger seat. He reached into the glove box and retrieved his phone and the tracker.

“Where’s my phone?” asked Charles from the back seat. “I swear I left it on the seat.”

“I’ll check under the seat.” Hudson opened his door and got out. He leaned down and reached under the seat. There wasn’t much room for his big arm, and he cut his forearm as he shoved his hand as deep as possible. He found the phone and pulled it back, being careful no pull it all the way out.

“Did you find it?” John asked as he searched under his seat.

Hudson pushed the tracker plug into the cell phone charging port. He remembered Raven saying it took twenty seconds for the device to install the tracking virus.

“I can never figure out how to turn the flashlight app on my phone on,” he said.

He fiddled with his phone. Twenty seconds seemed like an eternity.

“It has to be here somewhere,” said Charles.

“Swipe up and tap the flashlight icon,” said John.

“Right, of course.”

With the light beaming from his phone, he looked under his seat again. “Hang on. I think I see something.”

Charles was looking under the seat from the back. Hudson quickly unplugged the tracker and pulled out Charles’s phone. “Got it!”

He handed it to Charles.

"Thanks. I don't know what I'd do without it."

Hudson smiled and nodded, while John looked at him with an unreadable expression.

Moments later, they were driving through the tunnel towards the exit. Hudson tried to control his nervous breathing and calm his racing heart.

"That's strange," said Charles from the back seat.

"Is everything okay, sir?" John asked.

Hudson turned to find Charles staring at his phone. "I'm sure it's nothing," he said and pressed a button on the seat in front of him. The tinted privacy window rolled up, obscuring him from view.

"What are you up to?" John asked as they reached the end of the tunnel.

"Nothing. What do you mean?"

The massive door blocking the tunnel opened, and they rolled through.

"I don't know yet." John stared forward.

The man would have made an excellent poker player. His tone and expressions never changed. Either he was in total control of his emotions, or he was a robot.

Hudson tried to remember if any of Sophie's conspiracy theories involved robots or androids. He couldn't think of any.

In his mind, he played out various scenarios. He could ask for his pen back. He could say he had leant it to Charles earlier in the day. However, Charles didn't become a billionaire by having a bad memory. He would know Hudson was lying.

If Charles made it back to the hotel room with the pen, he might get changed and not realize the pen was in his pocket. The following morning, Hudson would sneak into his room while he was having breakfast and find the suit jacket. Too many things could go wrong with that plan. What if Charles found the pen when he removed his jacket before going to bed? If he looked close enough at the pen, he might see the camera. But would he suspect Hudson planted it there? Even if Charles didn't know whose pen it was, Hudson still wouldn't have the pen or the valuable footage on it. Also, John knew something was wrong. He had to get the pen back tonight…somehow.

CHAPTER 31

Back at the Luxury Grand Hotel, John and Hudson flanked Charles as they rode the elevator. As Hudson inched his hand towards Charles' pocket, John turned to look at him. Hudson stared forward and brought his hand back and clasped his other wrist.

Above the doors, the LED blinked from five to six and dinged. The doors slid open, and they stepped out. John led the trio down the hallway. Charles' room was the second door on the right. John stepped aside as Charles swiped his card at the door.

"Do you have my pen?" Hudson blurted out.

"Pardon?" Charles turned to him.

John squinted at him.

"My pen." Hudson's heart felt like it was about to beat out of his chest. He tried to make his voice sound natural but was sure he sounded like a shy teenage boy asking a pretty girl to the prom. "I lent you my pen earlier. It was a gift from my late wife, and I don't want to lose it."

Charles' brow creased as he reached into his pocket. "You didn't —"

His hand returned from the pocket with the pen. "When did you give me this?"

John leaned forward, staring at the pen. "Let me see that." He reached toward the pen.

Hudson tried to grab it, but John snatched it from Charles' finger first.

He held the pen inches from his face, studying it. "Is that a—?"

Before he finished, Hudson swiped the pen out of his hands and bolted down the hallway. Behind him, John yelled. As Hudson reached the door to the stairwell, a gunshot rang out. The bullet pierced the drywall beside him, spraying gypsum dust into the air.

Charles yelled something as Hudson flung the door open. He flew down the stairs, leaping down each flight with giant leaps. On the ground floor, he opened the door and stepped out. With a steady gait, he walked towards the lobby. At the front desk, he saw the man behind the counter talking on the phone with a concerned expression. He pressed a button under his desk and scanned the room. Hudson ducked behind a fake tree. Peering out, he saw a security guard reach under his jacket as he moved towards the front entrance.

Another guard appeared from the restaurant and walked towards him. With nowhere else to go, Hudson retreated into the stairwell. He listened for a moment before climbing back up. As he reached the second level, the door below him opened. Above him, footsteps echoed off the concrete walls. The sound of doors to other levels opening and closing echoed through the stairwell. They were closing in on all sides.

Hudson shoved the pen in his pocket and unholstered his pistol. He cautiously ascended the stairwell. Someone ran down from the flight above, and Hudson pointed his gun at the incoming figure.

“Don’t shoot!” Reggie stood on the stairs in his boxers and t-shirt.

“What are *you* doing here?” Hudson lowered his gun.

“Like everyone else in this hotel, I heard the gunshot. What happened?”

“I got it!” Hudson held up the pen. “I have the proof of the IEC’s secret meeting.”

Reggie’s mouth dropped. “No way! What’s on it? Are they planning on installing a new socialist world order?”

Rapid footsteps from above a below increased in speed and volume.

“They know I have it,” Hudson said in a serious tone. “And they’re coming after me. The lobby is crawling with guards, and all of Charles' security detail are searching for me."

Reggie beckoned him to the doorway. "Come on."

A few guests peered into the hallway from their open doorways. Two armed men in suits that Hudson didn't recognize stood outside a room at the far end of the hallway. Hudson quickly shoved his pistol back into his holster and covered it with his suit jacket.

"My room is right here," said Reggie, swiping his card.

"What about your father?"

"His room is on another floor."

Hudson followed him inside, and the door shut behind him.

"You have separate rooms?"

"Yeah." Reggie held out his hand. "Let me see the pen."

Sirens wailed outside. Hudson handed him the pen and walked to the window. White and orange police cars converged in the parking lot below. Their blue and red strobes lit up the darkness in a colourful flashing display.

"I can't stay here," said Hudson. "You take the pen. I'll surrender to the police, and you can take the footage to the press."

Reggie opened his laptop. "That's a stupid plan. You are going up against one of the most powerful organizations in the world. How long do you think it would take for them to connect us?"

They froze at the sound of three loud knocks on the door.

"That was quick," said Reggie.

Hudson pulled out his gun. "Give me the pen back."

Reggie screwed the pen back together and handed it to Hudson.

"Reggie, are you in there?" It was his father's voice from outside the door. "Are you okay?"

"Hide!" Reggie shooed Hudson behind the bed and pulled the door open.

"Dad, what's going on? I thought I heard a gunshot."

Lawrence Hargreaves pushed his fingers through his bedraggled hair and rubbed his eyes. "I'm sure the police have everything under control. They're telling everyone to stay in their rooms."

"Okay. I think I'm going to get a few hours of sleep before morning."

Lawrence scanned the room. "Have you seen Hudson?"

"No. Why?"

"Just wondering. I'm heading back to my room. I have some things to take care of. Lock the door behind me and don't sleep in too long tomorrow. Your flight back leaves at nine."

"What about you?"

"I have another matter to take care of, but I'll be home in a few days."

Reggie pushed his glasses up his nose and put on a fake smile. "Okay."

After he left, Reggie pulled his clothes on.

"What are you doing?" asked Hudson.

"I'm coming with you."

Hudson shook his head and looked back out the window. "It's too dangerous. You should stay here."

"Not a chance."

Reggie finished dressing and shoved his laptop in a backpack and shouldered it. "What's the plan?"

"I don't have one. This place is crawling with security guards and now cops. There's no way out."

Reggie opened the door and looked into the hallway. More guests stood outside their rooms, talking excitedly amongst themselves.

"I have an idea." He walked into the hallway as Hudson watched him from the door.

"What are you doing?"

Reggie did not answer. Instead, he walked towards the elevator. He looked in both directions before pulling the fire alarm.

A high-pitched tone screeched, and strobes blinked across the hallway. More guests came out of their rooms, joining the people already gathered in the hallway. A man in a bathrobe pushed the elevator button, but nothing happened. They began filing to the stairwell as Reggie pushed his way through the people back to his room.

"Now we can leave," he said, smiling.

"Please remain calm," a voice boomed over the hotel intercom.

"Take the nearest stairwell to the main floor and your nearest emergency exit."

The people in the hallway shuffled towards the stairwell, but Hudson held a hand up to Reggie. "Wait. Let the others go first."

"Why? Don't we want to blend in with the crowd or something?"

"They will be searching for me when we reach the lobby. It will be easier to blend in with a panicked mob."

Reggie looked at the group filing into the stairwell. "They don't look panicked."

"Not yet." Hudson waited until the last person got into the stairwell and pulled out his pistol. "Get ready to run."

He fired a deafening shot into the wall. "Go!"

Reggie opened the door. "You first."

"Why—?"

"Trust me – hurry!"

Hudson stepped into the stairwell and joined the back of the noisy crowd descending the stairs.

"What was that?" asked the woman in front of him.

"I don't know," Hudson answered, "and I don't want to stick around to find out."

"HE'S GOT A GUN!" Reggie shouted from above them. "RUN!"

The worried throng quickly morphed into a panicked mob. Reggie and Hudson joined them as they raced down to the ground floor. A woman screamed as she fell onto the landing. Hudson hoisted her up.

"Are you okay?"

"I hurt my foot," she whimpered.

Hudson picked her up and cradle-carried her to the main floor. They ran down a short hallway to an emergency exit. Hudson cursed himself for not finding it previously.

Outside, police and security guards guided everyone to a growing crowd in the snowy, dark parking lot. Some found their cars and got inside to keep warm.

"Are you hurt, ma'am?" a policeman asked the woman Hudson still held.

"Just a sprain," she answered.

"Take her with the others over there," the man instructed Hudson. "Medical personnel are on their way."

A burly man from Charles Porter's security detail watched the people exiting the hotel. Hudson turned his face away and pushed into the crowd.

"I'm a doctor," said a woman in a winter coat. "Can I help?"

Hudson set the injured woman on the hood of a car. "She hurt her foot."

The woman thanked him as he smiled and backed away. He turned to Reggie. "You stay here."

He walked out of the parking lot with his head down.

"Hey, you!" someone shouted behind him.

"That's him!" another man yelled from his left.

Hudson sped up and debated whether to pull his gun as his former fellow security detail closed in. Flashing emergency lights from nearby police cars lit up the night. Blue and white light flickered off the reflective snow as he ran. A neon green and orange firetruck blared its horn as it rumbled past him. The truck temporarily obstructed the view of his pursuers.

When Hudson reached the road, a sliver sedan slid to a stop in front of him. Hudson reached for his gun as the window slid down.

"Get in!" yelled Reggie from the driver's seat.

Hudson ran around the car and opened the door. "Move over."

A gunshot rang out as he ducked inside. He slammed his foot on the gas. The tires spun for a few seconds until they found their grip. They flew out of the parking lot, leaving the mayhem behind them.

The car's headlights glistened off the thin layer of snow on the roads.

Reggie's phone rang. He pulled it out of his pocket, tapped at the screen and returned it to his pocket.

"Who was that?" asked Hudson.

"My dad."

"You should talk to him."

"I texted him I was okay."

A siren wailed as a bright yellow ambulance drove by. Hudson slowed and pulled to the side of the road to let it pass.

"Hurry!" yelled Reggie, "They're catching up!"

Behind them, a black SUV spun out of the hotel parking lot.

Hudson kept his foot on the brake. "You should get out."

"What! Are you crazy? They're right behind us."

"It's me they want, and they have guns. I can't let you get hurt. You should go back to the hotel and your father."

"If I get out now, what's stopping them from shooting me?" Reggie crossed his arms and stared forward. "Just drive."

"Keep your head down." Hudson slammed the gas pedal, and the car fish-tailed for a few seconds before speeding away. Bright headlights shone behind them as the black SUV caught up.

Years of driving through Michigan snowstorms gave Hudson considerable winter driving skills. He slowed to almost a stop before taking a sharp right onto a shadowy side street. The incoming SUV almost crashed into them before sliding across the road and slamming into the curb. The front right tire snapped off its axle.

"I think we lost them," said Reggie as Hudson turned onto another street.

They returned to the main road and drove north, passing a few smaller hotels, chalets, a train station and a restaurant before emerging from the town of Sovad. The lights from the city faded behind them, and dark forests and looming mountains surrounded them on both sides.

"Where are we going?" asked Reggie.

"There are only two ways out of Sovad," Hudson replied. "North and south. We are going north."

"Great. What's the plan?"

"Plan? I don't have a plan. Right now, I'm just trying to keep us alive."

As they turned out of a wide curve in the road, the road ahead lit up with flashing blue and white lights. Hudson slowed to a stop and stared at the police cars blocking the road.

"This isn't good," he said, turning around.

"Do you think they're looking for us?"

Hudson performed a quick three-point turn and drove back towards Sovad.

"I'm not willing to find out."

"Where are we going now? Won't the cops have the south road blocked too?"

"Probably."

Reggie shook his head. "I knew Charles Porter and his deep state elites were up to something. There must be real evidence on that pen that they don't want the public to find out. We need to look at the footage and upload it to the cloud as soon as possible."

Reggie opened his backpack and reached for his laptop, but Hudson shook his head.

"There's no time for that. We need to get out of this town as soon as possible."

He drove the car into a small parking lot and turned off the ignition.

"Where are we?" Reggie looked around at the almost empty parking lot and a small wooden building.

"The train station."

A single track ran in both directions. The platform was quiet, and the single bench sat empty. Inside was just as quiet until they stamped the snow off their shoes. An older woman behind the counter put her phone down and smiled.

"Guten Morgen."

"When is the next train out of here?" asked Hudson.

"We have a train leaving for Zurich at 5:30 am." She looked at the clock on the wall. "That's two and a half hours from now."

Hudson reached for his wallet, then looked at Reggie then out the window.

"No!" said Reggie as if reading his mind. "I'm not going back. We're in this together. You need me, and we're a team."

After paying for two tickets, Hudson walked outside the station.

"Why are we waiting outside?" asked Reggie.

"That's why." Hudson pointed at a black SUV pulling into the train station parking lot and stopping beside the sedan.

"Why don't you just shoot them?" asked Reggie.

"I'm not murdering anyone." Hudson led them around the far side of the building and watched the men exit the SUV and peer into the sedan windows.

"It's not murder if it's self-defence," whispered Reggie. "They already shot at you, so shooting them would be justified."

"Yes, but the cops would still arrest me for murder."

"The cops are already looking for you."

Hudson watched the two men walk towards the station. When they disappeared around the corner of the building, Hudson and Reggie ran to the sedan.

He started the car and drove away before the two men returned.

"You know why the cops are after you, right?" asked Reggie as they drove into a restaurant parking lot.

"Because Charles Porter told them I stole something?"

"The cops wouldn't setup a roadblock for a stolen pen. The cops are a pawn of the powerful elites who control governments, police and the media."

"But they don't control me. Why don't you get your laptop so we can look at the footage?"

Reggie pulled out his laptop. "The battery is dead."

Hudson pushed the lever under his seat and leaned back.

"What are you doing?"

"I'm exhausted. I'm taking a nap."

"How can you sleep now?"

"Like this." Hudson closed his eyes. "In a couple of hours, we'll go back to the train station and catch the train to Zurich."

CHAPTER 32

The temperature dropped several degrees while Hudson slept, and he woke several times to turn the car on and run the heat. At 5:25 am, it was still as dark as night as they returned to the train station. Five vehicles sat in the parking lot, but not the black SUV.

"Keep a lookout," said Hudson. "They might still be waiting for us somewhere."

The snow crunched loudly underfoot as they walked towards the platform. Two men and a woman stood on the platform, waiting for the train. None of them looked like police or Charles' security detail.

Just as Hudson breathed a sigh of relief, the door to the station opened and two men in dark suits and overcoats stepped out. One of them was John. All four of them stopped in their tracks. John looked around as if deciding to pull out his gun in front of bystanders. Hudson felt for the gun under his coat and debated the same thing. Reggie's breath caught in his throat, and he almost screamed.

In the distance, a train clacked towards the station.

"Go back," whispered Hudson as he pulled Reggie's arm. "And pull up your hoodie."

Reggie complied as they speed walked towards the parking lot. When they reached the sedan, John shouted behind them.

"Stop, or I *will* shoot!"

Reggie's arms flew up, but Hudson remained in place. His hand slid under his coat, and he grasped his pistol.

"Don't do it, Hudson," said John. "There are two guns pointed at you. You won't have time to shoot both of us."

He left the gun in its holster and slowly raised his hands.

The train squealed to a stop in front of the station.

"All we want is the pen," said John.

"And then you'll let us go?" asked Hudson, with a sarcastic tone.

"And then I won't shoot you on the spot. If you hand over the pen and come with us peacefully, no one will get hurt."

Hudson turned to face them. Both pointed their pistols at him.

"Who's with you?" John pointed at Reggie with his gun.

"No one," said Hudson, and stepped forward. John's gun moved back towards Hudson.

The train doors hissed closed.

"Don't shoot." Hudson slowly reached into his jacket and pulled out the pen. He held it in the air with his left hand. "Is this what you want?"

"Get the pen, Frank," John ordered his sidekick.

As Frank moved towards him, Hudson threw the pen. Both men turned to look as it flipped end over end towards a large snowbank. As Frank dove to catch it, Hudson drew his pistol and fired before John had time to react. The bullet pierced his arm, and John fell back as his gun dropped to the ground. Meanwhile, the pen disappeared into the snowbank as Frank landed face-first.

"Go!" yelled Hudson as he pulled at Reggie's sleeve.

John glared at Hudson with a painful grimace as Hudson kicked his gun away. Reggie followed Hudson towards the train platform as Frank dug frantically through the snowbank.

The train gained speed as it pulled away from the station.

"Hurry!" yelled Hudson.

They ran alongside the tracks, trying to match the speed of the train before it was too late. Just as the last car threatened to pull away, Hudson jumped on. He reached back to a struggling Reggie. Grasping his hand, Hudson yanked Reggie onto the train.

An angry ticket collector let them inside and gave them a stern scolding before letting them find a seat.

"Wow!" said Reggie, panting as they sat down. "You shot that guy. Is he going to die?"

"Keep your voice down," said Hudson. "I only shot him in the arm."

"I can't believe we made it."

"Yes, except now we lost the pen."

"It doesn't matter."

Reggie pulled out his laptop and plugged it into the outlet beside the seat.

"Of course, it matters." Hudson rubbed his temples. "We lost our only piece of evidence, the security team of one of the richest people in the world are after us, I shot a man and the cops probably have a warrant for my arrest."

"All of that is true except for one thing." Reggie logged into his laptop.

"Oh, yeah? What's that?"

Reggie reached into a side pocket of his backpack and pulled out a tiny white card.

"I removed the SD card from the pen."

"No..."

"I said you needed me."

Reggie pushed the card into a slot on the side of the laptop and used the touchpad and keyboard while Hudson watched.

"Are you going to open it?"

"First, I am making a copy in case the elites shoot a space laser to kill us on this train."

"A space laser?"

"Okay, what about a drone strike?"

Hudson looked out the window but didn't respond.

"Okay, here we are," said Reggie. "With one click of a button, we can see the first ever video footage smuggled out a secret meeting of the global elites in the secret location deep in the mountains of Sovad, Switzerland."

"Great, click the button already."

Reggie held his chin in the air. "Not until you thank me for saving the footage."

"Thanks."

"That's it? No *great job, buddy*, or *you're a valuable part of the team*, or *I couldn't have done it without you*?"

"Just open the stupid file, already."

He clicked on the file, and the screen filled with a dark grey, blurry image.

"What is that?" asked Hudson.

"Where was the pen?" Reggie asked.

"I slipped it in his side pocket."

"That's what we're seeing – the inside of his pocket." He moved ahead on the video timeline, and the image changed slightly but was still dark and blurry.

"Wait, I bet there's audio."

He turned on the laptop volume, and a jumble of staticky voices came on.

"What are they saying?" asked Hudson.

Reggie reached into his laptop, pulled out a set of earbuds, and handed one to Hudson.

They each put an earbud in, and Reggie started the video from the beginning. After what sounded like vague opening remarks, the meeting began. Some voices were not English, and others were difficult to hear. Charles' voice was the only one barely decipherable.

"This is useless," said Hudson. "I can't hear anything."

"I'll send the file to Raven and see if she can enhance the audio."

Hudson handed his earbud back. "In the meantime, I have to plan our next step, now that we're fugitives."

He stared out the window. A faint glow behind the looming mountains hinted at the incoming sun. Snow-capped evergreens dotted the endless rocky foothills. A herd of ibex leapt down the craggy slopes like graceful, wild traceurs.

Hudson's eyes drooped, then closed before he drifted to sleep.

It felt like five minutes had passed when Reggie nudged him awake.

"She found something!"

Hudson rubbed his eyes. The bright morning light was evidence that his nap was longer than five minutes.

"Is it coffee?"

"Raven found something. She listened to the recording, and there was a strange word that they kept repeating."

"What word?"

"Kembato," Reggie announced the word as if it were the holy grail of words.

"Isn't that a country in Africa?"

"That's right."

Hudson held out his hands and raised his eyebrows. "What else?"

"That's it, just Kembato."

"I thought Raven was a computer whiz or something. The only thing she got off that recording was *one* word?"

"She's a hacker, not a sound engineer. Also, she could make out a few other things, but Kembato was mentioned a few times."

"Great! All that work and we got nothing but the name of a country."

"Not necessarily. She said it sounded like they also said *phase two* a few times."

Hudson leaned back and closed his eyes. "I'm going back to sleep to dream of an alternate reality where I made better life choices."

"Kembato does not have any representatives at the Sovad conference," Reggie continued.

"Uh-huh," Hudson muttered.

"Now we know that the global elites are planning a phase two, and it's going to start in Kembato! We should get off this train in Zurich, go to the airport and catch a plane to Kembato."

"No. We shouldn't." Hudson's eyes were still closed.

The phone in Reggie's pocket chirped. His eyes widened when he looked at the screen.

"Hey, check this out." He elbowed Hudson. "Raven just texted me. She heard from the Sentinel."

Hudson opened his eyes and read the screen.

Just received this message: Have your people meet in Abena, Kembato - memorial square – Tuesday @ midnight. I have more info – The Sentinel.

"This is incredible!" shouted Reggie. "We can finally meet this mysterious Sentinel, *and* he wants to meet in Kembato *and* he has info!"

"Huh," Hudson grunted.

"Now, can we go to Kembato to uncover the phase two plot of the global elites?"

"Okay, but you're buying."

"Yes!" Reggie smiled. "I'm going to see if they have food on this train."

"Bring me back something," said Hudson as Reggie got up. "But not one of your stupid health foods. I want something that once had a beating heart."

"That's gross."

After he left, Hudson stared out the window at the snowy trees rushing by.

Based on his limited geographical knowledge, Kembato was somewhere in the centre of Africa. Like almost all other countries in Africa, it was a poor country. He wondered if they had elephants.

His mind wandered to several years earlier and his scuttled plans to take Sophie to Africa.

When they met, Hudson knew about Sophie's obsession with elephants. However, it wasn't until their trip to California that he truly understood her deep connection to the gentle giants.

It was a few years before Covid. Sophie wanted to spend their week of holidays going to an elephant sanctuary in California. Hudson told her about the many closer zoos that all had elephants, but she insisted on the sanctuary. The elephants in enclosed environments in tiny zoos were unnatural, and even thinking about them trapped in the zoos made her angry.

The rescue sanctuary in California was thousands of acres where elephants, big cats and bears roamed freely in natural habitats. Many were previously neglected, retired, or the result of changing zoo legislation. It was one of only a few sanctuaries in the States to allow elephant viewings. They took the seven-hour flight to Sacramento and stayed at a hotel near the airport. The next morning, they drove a rented car through a landscape filled flat fields with rows of grapevines and dotted with wineries. An hour later they reached the sanctuary. Sophie was giddy with excitement the entire trip.

The sanctuary tour itinerary included a short jeep excursion to see the elephants. Finally, the jeep stopped near an open field next to a parade of elephants. Sophie stared wordlessly at the massive beasts, ignoring the tour guide's endless chatter. Afterwards, they sat in the pavilion eating a light lunch with a view of the elephants grazing in the distance. Sophie didn't touch her food. Instead, she sat staring at the elephants. When Hudson returned from a washroom break, she was gone. Only her uneaten lunch remained on the picnic table. He searched the pavilion and checked the washrooms, but she disappeared. He stood at the table and looked into the grassy fields where the elephants grazed. A muddy river wound its way along one side of the field, and a stand of gargantuan cottonwoods stood guard on the other.

Hudson made sure no one was looking and dashed into the trees. Sticking close to the field, he ran through the forest. Almost ten minutes later, he found her sitting on a thick cottonwood branch, staring into the field. After catching his breath, he climbed the tree and sat beside her.

"They're beautiful, aren't they?" she asked.

He looked into the swaying grass. Two massive grey pachyderms and a calf grazed less than twenty feet away.

"Yes, but what are you—?"

"Did you know elephants are one of only a few species that recognize themselves in a mirror? They are one of the most highly sensitive and caring animals in the world. After a two-year pregnancy, when their baby is finally born, the herd celebrates the birth with a ceremony involving trumpeting and touching. Also, when the baby cries, the herd will caress the baby to soothe it."

"I didn't know that."

"Look at that elephant." She pointed at a third elephant, who stood away from the pack. Its trunk swished back and forth as it looked down at a spot on the ground.

“I wonder if a loved one died there.” Her voice was quiet and serious.

“Why do you say that?”

“When an elephant passes a spot where a loved one died, they will pause for several minutes at the same location in a moment of silence - sometimes, even years later. They always remember.”

Hudson did not know how to respond. Instead, he sat on the branch with her, watched the elephants and listened.

“When I die,” she continued, “I want my ashes spread across the fields where elephants roam -over the savannas of North Africa or the rainforests of West Africa.”

They sat on the branch of the cottonwood tree watching the elephants for almost an hour before Hudson convinced her they had to leave.

When they returned to Michigan, Hudson opened a savings account with plans to surprise her with a trip to the Savannah in Africa. He deposited all his overtime pay, tax refunds and part of his Christmas bonuses into the secret fund. By the time he had almost enough money in the account for the plane tickets for an African elephant safari, the Covid pandemic hit. The ensuing lockdowns put his plans on hold, and her death made his big surprise wilt before it bloomed.

Now he was going to Africa – without her.

CHAPTER 33

They got off the train in Zurich. Hudson put his bullets and pistol in separate trash cans before they hailed a taxi and went to the airport.

As they stood in line to buy their tickets to Kembato, Reggie turned to Hudson. "I would love to see Charles Porter's face when he sees the SD card missing from the pen. He's going to be *so* mad."

"He'll only be mad if he thinks there's something useful on it," Hudson replied.

"What do mean? We have proof of the social elite's phase two!"

"Not really. All we have is bad recording."

"Yes, but they don't know that. They *think* we have a recording of their secret meeting – which we sort of do..."

"If they discussed plans, they don't want the world to find out, they'll come after us with everything they've got."

Reggie looked around nervously. "I shouldn't buy the tickets with my credit card. They could use the transaction to track us."

"You're too paranoid. Besides, they still don't know you're with me. Wait! What about your father? Won't he be looking for you?"

"No. He's out on another business trip and probably thinks I'm home by now. Besides, he doesn't care about what I do."

Before Hudson could respond, Reggie stepped up to the counter. As he discussed flights to Abena with the man behind the counter, Hudson scanned the area. Hundreds of travellers filled the airport, and half of them looked suspicious. He wasn't expecting to see a tall man in a trench coat pretending to read a paper, but perhaps one of Charles' security detail or a cop in search of a fugitive. A man in a dark suit watched him from an escalator, but when he reached the bottom, turned and walked in the opposite direction.

Minutes later, they waited in line at security, boarding passes in hand.

"You keep looking around," said Reggie. "Do you think they're following us?"

"We have a small head start, but they *will* come after us."

"Now who's getting paranoid?"

"I shot John. He didn't like me before. Now he probably wants to kill me."

"We have more to worry about than an angry bodyguard. We just infiltrated a secret meeting of the world's most powerful elites. If we don't expose their plans soon, they'll send a squad of mercenaries to liquidate us."

Hudson looked at him with raised eyebrows. "Liquidate us?"

Reggie shrugged. "I heard it in a movie once. How about terminated? Eliminated? Deleted? Oooh…what about erased?"

"Hey! This is serious, Reggie. If anything happened to you…"

Reggie pointed at him. "You would miss me, wouldn't you?"

"A lot of people would miss you."

"Not likely. The only people that would miss me are Aunt Sera and maybe my friend Carter."

"And your dad."

"Ha! I doubt that. He hates me."

"No, he doesn't."

"If I died, would you say something at my funeral?"

"If assassins erased you, they would erase me at the same time. I can walk with you to the gates of St. Peter if you want."

"Thanks. Do you think Raven would miss me?"

"She would cry a thousand tears for her lost love."

"You're mocking me."

"Yes, I am."

"Please place your valuables and shoes in the tray and step this way, please," said the security guard.

As they passed through security, Hudson watched a man in the tan suit glance in his direction before entering a washroom. He looked like the same man he saw by the ticket counter but wasn't sure. The terminal was filled with many businessmen in tan suits.

Once in the secure portion of the airport, they walked the long corridor towards their terminal.

"Are private jets faster than commercial ones?" he asked Reggie.

"For sure," Reggie answered. "They're lighter, faster and there is less waiting time at the airport. Although some of the smaller jets have less range. Why?"

"If Charles sent his security team after us, they could charter a private jet, beat us to our destination and be waiting for us when we arrive."

"The only way they would know we're going to Kembato is if we're right and they are planning their second phase there."

"If we're right, they'll kill us when we arrive, and if we're wrong, we're safe."

"I'm too clever, and you're too strong to let that happen. We are a formidable spy team on an impossible mission to expose the plans of the global elites to create a New World Order—"

"Simmer down, Mr. Bond. First, we have to find our gate."

"Okay, but I need to find a bank machine. I looked it up, and Kembato doesn't take credit cards. We need cash."

Hudson did not see the man in the tan suit again, and they boarded their flight an hour later. During the fifteen-hour flight, Hudson slept, ate, worried and tried to watch an in-flight movie. Meanwhile, Reggie described his conspiracy theories, played video games, texted Raven and slept. They got off in Paris to catch a connecting flight to Kembato's capital city, Abena.

Stepping off the plane was like getting hit with a hot, wet blanket. The contrast from the cold, crisp air of the Alps to the warm, humid air of Kembato was intense. The weather wasn't the only difference between the two countries. Instead of walking into a modern airport, they remained outside. They descended the passenger stairway onto the tarmac, then followed the line of passengers to an outdoor security checkpoint.

Hudson's shirt stuck to his chest and back and sweat beaded on his forehead.

"I need some summer clothes and a shower."

"I already booked a hotel on my phone," said Reggie.

Hudson looked around for anyone following or watching them but saw no one suspicious. Other than a few other European travellers, Hudson and Reggie were the only white people. Kembato was not a big tourism destination.

"Parlez-vous français?" asked a man leaning against a yellow taxi.

"English?" asked Hudson.

"You must be Americans, no?" The man's thick accent was a blend of French and West African.

"Yes. We need a ride to the Abena Royal Hotel," said Reggie.

"You have American dollars?"

Reggie held up a small wad of cash.

"Get in, my friends," he said with a wide smile. "My name is Michel. I will take you anywhere you want. You need something, you let Michel know."

"Don't do that again," Hudson whispered to Reggie as they stepped inside.

"What?"

"Flash your money. Look around you. This is a poor country, and unless you want to get robbed, don't wave around your cash."

"Okay, sorry," said Reggie, and they climbed into the back of the cab.

"Straight to the Abena Royal?" asked Michel. "There is lots to see in the city. I give great tours."

"We need to stop to buy some clothes first," said Hudson.

"No problem. I know a great place. My cousin works there."

Yellow taxis and motorbikes filled the busy streets of Abena. The taxi did not have air conditioning, and heat poured through the window.

Reggie looked at his phone. "Raven found something."

Hudson wiped the sweat from his brow. "What?"

"There is a Virology Institute in Abena, and guess who funds it?"

"Charles Porter?"

"Yes. In 2012, the Porter Foundation founded the Kembato Virology Institute."

"I know that place," said Michel from the front seat. "It's on the north end of town, past the football stadium. They research all the nasty diseases that come from the jungle. My cousin works there. He says they deal with some dangerous viruses. Worse than Covid. Did you guys get the vaccine?"

"Yes, we got the vaccine," answered Hudson.

"You're lucky. Almost nobody here got the vaccine or the booster."

"Are people still dying from Covid?"

"No. Not too many people died from Covid here. My cousin had Covid. He was sick for a week, but got better. A few people got it, but it seemed to go away."

"Of course it did," Hudson mumbled.

"Okay, we are here!"

He stopped outside a busy outdoor market. Clothes hung from racks or were piled on tables. Men, women and children milled about, many shielding themselves from the scorching sun with umbrellas.

"I will wait here," said Michel.

They waded through the small crowd of shoppers to the men's shirts and shorts.

"How much for this one?" Reggie held up a brown short-sleeve shirt.

The woman behind the table smiled and nodded.

"How much?" he repeated.

"I don't think she speaks English," said Hudson.

Reggie pulled out a thick wad of cash from this pocket, then quickly stuffed it back in. He smiled at Hudson and separated three five-dollar bills.

The woman smiled and pointed at the money.

"Fifteen dollars?" Reggie asked.

"Have you never bartered before?" asked Hudson.

"No. I've never had to."

"Hold up the five."

The woman shook her head.

"Now shrug and walk away," Hudson instructed.

"But I need the shirt."

"There are lots of shirts here and lots of vendors. Besides, she'll call you back."

Reggie did as he asked. After walking three steps, the woman yelled something in French to them. Reggie stopped and turned around. She held up the shirt, nodded and pointed at them.

"Wow, that worked!" Reggie exclaimed.

After a few more lessons in bartering, they left the market with lighter, cooler summer clothes. They returned to the taxi, and Michel drove them to the Abena Royal Hotel.

Michel parked at the entrance and handed them a business card. "If you need a ride anywhere, you call me. I know everything about this city. It's not too safe here. Don't go anywhere alone. We have lots of kidnappings, and you two are big white targets. Also, many people are unhappy with the government and are taking to the streets."

"You mean like protests?" asked Hudson.

"Not just protests. There is talk of a big demonstration. The government does not like demonstrations and will use brutal tactics to stop them."

"Thanks, we'll be careful," said Hudson.

"How much for the ride?" asked Reggie.

"For you – twenty dollars."

Reggie handed him forty.

"What did we just learn about bartering?" asked Hudson.

"Sorry," Reggie apologized. "It's something my father would do."

"You are very generous." Michel bowed his head. "Thank you."

CHAPTER 34

"What is this crap?" asked Hudson, as he pulled another dish of food from the plastic bag.

"I found a local restaurant that serves authentic African dishes," replied Reggie.

"This is Africa. Isn't everything authentically African?"

Reggie handed him plastic utensils and a napkin. "It's egusi soup. The one with the red mark on the top is vegetarian, and the other has crayfish and beef."

"That's my kind of meal!" Hudson ripped off the lid and scooped up the colourful soup.

"Wait! You're supposed to dip the fufu in it."

"The what?"

"Fufu. It's made from Cassava." Reggie pointed at the doughy white balls.

"It looks like a bun." Hudson picked one up.

"It's not a bun."

Hudson shrugged and took a bite. "Not bad."

As they ate, someone knocked on the door.

Hudson swallowed another bite of fufu and got up.

"Wait!" said Reggie. "No one knows we're here. What if they've come to kill us?"

"Don't be so paranoid. Assassins don't knock first."

Hudson peered through the peephole before opening the door.

"Michel? We don't need a ride till later tonight."

The taxi driver looked back into the hallway and dashed inside.

"You are in danger," he said, running to the window and closing the curtains.

"What are you talking about?" asked Hudson. "Nobody knows

we're here."

"Somebody knows you're here, and they want you dead. Pack your things. I can take you somewhere safe."

"We're not going anywhere until you tell us what's going on," said Hudson.

"My cousin who works at the shipyard told me there was a hit on a big white guy travelling with a skinny white kid."

"I'm not that skinny," said Reggie.

Suddenly, the window shattered, spraying shards of glass into the room. Reggie dove under the bed, while Hudson ducked behind it.

"Let's go!" Michel shouted from the door.

"Wait!" Hudson wriggled across the floor to the laptop. He pulled the SD card out of its slot and stuffed it into his sock.

"Okay, now we can go!" Hudson yelled at Reggie.

He nodded, and they crouch-walked to the door. Michel led them down the hallway to the stairs. They ran down two flights of stairs and waited as Michel peered out the doorway at the bottom.

"Where are we going? Won't they be waiting for us?" Hudson asked.

"They aren't professionals. We can make it out."

"How do you know they're not professionals?" asked Hudson.

Michel smiled at him. "Because you're not dead yet. Follow me."

He opened the door and speed walked through the hall to a side door exit.

Again, he opened the door and peered out. "Uh-oh."

"What do you mean, uh-oh?" asked Hudson.

"There is someone out there waiting for us," he replied.

"I told you!"

Michel shook his finger. "No-no. This is a different assassin. He isn't a professional either – I think."

"What do you mean *you think*?" asked Reggie.

"What do you mean, *a different assassin*?" asked Hudson.

"There is no time to answer your questions. We are going to run. Follow—"

Hudson grabbed his elbow. "If we run, aren't they going to shoot us?"

Michel shook his head. "They are too far and probably have poor aim."

"What if they're professionals?" asked Hudson.

"Then you will die."

"I don't like it," said Hudson.

"The longer we wait, the more assassins will show up and soon it will be dark."

"More assassins?" asked Reggie. "That sounds bad. How many are we talking about?"

"All of them," Michel answered. He pushed the door open again. "Okay, now's our chance. Run!"

Before either of them could object or ask more questions, Michel took off.

Reggie looked at Hudson with scared, questioning eyes.

"I guess we run," said Hudson.

They dashed after Michel, who bolted down the alley. Shots rang out behind them. Bullets pockmarked the red brick as they sprinted towards a pile of garbage.

Michel took a quick left and smashed through a wooden door. Hudson and Michel followed close behind as they ran through a dark, boarded up restaurant. The faint orange glow of the recently set sun filtered through the space between the boards on the windows. Reggie slipped on a pile of broken plates and almost landed on an overturned chair. Hudson slid to a stop, whirled around, and hauled Reggie back to his feet.

"Are you okay?" he asked.

"I hurt my ankle again."

Hudson scooped him up and carried him out the front door behind Michel as their pursuer fired more gunshots.

On the street, Michel opened the rear door to his waiting cab and dove into the front seat. Hudson threw Reggie into the backseat and jumped in after him. The car sped off before Hudson could close the door.

"Are they coming after us?" Hudson looked out the back

window.

"I don't think so," said Michel.

He took a few fast, tight turns, dodging through traffic, before he finally slowed to a normal speed, five minutes later.

"Okay, we're safe - for now."

Hudson took a deep breath. "*Now*, can you answer a few questions?"

"My ankle is only twisted, if anyone cares," mumbled Reggie.

"Why are there amateur assassins trying to kill us?" asked Hudson.

"There are more than just amateurs after you. Those were just the ones in the area when the call went out."

"Call? What call?"

"As I said before, my cousin told me."

"You said a big white guy travelling with a younger, better looking white guy," said Reggie. "Is the hit on just the big guy or both of us?"

"Who put out this hit?" asked Hudson.

"I don't know. Normally I don't hear about these things, but my cousin was bragging about how he was about to make a hundred thousand dollars for offing a couple of stray Americans. I assumed he was talking about you."

"How many cousins do you have?" asked Hudson.

"A lot."

"Why are you helping us?" asked Hudson.

"You seem like nice people, and you gave me a big tip."

"I told you." Reggie pointed at Hudson.

"We appreciate your help, Michel," said Hudson. "Where are you taking us?"

"There is a small farm outside the city where you can spend the night."

"No!" yelled Reggie. "We have to meet the Sentinel."

"You have a sprained ankle, and every mercenary in Abena is trying to kill us. We should lie low for a while."

"My ankle is fine. They're after us because we are close to the truth. The only way out is to finish what we started. They found us at the hotel – they can find us anywhere."

"How do we defend against an army of assassins?"

"I can help you with that," said Michel. "Do you know how to use a gun?"

"Yes, but I dropped mine in a garbage bin in the Zurich airport."

Michel looked back at them in the rearview mirror. "If you have money, I know a guy..."

"Let me guess," said Reggie. "He's your cousin?"

"Not everyone I know is my cousin." There was a brief pause before Michel spoke again.

"But yes, he's my cousin."

CHAPTER 35

It didn't take long to leave the bustling city. They left the big buildings, bustling streets and bright lights behind them. Michel drove them down long, dark dirt roads through the quiet countryside.

Ten minutes later, they drove into a short driveway to a set of interconnecting shacks and ancient concrete buildings. A group of three men talked and drank beside a barrel fire in front of the doorway to the main building. The yellow flames licked at the air, sending flickering shadows across the concrete block wall behind them. They looked up when Michel parked in front of them.

"Wait here. I have to talk to Gorilla first," said Michel, and exited the car.

"Did he just say Gorilla?" asked Reggie.

Hudson nodded.

The men around the fire glared at them. One yelled something in French, and the others cackled.

"Is this a good idea?" asked Reggie.

"Which part? Going to Switzerland to infiltrate a secret international organization, running from an angry billionaire or flying to a third world country?"

"I meant buying guns from a guy named Gorilla in creepy neighbourhood."

"Probably not, but you're the one who refused to lie low."

Despite the sun setting, the African heat was relentless. Sweat soaked through Hudson's new clothes.

A few minutes later, Michel returned. "Okay, he's agreed to meet you."

"What did you tell him?" asked Hudson as he got out of the car.

Michel smiled. "I convinced him not to kill you."

"Oh, good..." said Reggie.

The men at the fire, eyed them suspiciously as they passed.

A short, balding man with an AK-47 greeted them inside the door with a grunt. Michel nodded at him before proceeding down a dark, narrow hallway. They walked towards the single incandescent light at the far end. It was too dark to see into the other hallways and rooms they passed. Either nobody lived here, they were all sleeping or were hiding in the dark.

Michel knocked on the cracked wooden door beneath the single light.

"Gorilla? Open up."

The door swung open, revealing a giant man inside. He was slightly taller than Hudson and barrel-chested. His python arms protruded from a grimy, sleeveless shirt and his skin glistened like motor oil. Gorilla glared at them from fat, glowing eyes and rubbed his massive bald head.

"I hear you want to buy guns from me."

He adjusted the gigantic chrome pistol tucked into his jean shorts.

"Do you have any long guns?" Hudson tried to sound more fearless than he felt. "Like a sniper rifle, or at least a hunting rifle with a scope."

Gorilla threw his head back and bellowed a thunderous and unsettling laugh.

"How will you aim a sniper rifle while you are running?" he asked.

"I'd like to dissuade my pursuers from getting too close," argued Hudson.

Gorilla leaned close to Hudson, his face just inches away. His hot breath smelled of ginger and mace.

"What makes you think your pursuers aren't already close?"

"Stop it, Gorilla," Michel interjected. "You promised not to hurt them."

"That is a limited-time offer," Gorilla answered, still staring at

Hudson.

After a moment, he broke his stare and sauntered across the room to a small table lit by a kerosene lantern. Hudson and the others followed.

"This is what I'm offering." He waved his hand like he was showing off a set of steak knives on an infomercial. Five small pistols lay in a line beside the lantern.

"That's all you've got?" asked Hudson.

"This is what I'm offering you."

Gorilla picked up the largest of the tiny guns. The Sig P365 disappeared in his giant hands.

"Do you have anything bigger?" asked Hudson.

"Not for you."

"We have money," added Reggie.

"Not enough." He stared at them with unblinking eyes as if sizing them up.

"How much for the Sig?" asked Hudson.

"Five hundred."

"We'll give you two-fifty."

"You're wasting time. Either buy one or start running."

"What do mean start running?"

Gorilla looked at Michel. "You didn't tell them?"

"Tell us what?" asked Reggie.

Michel gave an apologetic smirk and shrugged.

Gorilla looked at an invisible watch on his wrist. "You now have a twenty-five-minute head start, before I come after you. The only reason I don't kill you where you stand is a favour for my cousin, Michel."

"We appreciate your generosity," said Hudson, rolling his eyes. "We'll take it for four hundred."

"Deal."

Reggie counted out the bills and passed them to Hudson.

"Can we offer you more not to come after us?" he asked, holding up the money.

"You can't hold that much money in your pocket." Gorilla snatched the cash and handed Hudson the Sig P365 and a small box of bullets.

"We should go." Hudson stuffed the gun in one pocket and the ammo in the other.

"You should be impressed with yourselves," said Gorilla as they left. "You're worth a *lot* of money."

They hurried through the hallway, past the short man with the big gun and out the front door. "Why did you bring us here?" Hudson asked angrily. "These people want to kill us."

The men around the fire looked up as they dashed past them back to the car.

"Everyone with a gun wants to kill you. At least now you have a gun."

"This thing is barely a gun," complained Hudson.

They jumped in the car and drove away.

Hudson looked behind them, but nobody pursued them.

"It's almost time," said Reggie. "We need to get to Memorial Square to meet the Sentinel."

Twenty minutes later, they were back in the centre of downtown Abena. Michel parked beside a nightclub. The thumping bass inside rattled the windows.

Michel pointed across the intersection ahead of them. "Memorial Square is up there. Be careful and good luck."

"Will you be here when we return?"

Michel shook his head. "No. I've taken you as far as I can. I have a family to get back to."

"Wait! You're abandoning us?" asked Reggie.

"Don't worry, my friend. I will say nice words at your funeral."

"That's a comforting thought," said Reggie.

"Thanks for your help," said Hudson. He loaded his pistol and got out of the car.

They stood outside the nightclub and watched Michel drive away.

"Have you heard from the Sentinel?" asked Hudson.

"My laptop is still at the hotel."

"Why didn't you bring it?"

"I was too busy trying to dodge bullets to think about packing my laptop."

"What about your phone?"

"Cell service in this city is spotty. Also, the battery is almost dead."

Hudson looked around the street. A homeless man lay in a heap on the sidewalk across the street. Behind them, an older woman lumbered across the road carrying a bulging burlap bag. Two drunken teenage girls staggered out of the nightclub. They giggled and pulled out their vapes. A motorbike let out a throaty growl as it drove by. Streetlights lit up the square across the intersection.

"This could be a trap," said Hudson.

"Perhaps, but it's our only option."

"You should wait here."

"Not a chance."

They tread cautiously down the street and across the intersection. It did not appear they were being watched or followed. Hudson's hand firmly clasped the pistol in his pocket as they neared Memorial Square. A twenty-foot-high concrete memorial sat on the corner overlooking both streets. The streetlights lit up the large granite structure, which resembled an oversized tombstone. A winding dirt and stone path led from the memorial to a darkened area with long brown grass and tall raffia trees.

Hudson looked around, searching for anything suspicious, but everything looked suspicious. A curtain moved in a second-storey apartment window. The homeless man sitting next to the light post shifted his position and glanced in their direction. Two men smoked and laughed as they leaned on the hood of an old pickup.

"I don't like this," he said.

"You have your gun, right?" asked Reggie. "Just shoot anybody that comes after us."

"This peashooter won't help against a sniper."

"I see someone!" Reggie pointed at a shadowed figure under a raffia tree in the park.

"Don't point. Just keep walking."

The figure stood motionless under the branches. The arching raffia fronds spread over him like a protective hand. Although they could not see his face, it appeared like he was watching them.

"This is exciting," said Reggie as they passed the memorial. "We finally get to meet the Sentinel. He must be an insider. Someone with knowledge of the—"

"Stop talking and watch your surroundings."

As they neared the figure, he leaned forward, as if trying to get a better look at them.

Without warning, the man turned and ran down the dark trail.

"No, wait!" yelled Reggie.

"Come on!" Hudson took off after him, with Reggie close behind.

The figure veered off the path into the darkness. The long, dead grass brushed against their knees as they gave chase. Light from the adjacent street filtered through the trees, spraying sparse light into the park.

Suddenly, the figure ahead of them dropped from sight.

They stopped running and looked around.

"Where did he go?" asked Reggie.

"I don't know. I can't see anything. Turn on your phone light."

Reggie pulled out his phone. The bright LED illuminated a rusty, dilapidated swing set.

"What are you doing here?" asked a voice from the ground.

"Is that...?" Reggie began. He stepped forward and shone the light on the man on the ground holding his ankle. The man looked up at Reggie with an anguished look.

"Dad?"

"What are you doing here, Reggie?"

"I'm meeting someone—wait, are you the Sentinel?"

Lawrence Hargreaves held up his hand. "Help me up. I think I sprained my ankle."

Hudson grabbed his arm and pulled him up. "Bad ankles must run in the family."

A noise came from the direction of the memorial. Hudson

whirled around to look. Three men strode towards them, and they were carrying guns.

"Get down!" Hudson shouted.

He and Reggie dropped beside Lawrence in the grass. Hudson's gun was out before his knees reached the dirt. His little Sig wasn't powerful enough to hit them from this range, but it might slow them down.

"No, no, no. This can't be happening." Lawrence cried into his hands.

The men fired back but retreated behind a raffia tree.

"We have to get out of here!" yelled Hudson.

"Just go," said Lawrence. "My ankle is sprained. I'll only slow you down."

"We're not leaving without you, Mr. Hargreaves."

"I'm so confused," said Reggie. "How can you be the Sentinel?"

"Stay down!" Hudson ordered. "And get ready to move."

He fired three more shots into the darkness.

"Do you have a gun, Mr. Hargreaves?"

When he didn't hear a response, he asked again, "Do you have —?"

He stopped mid-question, when he saw Lawrence's hand over his chest. In the darkness, the blood leaking between his fingers looked like black oil.

"Now you'll have to leave without me," he said.

"Dad? What's wrong?"

Lawrence grabbed his son's hand and squeezed. "I'm sorry, Reggie – for everything. I know I was an inadequate father and —"

"What? No, it's okay, I..."

Hudson fired three more shots. "We'll get you to a doctor..."

"Hudson?" Lawrence mumbled. He struggled to keep his eyes open, and blood oozed out the corner of his mouth. "Take care of my boy."

"Dad? Wait I—" Reggie gasped.

The men moved from their position. One crept closer as the others attempted to flank him on either side.

Hudson grabbed Reggie's arm. "We have to go."

"I'm not leaving him!" Reggie screamed.

Hudson looked at him, kneeling beside his dying father. An image of Sophie reaching out from the tablet flashed through his mind.

"Okay."

He fired twice before diving and rolling forward. As he came up, he fired three shots into the first man's chest. He bolted past him and made a wide arc to the pursuer on the right.

"Alain, est-ce que vous?"

Hudson answered with four quick shots at the dark form. The man collapsed to the ground. Looking back towards Reggie and his father, he saw the third man twenty feet from them.

As he ran, Hudson fired as quickly as he could squeeze the trigger. The man fell backwards as the Sig clicked on an empty chamber.

"Okay, *now* we have to go!" yelled Hudson.

Reggie wiped his eyes and shook his head.

"I didn't know it was you," said Lawrence, bloody spittle dripping from his chin. "I thought it was Raven..."

"Wait, if you're the Sentinel...What is the information you wanted to give us?"

Lawrence coughed blood into his hand and took a raspy breath. "Stop neepahbum . . . tomorrow..."

He reached into his pocket, pulled out a keycard and handed it to Reggie.

"What is this for, and who is Neepabum?"

A sad smile formed on Lawrence's face. "I'm coming, Deborah..."

The last of the air in his bloody lungs escaped in a final sigh, and his body went limp.

Reggie stared down at his father.

Hudson heard voices from beyond the trees, and he ran to get a better look. A group of ten heavily armed men strode from the memorial in his direction. The silhouette of the lead figure was unmistakable. He ran back to Reggie, who still sat in stunned silence beside his dead father.

"Time to go!" he said, lifting Reggie. "Gorilla and his gang are here."

Reggie nodded and followed Hudson as they ran from the park. They emerged from the other side and bolted across the street. A motorbike beeped and swerved around them. Hudson scanned the area, looking for threats and a means of escape, while Reggie followed in a stunned trance.

Gorilla and his gang stormed out of the park as Hudson and Reggie dashed into a convenience store.

The bell above the door jingled as they burst inside. The woman behind the counter looked up from her magazine and mumbled something.

Hudson peered through the advertisements and flyers covering the front windows. Gorilla's gang split up, with half going west along the street and the others going east.

"Can you help us?" Hudson asked the cashier. "We need someplace to hide."

She responded in a foreign language.

He looked for a back door but found it locked.

Reggie stared at the magazine rack. "He's gone."

"Yes, I know, and we will be too if you don't snap out of it. Gorilla's men are searching the stores on this street, and we have no way out."

"Those." Reggie pointed at a hat rack.

"Good thinking. We'll buy some hats and sunglasses."

The bell above the front door jingled as two men stormed into the store. Hudson ducked behind the row of candy, pulling Reggie down with him.

The men yelled something, and the woman yelled back. After a half-minute of loud arguing, the store fell silent.

Hudson peered around the corner. A short man with a bandana and a massive black pistol crept slowly towards them. The second man was not visible. Hudson grabbed a chocolate bar and threw it over the shelving. As soon as it landed, he dove at bandana man. His shoulder impacted the man's chest with a thud, and he grabbed at the pistol. They both fell to the floor, but the man kept hold of his gun. Hudson held his gun wrist and slammed it onto the floor. The man cried out in pain, and the pistol slid across the floor.

Straddling his gunless attacker, Hudson punched the man hard in the face twice. The first punch knocked him out, and the second bounced his head off the tile floor.

A gunshot rang out behind him, and Hudson turned in terror, expecting to find Reggie with a bullet in his chest. Instead, a thin man wearing fatigues, carrying a machete stood in front of Reggie with mouth agape. Blood poured out of a hole in his forehead, and he toppled to the ground. Reggie still pointed the big black pistol at him.

Ducking behind the counter, the cashier screamed.

"Good job, buddy." Hudson pulled the pistol from Reggie's hand and stuffed it in his pocket.

"Do you think he's the one that shot my Dad?" Reggie asked.

"Yes, I'm sure he was."

Hudson pulled the army coat and hat off the tall, dead man and put it on. He grabbed the colorful shirt and bandana off the other dead man, and Reggie put them on.

With their new disguises, they ran out of the store and hurried down the street. Sirens wailed in the distance. Two more of Gorilla's men stalked by them on the opposite side of the street but didn't recognize them in the darkness.

Hudson led them down a few side streets till he was sure they were out of range of their pursuers. They leaned against a brick wall in a short alley, trying to catch their breath. The muted sounds of electronic music reverberated from behind the wall.

"Now we're screwed," said Reggie. The tears on his cheek dried, and he seemed to have awoken from his trance. "We are in the middle of an African city with an army of assassins chasing us, our hotel is probably being staked out, our taxi driver abandoned us and we've failed in our mission to get intel from the Sentinel."

"And your father died..." Hudson added.

"That's okay. He was a jerk."

"Reggie, he—"

"Do you still have the SD card?"

Hudson checked his sock. "It probably smells funny, but it's still there."

Another police siren wailed in the distance.

Reggie pulled out the swipe card his father gave him and looked at it. It was plain white on one side. He turned it over to inspect the other side, and it slipped from his hand. The card fell to the sidewalk. When he bent over to retrieve it, a hole appeared in the brick previously behind his head. Mortar dust sprayed into the air.

"Sniper!" yelled Hudson.

They ducked and ran further into the alley.

"Keep your head down!" he screamed as they reached a steel door at the end of the alley.

"I forgot the card," said Reggie, turning and running back.

"Wait!"

Hudson looked out of the alley and across the street. A man crouched behind a park bench with a long rifle pointed in their direction.

As Reggie ran back for the card, Hudson whipped out the big black pistol and fired towards the sniper. He kept firing until Reggie returned.

"Got it!" Reggie held up the card.

Hudson shoved the gun into his pocket and pushed open the door.

The music increased in volume a hundred times. The rapid beats of a synthesized drum pounded as they moved through the small dark hallway. A girl burst from a washroom and almost ran into them. She slurred something in French before stumbling down the hallway.

They followed her into the main room. Hundreds of revellers bounced and danced to the music. Strobe lights flashed as coloured spotlights moved randomly across the throng of partiers. A DJ bopped his head from a booth on the far end of the dance floor.

Hudson led them around the outskirts of the dancers and past the long shiny bar along one side. A man turned from the bar and ran into Hudson. His drink spilled onto Hudson's chest.

"Je suis vraiment désolé," the man apologized.

"Bless you," said Hudson and shuffled away.

Eventually, they made it to the front door. The bouncer leered at them when they passed.

They stepped onto the sidewalk and saw a man glaring at them with one hand under his jacket. Hudson pivoted to the left, and they hurried away.

"I think that guy behind us has a gun," Hudson whispered.

As they reached the next intersection, they both stopped in their tracks. Gorilla grinned at them from across the street. Two henchmen stood on either side, and they all held guns.

Hudson looked behind them and saw the man with a gun in his jacket still chasing them. There was nowhere to go.

Suddenly, flashing red and blue lights lit up the street. Sirens wailed as two police cars screeched into the intersection.

A cop jumped out of the car, pointing a gun at Hudson and Reggie. They raised their hands in surrender.

CHAPTER 36

"I've never been in jail before," said Reggie. "This is kind of cool."

Hudson sat on the cot and rubbed his wrists where the cuffs had dug in.

"Don't get too excited. Kembata is not a country known for its gleaming human rights record."

"We won't be here long. I'll call my father—." Reggie held onto the bars and stared out.

"Are you okay?" asked Hudson.

"Of course."

"Reggie, you watched your father die. It's okay to be sad."

"Ha! The man was a total scumbag. He talked down to me, insulted me, abused me and blamed me for my mother's death. I'm *glad* he's gone."

"He was still your father."

"I don't have a father and I never have."

Hudson lay on the cot. "I'm going to sleep. You should rest too. We need to figure out what we're going to do next."

Hudson woke to the screech of ancient hinges as the prison door opened. A serious guard with a bulldog face stood outside their cell and grunted.

"Hudson, wake up." Reggie slapped his shoulder.

Hudson sat up. "I'm awake."

"How can you sleep?" Reggie asked.

"I was tired."

The guard grunted again. "Il est temps de laisser aller."

"I don't know what that means, but we're coming."

Hudson stood up and exited the cell with Reggie close behind. They walked past a long line of jail cells.

"Tu ne peux pas nous garder pour toujours!" a man yelled through the bars. He glared at the guard as they passed.

"Le gouvernement est corrompu," called a prisoner from the other side.

"Allez!" the guard barked, and Reggie and Hudson continued to the door at the end of the corridor.

The door buzzed open, and the guard led them into a noisy police station. Phones rang, people talked excitedly, and a young woman screamed. Their escort held his hand for them to stop while two policemen wrestled an angry teen to the ground in front of them. He grunted and directed Reggie and Hudson to give the tussling trio a wide berth.

He led them through another corridor to a small interrogation room and opened the door. A single table sat in the centre, with two chairs on one side and a single chair on the other. The guard grunted and left, closing the door behind him.

Hudson and Reggie sat down and waited.

A few minutes later, a lean man in a standard Kembato blue police uniform, including a beret, entered the room. He sat in the chair across from them and placed a manilla folder on the table.

"Good morning. My name is Sergeant Leon." His English had only a slight accent. "I will make this quick, as we are very busy today. Why are you here?"

"That French Bulldog made us come here," said Hudson.

He glared at them through round silver glasses. "Typical Americans – always making stupid jokes."

"Are we under arrest?" Hudson asked.

Sergeant Leon opened the folder and flipped through the pages. "It says here you were in possession of a concealed firearm."

"That was for self-defence. We took it from a man who tried to kill us."

"Do you mean the dead man in the convenience store? Did you kill him?"

"We're not answering that without our lawyer."

The Sergeant looked up and stroked his thin moustache. "If we didn't *arrest* you when we did, you would both be in the morgue this morning. Why is there a reward for your assassination?"

"You know about that?"

"Answer the question."

"Somebody wants us dead."

He pulled a white key card from the folder and placed it on the table. "Where did you get this?"

"My father gave it to me."

Reggie reached for the card, but Leon snatched it back.

"My condolences on your loss, but why did he give you this?"

"I don't know."

The sergeant leaned forward and spoke in a soft, serious tone. "I am trying to help you. If you continue to deflect my questions, I will dump you back onto the streets. You won't last five minutes out there. Right now, thousands of protestors are taking over the streets of Abena. Every available unit is working on crowd control. We can't keep you safe. The only reason you're still here is because I saw this."

He turned the keycard over revealing a logo with the letters *KVRI*. "This is a security card for the Kembato Virology Institute. Why do you have it?"

"I don't know," said Reggie.

The sergeant slapped his hands loudly on the steel table. The card fell to the floor as he yelled, "Why did you have this card?!"

Hudson held his hands up. "We really don't know. He gave us this card, but died before he could tell us why."

After taking a deep breath, Sergeant Leon lowered his tone. "My sister works at the institute. Kiara researches some *very* lethal diseases. If she or the institute are in danger, I need you to tell me *now*."

"Do you know Neepabom?"

"Is that a name?"

"We don't know," said Hudson.

"Is there anything you *do* know?"

"We came to Abena to meet Reggie's father. He had information for us, but they killed him before he could share it. We're telling you the truth."

Sergeant Leon shook his head. "We don't have the time or resources to pursue this any further. We will take you to the airport and send you home. I will arrange for your father's body to be sent back to America as well."

He stood up and slid his business card across the table. "Call me if you have any information on the Institute. If something happens to Kiara and I find out you withheld intel, I will press charges for carrying a concealed weapon and murder. I'm not sure what the punishment for murder is in America, but we still have the death penalty."

After he left, Reggie pushed his chair back and grabbed the card from the floor. He slipped it into his shoe before two policemen entered the room. The tall one wore a permanent stern expression, and the shorter man sported a recurring smirk.

"Come with us," said the smirker. "We're going to the airport. I'm Obi, and my grumpy partner is Badru. Stay close to us for your safety."

"Where's our stuff?" asked Reggie.

Badru pulled the phone from his pocket, handed it to him and mumbled something in French.

"What?" asked Reggie.

"He says your battery is almost dead," Obi replied.

Reggie rolled his eyes. "Thanks. Where's the cash you took from me last night?"

Obi translated his partner's response. "He says he didn't see any money."

"Of course, he didn't."

The policemen escorted them out of the interview room and into a raucous, frenzied reception and processing area. A man soaked in sweat and covered in grime screamed at the policeman. Beside him, a woman bleeding from her ear sobbed. Two women behind them wrestled each other. An older man in a drab military uniform by the front door argued with a policeman in the corner. None of their conversations were in English.

As they wove their way through the noisy mayhem, the front

doors opened. Five policemen escorted a dozen angry people inside. One cop yelled at Badru. He responded angrily in French, then said something to Obi. Badru grumbled and stormed away.

"Now it's just me," said Obi, and led them out the front doors into the stifling African sun.

The streets bustled with people, taxis, busses, a few trucks and a lot of motorbikes.

"Should we make a run for it?" Reggie whispered as they followed Obi to his cruiser.

"No. The assassins are still after us. It might be best for us to leave here while we can."

"You're giving up?"

"I never said that."

They got in the back of the cruiser, and Obi drove out of the police station parking lot. Reggie pulled the card from his shoe and slipped it into his pocket. Hudson watched him and nodded his approval.

"You should have left yesterday," said Obi. "The city is on the brink of chaos."

He stopped at an intersection, and a line of people with protest signs marched by. One of them slapped the hood and yelled something on his way by.

"What are they protesting?"

"The corrupt government postponed the elections because of Covid and still refuses to call an election. Our president is a greedy, selfish man who won't give up his power."

"We know what it's like to not trust the government," said Reggie as he turned on his cell phone.

A line of protestors filed across the road in front of their car. Obi slowed to a stop and waited before driving down a side street.

"We'll have to take the back way," said Obi.

Reggie tapped his phone. "I think Raven was worried about us."

"I think she was worried about you," said Hudson with a smirk.

"Whoa!" Reggie looked at his phone, then at Hudson.

"Whoa?" asked Hudson. "What's *whoa*?"

"She figured out what Neepabom means..."

"Who or what is it?"

Reggie read from his screen. "The Kembato Virology Research in Abena studies various viruses and diseases in Africa, including the Nipah virus. It can spread among animals and people rapidly and has a high mortality rate. Also, there is no vaccine."

"Wow, that sounds serious." Hudson looked out the window at the growing crowd of demonstrators. "But what is Nipahbom—"

"It's two words! Nipah bomb! My father's exact words were Nipah bomb, tomorrow."

"We need to call Sergeant Leon and warn him," said Hudson.

Reggie held up his phone, showing a black screen. "My phone is dead."

Hudson leaned forward in his seat. "Obi, call your superiors. There is a bomb at the Kembato Virology Research."

"Do you realize fake bomb threats are a 10-year jail sentence?"

"This isn't fake," said Hudson. "We have evidence of a bomb at the Institute."

"I bet they want to blow up the Institute and release the Nipah virus into the air," said Reggie. "This could be the next pandemic!"

They drove past the *Welcome to Abena International Airport* sign to the terminal.

Obi turned in his seat to face them. "How do you know about this bomb? Did you plant it?"

"No, but a reliable source told us."

"Did this reliable source plant the bomb?"

"No, but—"

"Who is your reliable source?"

"My father?"

"Isn't he dead?"

"Yes, but he told us about the bomb with his dying words."

"Why didn't you tell Sergeant Leon about this at the station?"

"We weren't sure that's what Mr. Hargreaves said."

Obi smiled. "To recap: a dying man mumbled something that you think sounded like there was a bomb at the institute. Your theory is that this bomb is supposed to blow up today and spread the Nipah virus and start the next pandemic?"

"I know it sounds crazy, but you have to believe us. Can't you at least check it out? Send a bomb squad to the institute to search for a bomb."

"We are a little preoccupied with a mass uprising. You two need to get on a plane and fly back home."

"At least call Sergeant Leon and warn him of a possible bomb," Hudson pleaded.

Obi opened his door and stepped out. He opened the back door and said, "I will call Sergeant Leon *after* I get you two on a plane."

"Thank you," said Hudson and got out.

As Obi escorted them towards the terminal entrance, his body crumpled to the sidewalk. A hole in his chest, the size of a shot glass, oozed blood. His face looked up at them with a dead smile.

"Sniper!" yelled Hudson. "Get down!"

A window in the airport terminal entrance exploded behind them. Reggie lay flat on the ground as Hudson crawled to the dead policeman. He fished out a ring of keys from his pocket and ran to the passenger side of the car with Reggie right behind him.

Hudson opened the passenger door and crawled into the driver's seat. Reggie dove in behind him.

"Keep your head down!" yelled Hudson.

Both the driver's side window and passenger windows shattered as bullets whizzed over their heads.

Hudson started the car and screeched away. Two more bullets dinged off the hood and trunk as they sped away from the airport.

"Are you okay?" asked Hudson.

"I'm not dead—wait, what happened to your face? Are you shot?"

Hudson touched his cheek and ear. It was wet and painful. "I think it's just glass from my window."

"Who do you think that was, and why couldn't we hear the shot?" asked Reggie.

"That was the professional assassin. Either someone with a long-range sniper rifle or a silencer. They were waiting for us."

"This is crazy. Are we going to die? How are we getting out of here? What about the bomb? I can't believe we stole a police car and professional assassins are trying to kill us. What do we do now?"

"Slow down...take deep breaths. Our options are limited. We can't go back to the airport, and it looks like we can't get back to the police station."

He pointed at the demonstrators filling the street ahead.

"Can we call someone with this thing?" Reggie pointed at the radio.

"Good idea," said Hudson and turned the radio dial.

The speakers blared a flurry of excited French chatter.

Reggie grabbed the microphone and depressed the button. "Hello? Is Sergeant Leon there?"

Nobody answered.

"Let me try," Hudson said, taking the microphone. "We have an officer down at Abena Airport, do you copy?"

After a brief pause, a voice crackled over the speaker. "This is station central. Who is this? Over."

"Officer Obi has been shot outside the terminal. He's dead, and the sniper almost killed us, too."

"Identify yourself. Over."

"My name is Hudson Finlay. Can I speak with Sergeant Leon?"

"Sergeant Leon is busy right now. Where are you? Over."

"We are trying to get back to the station, but the streets are too packed with protestors."

"Where are you? Over."

"It doesn't matter where I am. You can't get to me, anyway. I really need to speak with Sergeant Leon."

"The Sergeant is currently indisposed, but I can relay a message. Over."

"There is a bomb at the Kembato Virology Institute that will go off today."

"How do you know this? Over."

"We have a reliable source. Can you at least check it out?"

"All officers are currently busy. We can send someone out there as soon as one is available. Over."

"What!?" Hudson yelled into the microphone. "What if the bomb goes off before that?"

"Please hold the line, sir. Let me make a call. Over."

"Thank you," Hudson said with a sigh.

"Do you think they'll do anything?" asked Reggie.

"I hope so."

"Are you sure you're okay?"

"I'm sweating like crazy, but at least I'm not shot yet."

"Reggie, you watched your father die, you killed a man and a sniper almost shot you. It's okay to be sad or scared."

"I'm fine."

The radio crackled to life.

"Station to Hudson Finlay. Come in. Over."

"This is Finlay."

"We made some calls. Nobody is working at the Institute today because of the protests. There is no immediate danger, but officers will check the place before tomorrow morning. Over."

"That place is full of dangerous viruses. A bomb could spread one of them over the city."

"That's not likely sir. I have been assured that an explosion would likely destroy any viruses. Over."

"Likely? That's not very comforting."

"Please report to the station, Mr. Finlay and stay off the police band. We are busy responding to more urgent situations. Over and out."

"I don't want to put you in any more danger, but…"

"What else are we going to do? Wait here for the assassins to find us?"

"Do you remember where Michel, our taxi driver said the Institute was?"

CHAPTER 37

"I can't believe this car doesn't have air conditioning," said Reggie, pulling his shirt away from his chest.

The midday sun beat down on the police car, heating the interior like an oven. Behind them, the massive circular football stadium loomed like an alien ship. In front, a steel gate barred entry to Kembato Virology Research Institute. A lone guard manned the security kiosk beside the gate.

"At least we have water," said Hudson, dabbing his cut cheek and neck with a wet rag.

They found a water bottle in the glove box. After drinking most of it, Hudson used the rest to clean his wounds.

"The keycard won't get us past the front gate," said Reggie.

"I have an idea," said Hudson. "But you'll have to wait in the trunk."

"Are you kidding? It'll be like a furnace in there."

"It will only be for five minutes while I get through security."

"Okay, but if I die, it's your fault."

They removed the remaining broken glass from both windows, and Reggie climbed into the trunk.

Minutes later, Hudson rolled up to the kiosk.

An older man with greying hair and a slight limp ambled up to the driver's side window.

"Bonne journée, officier. Que puis-je faire pour vous?"

Hudson forgot that almost everyone spoke French or one of the many African dialects.

"Um...hi...Do you speak English?"

"A little," he said in a heavy accent.

"Can you do me a favour? I'm learning English, and I am trying to speak it as often as I can. It would be helpful if I could practice. Can we talk in English?"

The man looked confused. "Okay…"

"Did you hear about the bomb threat?"

"Yes, and I told the police that almost no one came in to work today. They are all at the protests."

"I understand that, but I am under orders to do a sweep of the property."

"Unless you have a warrant, I can't let you in."

Hudson held up the keycard. "We spoke to the Director of the institute. He gave me an access card and told us we could do a quick search, if we didn't enter any restricted areas. Which I don't want to, anyway. I hear there are some nasty diseases here."

The man squinted at Hudson. "I should probably call the director to verify—"

"Okay, but hurry. If that bomb is real, it could go off at any second."

The old man's expression changed from suspicion to worry. "Miss Kiara is inside. Do you think she's in danger?"

"I thought you said nobody was here today?"

"I said *almost* no one came in today. Miss Kiara is working in the lab. Do you think she's in danger? I told her about the bomb, but she said she was working on something very important."

"Would it help if I went inside and talked to her?"

The man nodded. "You had better hurry."

He returned to the kiosk and pressed a button. The metal gate rolled open, and Hudson drove inside. A line of dense Leucaena trees lined the perimeter fence, blocking the view of the security kiosk.

After parking near the front door, Hudson got out and opened the trunk.

"I need some water," Reggie gasped.

"Sorry, I used the last on my wounds. We'll find some inside."

Reggie clambered out of the trunk, panting. "What took you so long?"

"I had a pleasant chat with the security guard and found out that Sergeant Leon's sister, Kiara is inside."

"I thought nobody was here today." Reggie swallowed, trying to activate his salivary glands.

"So did I."

They walked to the front door and swiped the card. It beeped, and the door lock clicked. Hudson pushed it open, and they stepped inside. Reggie ran ahead past the reception desk.

"Where are you going?" yelled Hudson.

"I have to find some water before I die from thirst."

Hudson found the emergency plot plan on the wall and studied it while he waited for Reggie to return.

Most of the offices and administration rooms were on the first floor, and the research labs and storage were on the level below.

Once Reggie returned, they rushed to the elevator. Hudson pressed the *LL* button, but nothing happened.

"Try swiping." Reggie pointed to the card reader beside the buttons.

Hudson tapped the reader and pressed the button again. This time, the elevator obeyed and brought them to the lower level.

"Do you think the bomb is in the basement?" asked Reggie.

"I don't know, but we are going to talk to Kiara first."

The door slid open. They froze in place as they stared down the silver muzzle of a Smith and Wesson 686. Behind the shiny six-shooter stood a petite woman with a big afro and a determined face.

"Qui es-tu?"

"Don't shoot. My name is Hudson, and this is Reggie. We know your brother, Leon. You must be Kiara."

She lowered the gun a few inches. "Why are you here?"

"We're here about a bomb."

Kiara lowered the gun to her side. "Where is this bomb?"

"We don't know," said Reggie.

She rolled her eyes and shook her head. "Let me know when you find it. I've got work to do."

"You should leave," said Hudson. "What if we can't find it?"

"Ha! I have more important things to worry about than a non-existent bomb." She turned and walked down the hallway.

Hudson went after her. "How do know there's no bomb?"

"I don't have time for this. Leave me alone. I have critical research to complete."

Reggie caught up with them as they reached the lab door at the end of the hall. "Are you working on the Nipah virus?"

Kiara stopped, turned and pressed her Smith and Wesson against Reggie's forehead. "What do you know about the Nipah virus?"

"Please, don't shoot," Reggie's begged in a shaky voice. "My father told us about a Nipah bomb and gave us the keycard to this place."

"Are you working with the Porter Foundation?"

"No! We think Charles Porter is behind the bomb."

She pulled the gun away from his head, and Reggie let his breath out. "You're too late. Someone already stole it. That is why I am working to develop an antidote."

"What are you talking about? Who stole it?" asked Hudson.

"Last night, four men killed the security guard and broke into the lab. They stole five vials of the Nipah virus stored in the secure vault. They were professionals."

"How do you know that?"

"They had key cards to the institute, knew exactly where to go and somehow safely cracked the vault combination. That was supposed to be an uncrackable vault."

"Why would your father say Nipah *bomb*?" Hudson asked Reggie.

"I don't know."

"Why would anyone bomb this place?" asked Kiara. "An explosion would only incinerate the viruses inside."

"That makes no sense," said Reggie. "I thought the second phase would be a bomb that would spread a deadly virus and start another pandemic."

"A VDB," said Kiara.

"What is that?"

"My oldest brother used to be in the army. He talked to me once about a VDB. It was something the military was working on. They even tried to get the institute to collaborate on the project, but we refused. The Virus Dispersal Bomb is not really a bomb, but a theoretical weapon used to spread a virus over an enemy."

"That's what they're going to do with the virus!" Reggie exclaimed.

"The only way it would work properly is over a large group of people. They would have to be outside and..." Kiara's words slowed as she came to the same realization as the others.

"Like thousands of mass protestors on the street?"

"How is this bomb deployed?" asked Hudson.

"You don't think..." her words faded as she stared into the distance.

"How is the bomb deployed?" Hudson repeated louder.

"I told you, it's only a theoretical weapon."

"In *theory*, how would you do it?"

"I don't know, probably from a high altitude. The VDB's would be programmed to disperse the virus at around 200 metres – depending on the wind."

"Where's the closest air force base?" Hudson yelled.

"It's about 30 minutes north of here."

Hudson nodded at Reggie. "Let's go."

"I'm coming with you," said Kiara.

"Shouldn't you stay here and research the antidote?" asked Hudson.

"I am a long way from finding a cure. You need someone who can safely handle the virus."

"This is going to be dangerous," Hudson warned.

Reggie nodded. "He's right. Every assassin in Africa is trying to kill us."

"I don't care. If they successfully deploy a VDB with the Nipah virus, we'll all die, anyway."

CHAPTER 38

"I'm having second thoughts about the two of you," Kiara said from the passenger seat as they bumped along the road.

"We told you it would be dangerous," said Reggie from the back seat.

"You never said you'd be driving a stolen police car full of bullet holes. How many laws are you breaking?"

"We're too busy trying to stay alive to worry about that," said Hudson.

"I'd ask how a big man with sad eyes and an angry teenager ended up chasing a deadly virus in Africa, but it's probably a really long story."

"Yes, it is," said Hudson.

The road went from paved to hard-packed dirt as they left the city of Abena behind. The landscape reminded Hudson of the grasslands of Nevada. Patches of scrub grass dotted the khaki-coloured flatlands. A massive baobab tree reminded him this was not a road trip with Sophie to California. Its large bulbous trunk seemed cartoonish compared with the tiny branches and foliage on top.

"Are there elephants in Kembata?" he asked.

"Of course, but not in this area."

Kiara punched buttons on her phone with a stern look.

"Who are you calling?" asked Hudson.

"I'm trying to call or text my brother, but I can't get through. Things must be getting worse downtown."

"Why aren't *you* joining the protests?" asked Hudson.

"My brother made me promise not to go. He said it would be too dangerous."

"I'm not sure what we're doing is much safer."

On the road ahead of them, a cloud of dust appeared.

"What is that?" Hudson leaned forward and squinted.

"I don't know," Kiara replied.

Like a sinister brown tidal wave, a massive dust cloud rolled towards them, accompanied by the roar of a hundred engines.

"You should pull over," suggested Kiara. "I know what that is."

A drab olive jeep with a tall, flailing antenna emerged from the dust tsunami. Behind it, an armoured 4x4, an anti-riot water cannon tank and a parade of other army vehicles kicked up clouds of dust and dirt.

For a long time, they watched the long line of military vehicles rumble past them. Eventually, when it passed, and the dust settled, they resumed their drive to the army base.

Ten minutes later, Kiara pointed to a road on the right. Long grasses partially covered a faded sign, but it wasn't English.

"Is this the base?" asked Hudson.

"No, this is the housing complex for families," said Kiara. "My brother's family lived here when he was in the army."

Dilapidated shacks and shanties lined the road on either side.

Kiara pointed to the overgrown parking lot of a boarded up community centre. "Park here."

"Do people really live here?" asked Reggie.

"Not anymore. The army used to pay for housing for military personnel's families. The new president cut back on military spending and closed this place down. Now the families live in town, and the service members live in barracks."

"Why are we here?"

"I don't think they're going to let you in the front gate, but I know another way in."

They got out of the car and followed Kiara into the long grasses behind the community centre.

A light breeze rattled the wenge tree leaves above them. A blue turaco perched in the drooping branches of a coconut palm let out a rat-a-tat call.

"It's beautiful here," said Hudson.

"What are you talking about?" yelled Reggie. "The grass is cutting my arms; the heat is unbearable, and the mosquitoes are bloodthirsty."

"They also carry many viral diseases," said Kiara.

"Great!" Reggie swatted a mosquito on his neck.

"Shh. We're almost there." Kiara ducked low as they approached a tall chain-link fence. On the other side was the army base.

"How are we getting over *this*?" whispered Reggie.

"Follow me." Kiara waved them forward as they plod along the fence until they reached the chain-link personnel door.

A rusty padlock secured it shut. Hudson reared back and kicked it hard. The lock fell into the grass. He pushed the door open, and they went through.

An overgrown path led to a group of one-storey buildings. No guards or other army personnel were visible as they ran to the closest one.

They lined up along the wall, and Kiara peered around the corner. "The airstrip and hangars are on the other end of the base. We need to find a vehicle."

"And then what?" asked Reggie. "Do we have a plan?"

Kiara shrugged and looked at Hudson.

"Why is everyone looking at me?" he asked.

"This was your idea," said Reggie.

After a brief silence, Hudson said, "How big is this virus dispersal bomb?"

Kiara thought for a moment. "I've never seen one, but if they want to infect a lot of people, they will need either a lot of bombs. This would require a really big aircraft. Probably one of those giant planes with the big door at the back."

"Right. Here's the plan: we find a vehicle and drive it to the airfield. Then we look for a really big plane with a big door at the back."

"And then what?" asked Kiara. "How are you planning on stopping them? We don't even have any guns."

"Where's your Smith and Wesson?" Hudson asked her.

"I left it in the car. I don't have any bullets."

"We'll have to figure something out," said Hudson. "Let's go."

They waited till a group of officers walked by, then ran along the side of the building. They found a locked door and kept going. Keeping low, they ran behind a stack of green steel crates.

Reggie lifted the lid of one and looked inside.

"Whoa! Are these RPGs?"

"We can't use those," said Kiara.

"Why not?"

"If we shoot the plane out of the sky, the bomb might go off and release the virus."

"Right." Hudson frowned with disappointment.

They ducked low as a jeep rumbled by. After it passed, Hudson led them to the next building. A grey door sat between two massive overhead doors. They found this one unlocked and stepped inside.

Hudson flicked a switch, and fluorescent tubes crackled and snapped to life. Mechanic tools filled the steel benches lining one wall. The other wall contained shelving filled with spare engine parts, oils and lubricants. Two vehicle bays sat between them. In one, a light armoured vehicle with no tires rested on a hoist. In the other was a green truck with an empty rocket launcher in the back.

Hudson climbed in and pressed the ignition button. The truck roared to life, spewing black smoke out of the exhaust.

Reggie used the manual chain hoist to open the door before joining Kiara and Hudson inside the truck. They squeezed together in the front seat. The truck backfired twice as they rolled out of the shop. As Hudson attempted to change gears, the transmission complained with a loud grinding but eventually complied. Thick black smoke spewed from the muffler as they drove across the base.

Kiara pointed out the directions to the airfield, which they reached ten minutes later. Hudson rolled to a stop beside a maintenance shed at the edge of the tarmac.

Two hundred feet away, a hulking green twin-engine turbo prop Antonov AN-26 sat on the tarmac. Behind it, a heavy army transport truck hissed and shuddered as the diesel engine rumbled to life. The truck stuttered and jerked as it changed gears. It gained speed and drove away, leaving the aircraft alone on the runway. The rear hatch still hung open like a gaping mouth.

"I think we're too late," said Kiara.

"What if we drove in front of it? They would have to stop, wouldn't they?" asked Reggie.

"They would probably shoot us," said Hudson.

"I knew I should have grabbed the RPGs," muttered Reggie.

They stared in silence at the aircraft. A man in a jumpsuit pulled away the wheel chocks and ran into the back of the plane. A moment later, the rear hatch lifted shut like a closing mouth. The turboprops whirred to life, and the aircraft turned its nose towards down the taxiway.

"We *are* too late," said Kiara.

"What happens if they take off?" Hudson stared at the plane as it taxied down the runway.

Kiara shook her head. "They fly to Abena, and when they reach the proper altitude, drop the VDB. It will separate into about five or ten mini-bombs. At a lower altitude – depending on the wind conditions – they will disperse their contents into the air. By the time the droplets reach the crowds of protestors in Abena, they will be in a mist form. The demonstrators won't notice as they breathe in the virus. When the protest is over, and they go back home - or to jail, they still won't know. After a few days, they may complain of a headache, a sore throat or light fever. A couple of days later, the symptoms will worsen. From vomiting and difficulty breathing, to disorientation. Then, seizures, brain swelling and possibly a coma. Within two weeks, 40 to 75 percent will die."

"So, not everyone," Reggie interjected.

"That depends on which strain they have. I was not involved in the research of the Nipah virus. If they were trying to find a deadly variant, they may have found one. Some Nipah outbreaks have had a 100 percent mortality rate. Also, infections can lead to death years after exposure – known as dormant infections."

"How fast does it spread?"

"Normally, it spreads through direct contact or airborne droplets. However, they may have mutated it to create a true airborne spreading virus."

"How many protestors do you think there are?"

"The news said tens of thousands were on the streets."

The plane rolled slowly down the taxiway towards the main runway.

"Everybody out of the truck," Hudson ordered. "I have an idea."

"What are we doing?" asked Reggie.

"Now!" Hudson yelled this time. "Move!"

Kiara and Reggie exited the car. He turned to Kiara. "I need you to call your brother. Tell him to get here as fast as possible with as many police as possible."

"It's too—"

He didn't let her finish. Instead, he started the engine and looked at Reggie. "You're a good kid. I'm sorry about your father. We made a great team, and you're a good friend."

"Why are you saying—"

"Sorry, no time to talk. I going to stop that plane."

He shoved the gear into drive and slammed on the gas. The truck tires squealed as he tore away, leaving them in a cloud of blue smoke. His head slammed against the headrest as the truck rocketed forward. Within a few seconds, he was driving alongside the aircraft. The twin propellor blades cut through the air only twenty feet to his left. Hudson locked his gaze on the landing gear and chubby tires thrumming along the tarmac.

He maintained a speed to match the aircraft.

"Sophie, I'm sorry."

He grabbed the wheel and spun it to the left.

CHAPTER 39

Coach Benny used to say too much focus would get you hurt. When in the boxing ring, it wasn't just about hitting the other boxer, but also about predicting and blocking the opponent's punches. One unblocked punch could end the match in seconds. He watched his adversary's every move - the way the body swayed, the flexing of the biceps before a punch or subtle eye and head movement. Often, he was so focused on upper body signals, he would miss his challenger's feet. A step forward, sideways or back might signal an incoming strike.

Coach Benny warned him not to focus too much on just the upper body. A boxer's dance can predict his next move or show his weariness. Situational awareness meant not being too focused on only what is right in front of you.

Hudson tried to apply this to not only the boxing ring but to his life. He prided himself on being aware of his surroundings and planning accordingly.

However, while focused on speeding towards the undercarriage of a 15,000-kilogram aircraft with the sole intent of crashing, he had a critical lapse in situational awareness.

A jeep appeared in front of Hudson's stolen army truck as if it teleported there. It blocked his kamikaze path to the Antonov AN-26. He kicked the gas pedal to the floor. The engine roared, and the truck surged ahead. However, the jeep matched his speed and was still between him and the aircraft. Several yards behind them, the turboprop continued barrelling down the runway. The jeep bounced along beside him. A man with a submachine gun tried to aim his weapon, but the bouncing jeep threatened to throw him out of the vehicle. They flew down the runway at a dangerous speed. If either of them hit a crack in the concrete or turned a fraction of a degree too quickly, they would be instantaneously airborne. He steadily maneuvered the car towards the jeep.

In the passenger seat, the man raised his gun towards Hudson. A tiny bump in the road caused both vehicles to jump into the air. The man bounced in his seat, causing the weapon to fly out of his hands. It bounced along the runway, nearly hitting the wing of the aircraft. Impressively, the jeep driver maintained control of the jeep. The vehicles were only a few meters apart, and Hudson eyed them through his missing passenger window.

Like a professional fighter, Hudson was aware of every minute detail of his surroundings. He watched the head movements of the other driver, the speed of the aircraft behind them and the look of frustration and anger on the jeep passenger's face. After losing his gun, the man pulled something out of a pack in the jeep's rear. Hudson maintained his speed, clung to the steering wheel, and waited. The gunless passenger stood up in his seat. Like a professional pitcher, he threw a grenade out of the jeep, through the open window of the truck and off Hudson's shoulder. It bounced onto the empty seat beside him. Maintaining one steady hand on the wheel and his eyes on the runway ahead, Hudson reached for the grenade. He knew he had only seconds before the car transformed into a fiery furnace. However, he also knew that a minor jerk of the wheel would transform the car into a flying machine without landing gear.

After a few terrifying milliseconds of groping for the grenade, his hands wrapped around the small explosive. Although boxing was his favourite sport, he also played hockey in the winter and baseball in the summer. He wasn't a major league pitcher, but he knew how to throw a ball. The grenade was almost the same size and weight as a nine-inch hard ball but weighed considerably more. The distance between him and the jeep was almost identical to the space between the pitcher's mound and home plate. However, he was required to throw it from an awkward side stance, in a sitting position and through a one foot by two-

foot rectangular opening. His knuckles turned white, and his grasp on the wheel threatened to crush it.
Hudson took a quick look at the jeep, before tossing the grenade back. It shot out the window towards the jeep. The driver saw the incoming projectile and tried to steer clear. He knew as well as Hudson, that a quick jerk of the steering wheel or even a minor course correction could prove disastrous at their current speed. Instead, he turned slightly away from the police car. The grenade hit the door of the jeep with a clang and bounced on the concrete. Two seconds later, Hudson saw a yellow explosion behind him. Instinctively, he ducked as the blast wave knocked out the windows in his truck. Something clunked underneath the car, and he raised his foot off the gas. He moved his foot to the brake as the rubber from a rear tire disintegrated beneath him. His muscles flexed as he struggled to keep the car straight. With a shudder and screech, the car swerved suddenly to the left. The tires with remaining rubber shrieked and the rim of the fourth squealed as it scratched the concrete like fingernails on a chalkboard. Suddenly, the steering wheel felt loose as giving up the fight. Hudson realized he was airborne for a brief second before the car touched down, the airbag deployed and he lost consciousness.

CHAPTER 40

Everything felt strange and disorientating as Hudson struggled to open his eyes. His head felt heavy.

Years ago, Coach Benny convinced him to try mixed martial arts. He wrestled a lot in high school and had black belts in karate and jiu-jitsu. He also dabbled in kickboxing. It wasn't a stretch to move into the MMA ring. His first fight was against a hulking man from Canada named Tank. Two minutes into the first round, the big man smashed his fist into the side of Hudson's left jaw. He dropped to the mat immediately. When he regained consciousness, he was lying on his back, staring at the bright lights above the ring. He felt dazed, confused and in pain.

He had that same feeling now. Hudson fought against the blackness void of his unconscious attempting to close back in. When he finally pushed his eyelids open, he didn't see a man in black and white throwing his arms to the side, signalling he had lost the fight. Instead, he saw the white canvas of a deflating air bag. Hudson batted it away and discovered the reason for his heavy head and disorientation. He was hanging upside down. Blood dripped from his head and pain shot through his leg. He mashed at the seatbelt button until it relented, sending him headfirst into the roof of the car. Foreign voices yelled in the distance.

Pain in his head throbbed as crawled out of the wreck. His left leg throbbed in pain as he shimmied out the side window. Someone yelled at him in French. He looked up at the muzzle of an AK-47. The man in fatigues, holding the gun, looked like the passenger of the jeep. The one that threw the grenade. He must have either retrieved his lost gun or found another one. The man yelled something else in French that Hudson interpreted as *stand up*. Hudson got to his feet and shifted some of his weight to his left leg. It didn't feel broken. The man yelled at Hudson while jabbing his rifle in Hudson's direction.

When Hudson put his hands on his head, the man stopped yelling.

Behind his captor, the jeep driver yelled into his radio. Fifty metres behind him, the Antonov AN-26 idled on the runway. its chubby tires and landing gear remained intact, but black scorch marks covered the underside of the fuselage. Another jeep with four occupants rolled down the runway past the plane and stopped in front of the other driver, still on the radio.

The front passenger exited the jeep and walked over to the man on the radio. They yelled and argued with each other and the person on the radio for several minutes. The soldier pointing his gun at Hudson's face jumped when his radio squawked to life. When he answered the call, Hudson considered using the distraction to take him out. However, he was still too sore and not fully alert to trust his abilities.

The man motioned for Hudson to get up and walk. He struggled back to his feet and limped towards the man with the radio. They zip-tied his hands behind his back and pointed to the other jeep.

Dying with a bullet to the back of the head at the side of a runway in the middle of Africa was not how he pictured his demise. He was, however, already alive longer than he expected ten minutes ago.

It surprised him when they stopped at the 2nd jeep and knocked on the window. Another guard opened the back door, and Reggie and Kiara stepped out. Both had their hands zip-tied behind their back, and they both looked terrified.

"Are you guys okay? I'm sorry—."

"Come this way," said the soldier. "You have one minute to make your peace with God."

The guards led them led away from the jeeps. Reggie looked at

Hudson with pleading eyes. It was the same look Sophie gave him over the tablet.

His eyes begging, *don't let me die.*

A red and blue light flashed at the far end of the airfield. It was too far to see clearly, but they all recognized the three police vehicles and the accompanying siren.

"Leon!" yelled Kiara. "My brother must have got my text!"

The lead soldier yelled into his radio. After receiving a response, he barked new orders to the other soldiers.

They urged Hudson and the others on as they made a speedy arc around the paused aircraft. Its turboprops were still spinning.

Hudson fought through a pounding headache and a dense brain fog, trying to formulate an escape plan.

He mentally played out a leg sweep, followed by a head butt, stealing a gun and killing three men with his hands tied behind his back. A loud squeal of metal broke him out of his impossible scenario planning. The rear hatch of the Antonov creaked open. The soldiers led Hudson and the others towards the opening door. Beneath them, the ground vibrated with the whirring jet engines and Hudson's ear drums hurt from the noise.

Three police cars reached the edge of the runway, lights flashing, but were still several hundred yards away.

The hatch hit the pavement with a clang that was barely audible over the roar of the engine. Like a gaping mouth, the open door waited to receive them. One soldier yelled something over the noise and motioned for them to walk up the plank. They shuffled inside and sat at the end of a row of metal seats lining both sides of the plane.

The hatch closed, and Hudson felt like a beast swallowed him.

One soldier sat near them with an AK-47 on his lap while the others moved deeper into the aircraft.

A moment later, the plane taxied forward.

"I'm sorry." Kiara's voice was barely audible over the din of engines. "We didn't see them coming."

"Don't apologize to him," said Reggie. "He abandoned us."

"I was trying to stop this plane without endangering you guys."

"That was a stupid plan," mumbled Reggie.

Hudson looked at Kiara. "Why haven't they killed us yet?"

"They were about to when my brother arrived. I think they decided it would be easier to dump our bodies somewhere over the Savannah, where no one will find them."

"Won't your brother come after us if he knows we're on this plane?" asked Reggie.

"Believe me, he would, if it were possible."

"Is that it?" Hudson pointed to the large contraption on the floor in front of them. A dozen tubes were all connected by a metal rack. Each tube looked like a cylinder used for welding. At the end of each tube was a large nozzle. Thick wires led from the nozzles to a black box with an LED screen and a keypad. Rectangular bricks were fastened to each tube, and a small electronic device was strapped to each brick.

Kiara nodded.

"How is that thing supposed to fly?" asked Reggie.

"It's not." Kiara studied the bomb in the dim light. "They will simply dump it off the back of the plane. Each tube will separate shortly after they drop it and begin dispersing the virus from the nozzles at the end."

"What are those bricks?" asked Hudson.

"I'm assuming they're explosives."

"I thought this wasn't that kind of bomb," said Reggie.

"Maybe they don't want to leave any trace of the bomb. After they release the virus, the bricks of C-4 go off and destroy any evidence."

"Hey, be quiet back there!" yelled the guard.

They said nothing as the plane sped down the runway and lifted into the air. The engines rumbled loudly in the hold.

Hudson leaned close to the others and whispered, "I have a plan."

CHAPTER 41

Hudson looked out the window behind him. The edge of the city was in sight. They had little time to initiate his plan. He nodded at Reggie.

"I don't feel so good," Reggie groaned.

"What's wrong? Where does it hurt?" Kiara yelled.

Reggie fell to the floor, groaning.

"Help! There's something wrong with him!" she yelled again.

"Hey, shut up," said the guard.

Reggie convulsed on the floor of the plane. With his hands zip-tied together, he looked like a fish flopping on the beach.

"Oh no!" Kiara knelt and felt Reggie's brow. "This isn't good."

The guard stood up and pointed his rifle at Reggie. "We were going to kill you anyway…"

"Wait!" Kiara looked up at the guard with wide eyes. "These are symptoms of the Nipah virus."

"What? How's that possible?" The guard looked at the bomb.

She looked at Reggie, then the bomb, then back at the guard. "I think you have a leak."

"Captain!" he yelled as he ran to the front of the plane.

As soon as he left, Hudson stood up and held his zip-tied hands as far back as he could. Then he slammed them back towards his butt. The plastic dug into his wrists but didn't break. He tried again, and this time, they snapped.

He snatched the fire extinguisher off the wall and sprayed the end of a nozzle of one tube. Yelling from the front cabin echoed through the plane.

Hudson replaced the fire extinguisher on the wall, before looking at the bomb closer. He grabbed a wire connected to a tube and yanked it.

"Come on, they're coming back!" urged Reggie.

The soldiers' boots clanged on the floor as Hudson ripped out more wires.

He quickly sat down with his hands behind his back as the soldiers returned. Kiara still knelt over Reggie, who lay coughing and sputtering on the floor.

The guard returned with two other men.

One of them had stripes on his shoulder. Hudson assumed it meant he was a sergeant or something.

"What is going on back here? I was going to dump you deep in the desert after our mission, but if you feel the need to misbehave, we can dump you now."

Kiara nodded at the tube with the fire extinguisher foam on the end. "I think your bomb is leaking."

One guard gasped, and the other stepped back. The sergeant yelled something in French, covered his mouth with his shirt and ran towards the cabin. Yelling, running and panicked arguing filled the next few moments. Within a few minutes, all the guards wore face masks with large filters. Two of them removed the straps holding the bomb to the floor, one stood at the button to open the hatch, and the captain tapped at the LED screen on the bomb.

Hudson, Reggie and Kiara moved away from the hatch.

The sergeant stepped back and nodded at the guard next to the button. A bright red light flashed when he pushed the button, and the hatch started to open.

Suddenly, the sergeant uttered a muffled yell through his mask and held up his hand. The soldier looked at him, confused. Air rushed through the gap in the door, the noise akin to a tornado.

The sergeant yelled again and stormed across the plane. He slammed his hand on the button, and the hatch returned to the closed position. The cabin went relatively quiet again.

The soldiers gathered around as he pointed at the broken wires on the bomb. His gloved finger touched the foam on the nozzle and brought it close to his mask for inspection.

"Uh-oh," whispered Reggie. "I hope you have a Plan B."

The sergeant pointed at the foam at the end of the fire extinguisher nozzle before tearing off his mask.

"Enlevez vos masques stupides!"

The soldiers hesitated before removing their masks. One guard held his breath.

The sergeant unbuttoned the leather holster on his belt and strutted over to the prisoners. Hudson eyed the black revolver, knowing he needed a Plan B really soon.

His hand hovered over the pistol. "It appears we have a couple of saboteurs."

"Why are you doing this?" Reggie pushed himself up to his knees.

The sergeant backhanded him across the face. The slap echoed across the cabin. Reggie remained in place, glaring back at his abuser.

"That's all you got?" He spit a wad of saliva and blood on the steel floor. "My father slaps harder than you."

As the sergeant reared back for another slap, Hudson spoke up. "He asks a valid question. Why *are* you killing your own people?" Hudson's hands were still behind his back as he pretended to still be bound. The captain turned to Hudson, folded his arms across his chest and smiled. "I don't—"

Before he finished answering the question, Hudson's arms flew out from behind him. His right fist performed a quick jab at the man's trachea as his left hand snagged the pistol from the holster.

Most people buckle over and grasp their throat when punched in the neck. However, the sergeant was a hardened army veteran, and his instinct was to punch back – despite the sudden oxygen cutoff. Hudson easily ducked the punch and pulled the man into a chokehold. He stood behind him with the pistol pointed at his skull above his ear.

"Everybody, get back!" Hudson screamed.

The soldiers raised their rifles and pointed them at Hudson and his hostage.

"This is your Plan B?" asked Reggie.

"Tell your men to drop their weapons," Hudson ordered.

The man coughed as he struggled to suck in air. "You won't—"

"I won't what? Shoot you? You are about to commit mass murder on your own people. If I shoot you, my conscious will be as clear as a creek in northern Michigan."

His men kept their guns trained on Hudson, while Kiara and Reggie watched with worried expressions.

The sergeant struggled to speak through the choke hold. "This country is a mess. All the politicians are corrupt, the economy is in chaos, people are starving, and the rest of the world has forgotten about us. He might be right, reducing the population may be the only way to save us. Besides, we're getting paid a small fortune for a two-hour job."

"Who might be right?" asked Reggie.

Still in Hudson's chokehold, the lieutenant tried to shrug. "The boss."

"Enough talking!" yelled Hudson. "Tell your men to lower their guns, Sergeant!"

"It's Lieutenant Chuki, and I don't take orders from civilians and neither do my men."

"If you want to live, tell them to stand down!"

The captain smiled. "Shoot him. He doesn't have the—"

Hudson pointed the pistol at the captain's leg and fired. The gunshot echoed loudly through the cabin. Everyone, including Hudson, winced at the deafening shot. Lieutenant Chuki yelled as blood flowed out of the hole in his thigh. Hudson returned the barrel of the gun to the lieutenant's head.

"Tell them to lower their weapons, or I will shoot your other leg!" he yelled again.

Lieutenant Chuki nodded at his soldiers. "Lower your weapons, but if I die from blood loss, kill them all."

Hudson instructed them to lay their weapons on the floor and sit in the back of the plane. He then helped Kiara and Reggie cut their zip ties.

Kiara found a first aid kit and wrapped Lieutenant Chuki's leg while Reggie piled the submachine guns near the front of the plane. He kept one for himself. "This is so cool."

"No, it's not," said Hudson. "Go to the back of the plane and guard our prisoners. I'm going to have a talk with the pilot."

"We've taken over the plane," Hudson announced as he stormed into the cockpit.

The pilot checked a dial and flicked a switch but did not turn around.

"What are your orders?" he said in a calm, even tone.

"Did you hear what I said? Don't you want to know who is in charge?"

"Nope. I don't care. Just tell me where I'm going now."

"I realize this is my first mid-flight aircraft commandeering experience, but shouldn't you be scared or something?"

The captain finally turned to Hudson. "I've been doing this a long time. In the last twenty years since I've been a pilot, Kembata has seen five regime changes and most of them violent. During that time, armed insurgents, angry generals and violent terrorists commandeered my plane. I don't care who is the boss. I just like to fly. Please tell me where I'm going. We have enough fuel for about 2,000 kilometres."

"Do we have enough to fly to Europe?"

"No. That is too far."

"Where are we now?"

"We are currently flying over Abena."

"Turn around, for now. Fly over someplace less populated."

"That won't be a problem."

When Hudson returned to the hold, Reggie was yelling at the Lieutenant who sat on the floor. Blood seeped through the gauze wrapped around his thigh.

"Tell us who your boss is?"

"Or what? You are nothing but a spoiled American teenager. When I was your age, I enlisted in the Kembata Republican Guard."

Reggie held his hand back as if to strike.

"Do it!" the Lieutenant taunted. "Be a man."

Hudson couldn't tell if Reggie was about to kill him or cry. His face reddened, and he glared at Lieutenant Chuki with glassy eyes.

"I will tell you who my boss is, if you hit me."

Reggie's poised hand quivered. "I'll do it!"

Hudson watched but did not intervene.

"Come on!" yelled the lieutenant. "Fight back. Hit me with all that anger I see in your eyes."

Reggie slapped him. It was harder than a friendly cuff to the back of the head but lighter than the first jab in a sparring round.

"That's it? That's all you got?" Lieutenant Chaka shouted. "Hit me! Hit me hard. Hit me like your father hit you! Don't be such a pansy!"

With a wind-up like a baseball pitcher about to throw a fastball for the strikeout, Reggie smacked the man hard across the face. Lieutenant Chaka's head swung to the side and returned with a bloody lip and a scarlet cheek.

"*Now* you're almost a man," he said, spitting blood. "I don't know his name, but my boss is on the tablet in my pack."

Reggie rubbed his eye with the back of his arm before folding and unfolded his arms. He looked like he couldn't get comfortable.

Hudson stepped forward. "If you're done interrogating the prisoner, we need to discuss our next move."

They huddled beside the bomb with their prisoners still in sight but out of earshot.

"We did it!" said Kiara. "I'm not sure if I approve of your methods, but we stopped them."

"I got the big guy to talk," said Reggie with a swagger. He held up the tablet.

"The pilot will take us anywhere we want," said Hudson.

"Great, let's go back to the air force base," said Kiara.

"We just commandeered an army plane and took a lieutenant and his men hostage. They might not give us a hero's welcome at the base."

"What if we went to the Abena International Airport? We could call the police and my brother. They will arrest these men when we land."

"There is still a bounty on our heads," said Hudson. "I think everybody with a gun in Abena is looking for us."

"We could go to a different country." Reggie tapped at the tablet.

"Kembata isn't too friendly with its neighbours. They might shoot down an uninvited army plane from another country."

"We need to let the world know about this," said Reggie. "Charles Porter and his merry band of elites are about to be exposed."

"Are we sure he was involved?" asked Kiara.

"Yes!" they answered in unison.

"And I'm going to prove it," said Reggie. "We can use this tablet to call Lieutenant Chaka's boss - who we know is Porter. We'll get him to admit that he was the mastermind of this plan and send the proof to the world!"

"Yes, but we'll still have a price on our heads," said Hudson.

"If he's exposed, he might call it off."

"Maybe."

"Here it is," said Reggie, pointing at the tablet. "Chaka used this video conferencing app to talk to his boss."

"We should let Chaka do the talking," suggested Hudson. "We don't want him to know that we foiled his plans yet."

They returned to Lieutenant Chaka, who was sitting on the floor adjusting the gauze on his leg.

"We need you to call your boss," said Hudson. "Tell him your mission to drop the virus was a success."

Chaka shrugged. "Okay."

Reggie handed the tablet to Lieutenant Chaka.

Hudson, Reggie and Kiara watched over his shoulder, making sure they were not in the shot.

The app rang twice before someone answered. An older black man with glasses stared back at them.

"The mission was a success," said Chaka. "Please confirm my payment."

"You're lying. Why was the VDB not dropped?"

"Of course it was! We did everything you asked. Send my

payment now!"

"We have eyes everywhere, Lieutenant Chaka. You flew over Abena but did not drop the weapon. Now you are somewhere over the Savannah. What is the problem?"

"The problem is three civilians on board."

"What are you talking about? Who—"

"Where is Charles Porter?" Hudson snatched the table away from Chaka. "I hate these things," he mumbled under his breath.

"Mr. Finlay. We had our suspicions you might still be alive."

"Put your boss on."

"I *am* the boss."

"Let me speak with Charles Porter."

"I don't know who that is. Please return control of that airplane to Lieutenant Chaka. If you don't, the F15 fighter we scrambled will shoot your plane out of the sky in 10 minutes."

"What? You can't do that!" Lieutenant Chaka tried to grab the tablet, but Hudson pulled it away.

Reggie poked his head into view of the camera. "If anything happens to us, I've made arrangements for the recording of the IEC secret meeting to go public."

The man paused before responding. "Do you have the recording with you?"

"You don't think I'm that stupid, do you?" Hudson reached down and felt for the card in his sock. "We will make a deal, but only if we can speak with Charles Porter."

"Again, I don't know who that—hang on."

The screen flickered, and a grey-haired Charles Porter appeared on the screen. Dark circles hung beneath his eyes.

"Mr. Hudson Finlay. What do you think you're doing?"

"I'm stopping you from attempting genocide."

"You're being a little melodramatic, don't you think?"

"You loaded a virus onto a bomb and ordered these men to drop it onto the crowded streets of Abena."

"That's an incredible story, but you have no proof that I was in any way involved in such an unspeakable crime."

"We have proof!" yelled Reggie.

"Reginald Hargreaves, I'm sorry about your father. He stuck his nose in places it did not belong, and it appears you are just like him."

Reggie opened his mouth but couldn't decide if he should argue the point or agree.

Charles continued. "And your fate will not be dissimilar. In about 9 minutes, an A7 Sparrow missile will disintegrate that aircraft and all its occupants."

"If anything happens to us, this recording will go public."

"I don't believe you had the time or resources to set that up. Besides, without first-hand witnesses, your evidence will only be hearsay."

"What if we make a deal?" asked Hudson.

"I'm listening."

"We will give you the recording if you call off your assassins."

Reggie glared at Hudson with disapproval.

"And then what? I just let you go? How many copies did you make?"

"None."

"Even if that were true, it would be better to cut my losses now. I can eliminate you and the recording at the same time."

"We can prove that no one will ever hear the recording," said Hudson.

"How can you possibly do that?"

"Call off your assassins and meet us in Abena. We will give you the SD card and prove that nobody will ever know of any conversation at your secret meeting. If you are satisfied with our proof, you let us go, call off the hit for good and let us return home in peace."

"And what if I'm not satisfied?"

"Then you can take the SD card and shoot us yourself. Either way, you get what you want."

Charles thought about the offer for a moment before nodding. "Deal. I'll meet you where Reggie's father, Lawrence, met his end – at Memorial Square. Nobody will touch you till then. Meet me there tomorrow at noon."

"That's too dangerous," Kiara interjected. "Downtown is probably full of angry protestors and police."

"That protest will be over by then, doctor. I'm sorry, but democracy in your country will have to wait a little longer."

"How do you know—"

She stopped mid-question as Lieutenant Chaka pointed an AK-47 at them. He yanked the tablet out of Hudson's hands and threw it across the plane.

Hudson cursed himself for not watching the man. While they were talking, he snuck away and retrieved a gun.

"Drop the pistol, Mr. Hudson," Chaka said smiling.

The gun clanged to the floor, and Hudson raised his hands.

"Don't move, or I'll blow you away!" Reggie aimed his AK-47 at the lieutenant.

"You are almost a man," said Lieutenant Chaka. "But hitting someone differs from killing someone. Put the gun down, boy before I beat you with it."

"I mean it." Reggie jabbed the air with his gun. "I'll shoot you!"

"I can see why your father hit you. You're a scrawny, useless, spoiled brat who will never—"

Reggie squeezed the trigger for less than a second. Eight bullets pierced the Lieutenant's arm, shoulder and chest. He slumped to the floor with a wry grin.

"*Now* you're a man…" He exhaled his final breath.

Hudson and Kiara stared in shock.

Reggie glared down at the body. "You'll never hit me again!"

The plane lurched forward, knocking them all off their feet. A soldier ran uphill from the back of the plane. He stopped for a moment to look at his dead lieutenant before nodding at Hudson. The engines sounded like they were in overdrive, and the plane was diving at an unnatural angle. The soldier yelled something in French and climbed into the cockpit.

A moment later, the plane levelled off. He emerged from the cockpit yelling and walked to the rear of the plane to the other soldiers.

"Uh-oh!" Reggie pointed at the bullet holes in the cockpit wall.

Hudson ran into the cockpit and found the pilot lying dead on the floor with a bullet hole in his head. A large binder jammed between the seat and the yoke held the steering wheel in place. Reggie and Kiara joined him.

"This isn't good," said Kiara.

They heard a commotion in the back of the plane and went to investigate. The soldiers donned parachutes, and the rear hatch was opening.

"Can't any of you fly this plane?"

None of them answered. The wind blew in from the open hatch.

"Wait! You can't leave us here!" Reggie yelled.

One by one, the soldiers jumped out of the back of the plane.

The last soldier was a tall man with a stubby beard. He pointed to the compartment above their heads. "Find a chute, strap it on and jump. My name is Essam. I will help."

He helped them don parachutes and gave them a thirty-second lesson on skydiving.

"Wait! What about the bomb?" asked Hudson. "If the plane crashes, won't the virus be released?"

"Not if we set the C-4 explosives," said Kiara.

"Will that work?"

"I think so, but I'm not a munitions expert."

"Theoretically, the explosion will incinerate the virus before it reaches the ground," said Kiara.

"We don't have a choice." Hudson pointed to Essam. "Can you set the timers?"

"Yes, I can do that," he answered.

While the soldier programmed the detonator, Reggie stared wide-eyed out the back of the plane. His brown curly hair fluttered in the wind.

Hudson stood beside him. "Are you okay?"

"I'm about to jump out of a plane with a parachute strapped to my back that I don't know how to use."

"Is that really what you're thinking?"

"I'm trying to get the images of four dead men out of my head. Three of them I murdered, and the other was my father."

"I'd hate to be the one that pays your therapy bills."

Reggie smirked. "You have a strange sense of humour."

"Yeah. I don't know how to handle these situations. Sophie was better at the emotional stuff. I'm not your father or your therapist. I'm just your friend."

"Does this mean we're finally partners?"

"We've always been partners, Reggie."

"Really?"

"No, I'm just saying that in case we die, and this is our final conversation."

"Okay, it's all set!" yelled Essam. "Remember, after you jump, count to ten before pulling the ripcord. Bend your knees and roll when you hit the ground."

"How fast do I count?" asked Reggie.

Essam smiled. "One elephant, two elephants, three elephants..."

"I like it," said Hudson.

The plane jolted suddenly, almost flinging them out of the hatch.

"We better hurry." Essam looked at the timer on the explosives. "In less than thirty seconds, this plane will be a ball of fire."

Reggie stepped closer to the edge. "I don't know if I can do this."

"Say *one elephant*," the soldier instructed.

"But you said to count after we—"

"Say *one elephant*!" He yelled this time.

"One eleph—"

Before he finished, Essam shoved Reggie out of the hatch.

Hudson peered over the edge and watched as Reggie's chute billowed open.

He looked at Kiara. "Are you okay?"

"Ask me when we reach the ground," she said, and leapt out.

Hudson smiled and held his hand out to the soldier. "Thank you for your help."

"Thank you," said Essam as they shook hands. "You saved a lot of lives today."

Hudson stood poised at the edge of the hatch. "Hey Essam, you don't have a cousin named Michel who drives a taxi, do you?"

"No, why?"

"Just checking."

Hudson jumped out. Immediately, his brain seemed to inject a gallon of adrenaline into his bloodstream. His entire body went rigid in terror. He fumbled for the metal handle of the ripcord. Looking above him, the plane was already tiny. Below, the ground was approaching fast. Not knowing how many elephants he missed, he yelled, "Ten elephants!" and pulled the handle.

Nothing happened.

He pulled harder. Still, nothing. With a final panicked yank, the ripcord gave way. The parachute flapped wildly for a second before opening. Hudson let out the breath he didn't realize he was holding.

The ground approached fast, and he was heading straight for a grove of bushwillow trees. He was sure there was a way to steer, but Essam didn't give them navigation instructions, and Hudson didn't dare fiddle with a working parachute.

A distant explosion scared him till he realized it was the plane. When he looked down, a large bushwillow tree was coming towards him way too fast.

Essam told them to bend their knees and roll when they hit the ground, but didn't give instructions about landing in a tree.

Instead, he yelled and pedalled in the air. His feet broke through the first branch and bounced off the next one. His chest took the brunt of another one while leaves slapped him in the face.

He broke through another tree limb, and his trajectory slowed. His chute caught on a branch above him and, like a bungee jumper, he bounced a few times before hanging twenty feet above the ground. He struggled for a long time to extricate himself from the parachute harness without falling out of the tree.

As he descended the bushwillow, a flash of black and white fur streaked across his peripheral vision. Something rustled in the leaves, and he froze in place. Whatever it was, moved fast across the tree, before settling on a branch ten feet away. It looked like an oversized skunk, but he soon realized it was a monkey. The fur was mostly black, but a mantle of silky white fur hung on its back like a shawl, and a ball of dirty white fluff hung at the end of a long, thick tail. It gawked at him with mischievous, beady eyes. Three more monkeys appeared on branches all around him.

“Uh…sorry guys. I didn’t mean to invade your tree. I’ll be going down now…”

“Who are you talking to up there?” Reggie yelled from below. Kiara stood beside him, looking up as well.

“Kiara? Are skunk monkeys dangerous?”

“Those are guereza monkeys. And they’re not usually dangerous, but I’ve never fallen into a tree full of them before.”

As Hudson continued slowly down the tree, he wondered if jiu-jitsu techniques would work on a monkey. They snorted and cawed at him but didn’t engage in an MMA match.

CHAPTER 42

The evening was fast approaching when they found Essam, and the four of them walked across the hot savannah for two hours before reaching a small village. Essam had friends in the village who fed the group and found some dirty, thin cots for them to sleep for the night.

He arranged a ride for the three of them into Abena the next morning but did not go with them.

Hudson, Reggie and Kiara sat in the back of a rusty pickup truck as it bumped along a dirt road, leaving a cloud of dust in their wake. They sat wedged between crates of a root vegetables that looked like mutant potatoes.

Reggie held one up. "What are these things?"

"Cassava," said Kiara pointing at the crates. "They are an important crop in Kembata."

Reggie tossed the cassava from one hand to the other. "What happens next?"

"We meet Charles Porter and give him the SD card," said Hudson.

"Then what?"

"Then we convince him not to have us killed."

"What about after that?"

"What do you mean?"

"We stopped the elites from creating another pandemic, but we lost our only proof of their plans. Shouldn't we find out what they're going to do next?"

"Let's make our deal with Charles first. Then we'll go back home, and you can bury your father."

"I don't want to go home."

"I know, but you have to deal with his death."

"He was a horrible father who didn't love me. I'm glad he's dead."

"You shouldn't say things like that," said Kiara.

"In a way, he was a little like you," Hudson said in a quiet tone.

"I doubt that!"

"He may have been a terrible father, but like you, he tried to fight the system. He was feeding us information, like the secret meeting at the IEC and he told us about their plans with the Nipah virus. It might have been him who got us out of trouble at the underground lab at the Acor Army Base."

"But why did he send Riker and Deltoid to kill us?"

"I don't think they were trying to kill us. They were trying to recover the tracker, and we don't know that it was your father who gave that order."

The truck slowed to a stop at an intersection at the edge of downtown Abena. Hudson scanned the surrounding area.

"What are you looking for?" Kiara asked.

"The last time we were here, everyone with a gun was trying to kill us. Charles said we'd be safe, but I don't trust him."

Twenty minutes later, they arrived in the centre of town, next to a bustling market. They jumped off the truck as the driver began unloading his cargo.

"Memorial Square is three blocks that way," said Kiara.

"You don't have to come with us," said Hudson. "Charles is a dangerous man."

"I know, but I want to see this through."

The trio crossed the street, dodging three mopeds, a compact car and dozens of other pedestrians. Hudson looked around, searching for suspicious characters or men with guns. Just as they passed a small cafe, a group of six men rounded a corner and strode down the sidewalk towards them. As they neared, Hudson recognized the barrel-chested, bald man with motor oil skin.

"Is that Gorilla?" Reggie asked.

"You know that guy?" asked Kiara.

"He sold us a gun and then tried to kill us," said Hudson.

"Oh."

"Keep walking," said Hudson. "If they were trying to kill us, they'd have their guns out already. We have to hope that Charles called off the bounty on our heads."

Gorilla stopped and glared at them but did not reach for his gun. His men stopped behind him. "You're safe for now, Americans," he snarled.

"You killed my father!" Reggie screamed and attempted to punch Gorilla in the face.

The big man caught the fist mid-flight. Reggie grimaced in pain as Gorilla twisted his hand.

Hudson stepped forward, and the man let go. "We aren't allowed to hurt you, but that doesn't mean we can't defend ourselves."

"You murdered my father, and I'm going to kill you!" Reggie screeched.

Kiara watched on in silence.

Gorilla held his hands in the air and looked down at Reggie. "I am not that bad. Sure, my men may have killed your father, and we tried to kill you. However, if *we* didn't, then someone else would. You can be mad at me, but I am a mere puppet. I get paid to do a job, and I do it. Perhaps you should direct your anger and need for revenge at the puppet master."

Reggie seethed with rage. Slowly, he calmed his breathing. Then he blinked and widened his eyes as if he had an epiphany.

"You're not allowed to hurt us, right?" he asked.

"That's right."

Reggie pointed through the window of the café. "Can you and I have a quick, *private* conversation?"

"What are you doing?" asked Hudson.

"I don't think you should—" began Kiara.

"We still have a few hours before our meeting with Charles," said Reggie. "You two wait at Memorial Square. I'll be there shortly."

"I'm not leaving you alone with this—" Hudson began, but Reggie held up his hand.

"Please…let me do this."

"Do what?" asked Hudson. "What are you doing?"

"You said we were partners and friends. Friends trust each other.

Trust me now."

"Partners also communicate."

"I'll tell you later," said Reggie. He looked up at Gorilla. "Tell your men not to let anyone bother us."

Gorilla considered the request for a moment. "Okay." He nodded at his men and opened the door to the café.

"I'll meet you at the square in thirty minutes," Reggie said to Hudson. "If I don't return, avenge my death." He smirked and walked into the café with Gorilla following close behind.

"I don't like this." Hudson went to follow them, but two of Gorilla's men blocked his path.

Hudson sighed and looked at Kiara.

"Let him go. He'll be fine," she said.

Hudson peered into the café and saw Gorilla and Reggie sitting at a small round table. He turned on his heels and stormed away.

"He's not your responsibility," said Kiara when she caught up.

"Yes, he is."

"Did you force him to come here?"

"No, but he's just a kid and I—"

"But he's not your kid."

"I got him into this mess."

"Really? Last night Reggie told me about some of your many adventures. He also told me you tried doing much of it alone because you didn't want him to get hurt."

"That's true."

"After everything you've been through, he's still alive."

"I feel responsible for him."

"My father used to say that what doesn't kill you makes you stronger. I'm not sure that's always true, but what was Reggie like when you first met him?"

"He was a dorky, paranoid, rich brat."

"Has any of that changed?"

"Probably."

"Have you changed since you met him?"

"Probably."

"If your wife were still alive, what would she say?"

"She was more paranoid than him. Sophie would have loved Reggie."

"Do you love Reggie?"

"We're partners in crime and maybe friends, but let's not get ridiculous."

They sat together at the base of the memorial for a little over a half hour before Reggie returned. Hudson tried not to jump up in excitement when he saw him walking alone towards them.

"You're not dead," said Hudson.

"I missed you too."

"What did you talk about?"

"I'll tell you later."

The scorching, midday sun forced them into the nearby shade, where they waited until noon.

"Is he going to show up?" asked Reggie.

"He'll show," said Hudson.

"Do you trust him?"

"No, but he's our only chance to make it out of Kembata alive."

A few minutes later, Charles ambled into the square. He held his suit jacket over his shoulder and joined them in the shade of a sprawling raffia tree. Sweat stained his underarms, and his reddened face glistened with sweat. Hudson couldn't see John or the other bodyguards, but that didn't mean they weren't close.

Charles looked at each of them when he spoke.

"Mr. Finlay, you're fired. Reggie, I'm sorry for your loss. Hello, Kiara."

He rubbed his neck. "It is hotter than the ninth circle of hell. Let's get this over with. Hand over the recording."

Hudson reached into his sock, retrieved the card, and handed it to Charles.

Reggie folded his arms. "You had my father killed, and you tried to kill us."

"Some secrets are worth dying for, and some are worth killing for. I just want to make the world a better place. Your father stuck his nose where it didn't belong. You could learn something from that."

"You got what you wanted," Hudson snarled. "Now, promise you will leave us alone."

Charles rubbed his greasy hair. "How do I know you have no copies?"

"We didn't have time to make copies," said Hudson. "Also, there's nothing on the recording."

"What? You're giving me a blank card? You promised—"

"The recording is barely audible," said Hudson. "The only decipherable words were phase two and Kembata. The rest was unintelligible. Reggie's father was the one who told us about the Nipah virus bomb. Even if we made copies, there is nothing that would implicate you for anything."

Charles nodded. "Nicely played. You two are an odd but interesting duo, and I think I'll let you live – for now."

Hudson glared at him. "Why did you do it?"

"Do what, Mr. Finlay?"

"Why did you put a tracker in my wife and then kill her? Why are you trying to destroy the world?"

"This isn't the movies where the bad guy reveals all his evil plans. I am *not* the bad guy, and I will *not* reveal all my plans. As I said, I am trying to make the world a better place. There are those that may disagree with my methods, but someday humans will live together in harmony. One without wars, starvation, poverty—"

"...or property," added Reggie.

"I don't care about any of that," yelled Hudson. "Tell me why you killed my Sophie! You owe me that much," yelled Hudson.

Charles' tone remained calm. "Is that why you're doing all this? For vengeance? I don't owe you anything, but I can tell that I didn't kill her. Sophie came snooping around at a research facility."

"The old Acor Army base – we know about that," Reggie interjected.

"We could have charged her with breaking and entering. It was Reggie's father that insisted that we didn't. Instead, we used the opportunity to test a new device we were developing."

"You're a monster!" yelled Hudson. "You kidnapped her, injected a tracker in her arm, and sent her home!"

"It wasn't quite like that. Like you two, she was trespassing. We have trade secrets and proprietary research at the facility that we take seriously. She crawled through a duct and broke into a lab. A research scientist discovered her. When she attacked him, he grabbed a syringe with propofol and injected her with it. Because of the violent struggle, he gave her a *little* more than was necessary. Not enough to be dangerous, but enough to make her sleep for a long time. It was the perfect opportunity to test our new tracking device. Call it a compensation for our trouble instead of jail time for breaking and entering and possibly corporate espionage."

"She was only trying to expose your illegal research and the New World Order's goal of creating a totalitarian government and—"

Charles interrupted Reggie. "Whatever the reason she was there, she still broke the law. We inserted a harmless device in her shoulder. It's not our fault she contracted Covid and died. Maybe she should have stayed at home like the government advised."

Hudson's fists clenched, and he wondered if he could kill a man with one punch. "Don't you dare blame her! Sophie was a young, strong firefighter with no health conditions. And you're telling me she died from Covid – even after she got the useless vaccine?"

"It was my understanding that she died of complications due to Covid. It had nothing to do with the tracker."

"She probably died from myocarditis from the vaccine that *you* created to control the population," said Reggie.

"There is no significant evidence that any of the vaccines cause any significant harm."

"That's not true," said Reggie.

Hudson shook his head. "If the tracker didn't kill her, then why did you send your cronies to recover it?"

"First, it wasn't my men – it was Lawrence Hargreaves, and second, he was trying to recover proprietary research. I think he felt guilty about the whole thing, and that's why he went rogue."

"What about—"

"No more!" yelled Charles. "I got what I came for, and I'm about to die from heat exhaustion. No one will come after either of you, unless I hear about another recording. Good day."

As he turned to leave, Kiara called out. "What about the Kembato Virology Institute?"

"The Porter Foundation is pulling all funding. Sorry Doctor, but you're fired too."

Charles Porter walked away without looking back.

"I hate that man," said Hudson. "I should have killed him when I had the chance."

"There you are!" Sergeant Leon ran towards them and clutched his sister in a big hug. "Are you okay? What happened?"

His face was dirty, a bandage peaked out from under his service cap and his uniform was torn in three places.

"It's a long story," said Kiara. "What happened to you?"

"We had a crazy day of protests yesterday. The army came in and broke it up. I think it's over – for now. Why don't you come over for dinner and we can swap war stories. Reggie and Hudson, you can come too."

"Thanks for the offer, but we should get back to the airport and back home."

Kiara smiled and hugged them both.

Sergeant Leon drove them all to the airport. Once he and Kiara left, Hudson and Reggie went inside to buy tickets back to the States.

"You still didn't tell me what you and Gorilla talked about," said Hudson.

"I offered him a deal."

"What kind of deal?"

"Are you sure you want to know?"

"Friends don't keep secrets."

"So, we *are* friends!"

"We won't be if you don't tell me."

"Since my father is dead, I am about to inherit his house and a lot of money. I used some of my new wealth to do my own puppeteering."

"What did you do?"

"Remember how you said you wished you killed Charles Porter when you had the chance?"

CHAPTER 43

Six months later, Hudson drove a rusty jeep down a packed dirt road out of Abena. Beside him, Reggie bounced in his seat as they bumped over another rock in the road.

"You still haven't told me why we're back here again."

"Be patient. We're almost there. Why don't you eat your pretzels or something."

"I quit eating pretzels. They're full of gluten and sodium."

Hudson slowed as they passed a large wooden sign at the side of the road.

"Réserve Naturelle Kembato," Reggie read the sign with a horrible French accent. "I left my cushy mansion, housekeeping and food delivery for a road trip into the desert?"

"You're becoming a rich, spoiled brat again," said Hudson with a smile.

"Unfortunately, my dad's will states I don't get most of the money until I graduate high school and turn eighteen."

"At least he did something right."

"I convinced the lawyers in charge of his estate to donate enough money to keep the Kembato Virology Institute going for a few more years."

"That will make Kiara happy."

"Speaking of women, I hear my Aunt Seraphina is moving to Michigan. I'm assuming she wants to be closer to you?"

"Her company offered her a position for a Civil Engineer in Motor City."

"How do you know that?"

"We may have had dinner together a few times."

"Ooooh...so you two are..."

"Never mind that. I heard on the news the other day that Charles Porter is still missing."

A man in a small field beside a small shanty stopped hacking at the soil and watched them pass by.

"I heard that too," said Reggie.

"Are you still going to therapy?"

"Yes, are you?"

"I'm too cool for therapy. Your father's service was nice."

"I guess. It's more than he deserved. Speaking of dead people, I heard the mean old guy at your gym died."

"Coach Benny went out fighting. He insisted he was fine until the very end when he died of an aggressive colon cancer."

"Is the gym closed now?"

"Nope, I bought it. I had enough money saved up and took out a small loan. I am now the proud owner of Hudson's MMA and Boxing Gym!"

"That's amazing! I'd come down to visit, but I'm considering converting to pacifism."

"Good thinking."

"Okay, are we there yet?"

Hudson pulled over and parked in the shade of a looming kapok tree. Its branches spread out like a gargantuan umbrella.

"Are we here to reunite you with your skunk monkey friends?"

"Not quite." Hudson stepped out of the jeep and pointed at the dark shapes in the distance. He reached into the back of the jeep and grabbed a silver urn.

Reggie followed Hudson out of the shade and into the sunshine. Shading his eyes from the sun, Reggie looked at the grey shapes.

"Are those elephants?"

"Yes, they are."

Hudson walked towards them, with Reggie following a few steps behind.

"Where are you going?"

"I'm getting a closer look."

"Aren't they dangerous? That big one has tusks bigger than my car."

"They can be. Elephants are the strongest land mammal on earth."

One elephant stopped and looked up at them as they approached. It trumpeted twice before resuming its grazing.

"Did you know that when an elephant passes a spot where a loved one died, they will pause for several minutes at the same location in a moment of silence - sometimes, even years later. They always remember."

When they were within thirty feet of the herd, Hudson stopped.

"Those are Sophie's ashes," Reggie spoke softly and pointed at the urn.

"This is a very personal moment for me, Reggie, and I wanted only my closest friends here for this."

Reggie looked around. "I'm the only one here."

"I know, and thank you for coming."

Hudson took a deep breath. "Wait here. I'll be right back."

Hudson moved slowly through the tall grass towards the herd. The largest elephant perked its head up and stomped towards Hudson. Big, deliberate steps at first, but then it picked up speed. Its trunk swayed from side to side, and its ears flopped as it charged. The ground tremored with every step, but Hudson remained defiantly in place.

Several feet before it skewered Hudson with its ivory, the enormous pachyderm stopped.

Sophie told him once that elephants are smart enough to detect human emotion. He wasn't sure he believed it until that moment.

Hudson wiped the dusty tears from his cheek and stared into the honey-coloured eye of the beast. He realized the elephant's eyes were the same colour as Sophie's. The beast stared at him for a moment before pawing at the ground with its enormous feet before turning away. It trumpeted as it lumbered back to the herd.

Hudson removed the lid from the silver urn and dumped the ashes. A gust of wind picked up the grey dust and carried it over the herd of elephants.

Hudson watched silently through a blur of tears as it dissipated over the savannah and disappeared.
"Goodbye, Sophie."

EPILOGUE

The group of men sat around the large table. Some had earpieces with automated translators.

One man stood up. "Thank you all for coming."

He cleared his throat and continued. "Unfortunately, we have lost one of our members, but we must continue with our mission. As you know, our last test run failed. In the meantime, we have continued our research. Our AI has developed a better, more virulent strain of the Nipah virus. This one has a long dormant period and an even higher mortality rate. By the time the world realizes there's a virus, it will be too late."

A woman with a thick accent held up her finger. "Do you have a cure?"

"Not yet, but we are close."

"What if we lose control? Isn't there the possibility of an extinction event?" said a deep gravelly voice.

"There is little chance of that."

"Do we have a name for this new virus?" asked the woman.

"Yes, we call it the Scourge."

If you enjoyed this book, please give your support by leaving a review on Amazon, Goodreads or on your favourite social media.

This book is a prequel for the apocalyptic series that begins with: Black Flag – Surviving the Scourge. Be sure to check it out on Amazon to continue your adventures.

BOOKS BY THIS AUTHOR

Black Flag - Surviving The Scourge

As a mysterious disease wipes out most of humanity, the world falls into chaos and anarchy. But a group of survivors, led by a former marine, refuses to give up without a fight. As they journey across the country in search of safety and hope, they must brave the dangers of a post-apocalyptic world and confront the terrible truth about the origins of the virus. Filled with action, suspense, and unforgettable characters, Black Flag Surviving the Scourge is a thrilling must-read for fans of apocalyptic fiction.

Black Flag - Surviving The Invasion

A tenacious group of Scourge pandemic survivors must defend their homeland from the Chinese invaders. Joe and his friends emerge from the safety of the bunker to fight for their country against an overwhelming force. The group becomes separated as the children are kidnapped, Joe and Tank are captured and Monique and Camille become stranded in the wilderness. They battle against Chinese, rats, wolves, bullies and personal demons.
What they don't know is that the Chinese invaders have a secret.

Black Flag - Surviving The Apocalypse

The second wave of the Scourge threatens to kill more than half of the remaining population, including many of Joe's friends. Joe chases the formula, Tank loses a piece of himself and Camille fends for herself. All your favourite characters are back in this epic conclusion to the Black Flag Trilogy, but who will survive?

Search Engine (Black Flag Brigade Origins, Book 1)

In a world without internet, cell phones or Wi-Fi, one girl discovers a search engine.
A cataclysmic event wiped out much of the population, leaving the remaining survivors struggling to rebuild society. Technology that once connected the civilized world and provided a wealth of information has vanished.
This makes fifteen-year-old Ivette's search engine a valuable asset, and it makes her a target.
Camille is a violent, fearless, knife throwing Commerce City Enforcer, while Pitbull is a charming, brawny jock yearning for adventure and a good fight.
The young teenagers' lives converge in this action-packed post-apocalyptic adventure as they search for the origin of the mysterious search engine.

Road To Empire (Black Flag Brigade Origins, Book 2)

Three teens leave their peaceful home for a perilous expedition through a lawless, well-armed post-apocalyptic America.
In this follow-up to Search Engine, Pitbull, Ivette and Camille battle sickness, raiders, snipers, kidnappers, gangs and slave-traders. They trek south into the unknown in their quest to discover the origins of Ivette's implant, locate a secret underground compound while pursuing a gang of murderous lunatics.

Justice (Black Flag Brigade Origins, Book 3)

With the Executioners chasing them, the group steps into the extraordinary world of Empire City.
In the final chapter of the Black Flag Origins trilogy, Camille and her friends finally reach the underground compound. However, they discover an impassable entrance and must search for another way inside. They find old friends, make new ones and discover a strange city with its own challenges and secrets.